To order more copies of
this book log on to:
www.barbarapercival.com

BEYOND DAVINCI

THE NEXT CHAPTER

Barbara Percival

Copyright © 2006 by Barbara Percival

All rights reserved. No part of this book shall be reproduced or transmitted in any form or by any means, electronic, mechanical, magnetic, photographic including photocopying, recording or by any information storage and retrieval system, without prior written permission of the publisher. No patent liability is assumed with respect to the use of the information contained herein. Although every precaution has been taken in the preparation of this book, the publisher and author assume no responsibility for errors or omissions. Neither is any liability assumed for damages resulting from the use of the information contained herein.

This is a work of fiction. Names, characters, places, and incidents either are the product of the author's imagination or are used fictitiously. Any resemblance to actual events or locales or persons, living or dead, is entirely coincidental.

ISBN 0-7414-3336-2

Published by:

INFI∞ITY
PUBLISHING.COM

1094 New DeHaven Street, Suite 100
West Conshohocken, PA 19428-2713
Info@buybooksontheweb.com
www.buybooksontheweb.com
Toll-free (877) BUY BOOK
Local Phone (610) 941-9999
Fax (610) 941-9959

Printed in the United States of America

Printed on Recycled Paper

Published July 2006

"There are more things in heaven and earth, Horatio, than are dreamt of in your philosophy."

-Shakespeare in Hamlet

ACKNOWLEDGMENTS

I would like to thank Kirk Percival for his many insightful contributions to the storyline and his unending encouragement in bringing this novel towards a cohesive product and B. James Tank for his detailed editing and historical advice. I would also like to thank Bruce Raley for all his computer assistance.

Author's Note:

This story was meant to inspire, to encourage the dreamer who has a nobler vision. You are not alone. Cultivate your dreams. There is a better way. However, in order to have a new way of living, we must first have a new way of thinking. Dare to believe that mankind has the capabilities for a greater purpose. Be the light in a world darkened by ignorance and self-interest by pressing forward in hope, with a loving heart, to preserve the principles of freedom. For to do this in an environment where Nature is honored – lies the key to the fate of mankind.

PROLOGUE

The fire was reduced to a few burning coals, its glow still reflecting off the black marble hearth. As the sound of the late winter rains intensified, Bernadette pulled the burgundy throw that lay carelessly across her legs up around her body, her left hand maintaining its grip on the book she had just finished reading. It was a novel that revealed a secret ancient truth that had been cleverly veiled in Leonardo DaVinci's works of art. The book had been on the *New York Times* bestseller list for months, but Bernadette resisted reading it until now. She knew the real story published years ago in the research book *Holy Blood, Holy Grail*. Why read a watered-down version? Although she had to admit, it was a clever idea, and a fleeting pang of jealousy that she hadn't come up with it herself reminded her she was still unpublished.

The troubling sound of a limb as it scraped against the house momentarily distracted her. She shivered from the bone-chilling temperatures brought on by the fury of the gusting winds as they tore maliciously across the landscape. *Would there be no end to this storm?* In the closing darkness she could still make out a gnarled, old oak, stoically braving the elements. A lone raven perched at the top - a solitary lookout on the mast of a ship being tossed by a tempestuous sea. The California foothills that normally offered a palatable winter had unleashed one of the worst in recent memory.

Bernadette's thoughts were drawn back to the DaVinci book lying in her lap. It told quite a story, but most readers, in her opinion, were missing the point. In a burst of frustration, she pushed her short dark curls away from her face. *Why don't they get it?* Then laughing out loud. *Did she get it?* She had been studying the Holy Grail for years and she still had as many questions as she did answers. Although recently, she had begun to suspect that the Holy Grail was only the tip of the iceberg and the real story went much deeper.

Her hand brushed across the book in her lap. It had exposed information to the general public that was explosive, causing turbulent waves to stir the ranks of Christian circles, but it was nothing new to her. She had unearthed the same information on her own.

So why did she feel this strong compulsion to make contact with the author?

The answer came as quickly as the question was formulated in her mind. Perhaps he knew more than he revealed in his book.

With a fierce determination, Bernadette clutched the novel resting in her lap. She had to find a way to meet the now famous author, so she could talk to him and see what else he knew. Opening the back cover, she studied his picture with a grave intensity as if trying to read his mind, or more importantly his soul. Samuel Sinclair. *Why did his name ring a bell?* Dressed in impeccably casual attire, he had the look of an Ivy League professor. The picture appeared a bit too staged for her tastes, but his eyes held her interest. Curious blue eyes, that seemed to look beyond the surface. The cover didn't say much, only that he lived in Massachusetts. That lonely sentence gave her encouragement. She had been born and raised in Connecticut, and although life had propelled her to California, there was something deep inside of her that still felt a strong kinship to New England.

A spark burst from the burning coals and her attention was drawn back to the fireplace and her father's picture that sat center-stage on the mantel. Without warning, the last images of his life flashed in her mind. He was laying in a hospital bed dying. She was alone at his bedside, standing vigil. His face pale as the January snow clinging to the trees outside the window. She tried to warm his cold hand held tight in both of hers. Unexpectedly, he opened his eyes and motioned for her to lean closer. Through lips that were parched, he struggled with each word. His voice barely audible.

"Wall safe . . . marble box . . . read letters . . ." But before he could finish, he released a momentous rasping sound and heaved his last sigh.

Bernadette cried for days, the dark circles under her eyes revealing the depth of her loss. Memories of their life together haunted her. As a young girl, sitting on his knee while he read to her after work, the smell of the factory still clinging to his rough clothing; their hikes in nature where he taught her to recognize the tracks of the wild creatures and respect for their habits; days spent at the ocean searching for shells as the waves washed teasingly over their feet; his infectious laughter and abounding enthusiasm. Her world would never be the same without him.

It was nearly a week before Bernadette remembered her father's last words. "Wall safe . . . marble box . . . read letters. . ." *How could she have forgotten?*

The next morning she quickly showered and anxiously drove the short distance to her father's place. It was difficult stepping into his house again. It was a modest house, much like the man who occupied it. The stillness without his booming voice was uncomfortable. It was a voice that reflected the passion he felt for life. Overwhelmed by her loss, Bernadette sank into an old easy chair. It was dark green, faded, worn at the arms. This is where her father would sit in the evening watching the Discovery Channel or reading the *National Geographic* magazines he cherished. So many memories!

Eventually she would have to dispose of his things, but not yet. She would face that obstacle later. Blowing the dust off a picture, she fingered it affectionately. Daddy in his funny cap and brown work clothes. She was young, seven or eight, a kitten held tightly in her arms, her curly head nestled against her father's shoulder. Their bond had always been strong. They shared everything, or so she thought. *But a hidden wall safe with letters – did her father have a dark secret?*

Her search began with hesitation. *Perhaps this was something better left buried in the tombs of the past!*

But the intensity behind her father's last words came rushing back to her, pressing her into action. She began checking behind paintings, bookcases, tapping on walls. Nothing.

She was about to give up when she remembered her grandmother's tales of the stock market crash of 1929 and the subsequent Depression. How she had waited in line for hours to retrieve her money at the Mechanics Bank, only to be told there was none. Grandma learned her lesson. She wouldn't lose her money a second time to the ill doings of others. Her grandmother had a secret hiding place built inside the wall at the far end of the closet where she burrowed away her meager savings for the rest of her life.

Had her father done the same thing? Bernadette hurried into the closet. Pushing away the clothes, she anxiously ran her fingers across the boards. There it was! Barely visible to the naked eye, a slight seam in the planks.

She stepped back – hesitated. *Should she?*

Again her father's last words prodded her.

Firmly pushing on the seam, the door popped open.

Her heart racing, she warily peered into the darkness.

A magnificent white marbled box occupied the space, beckoning her with its dazzling beauty. She removed it carefully, struggling with its cumbersome size. In the light, she stared in awe for a long time before her hand was drawn impulsively to the exquisitely carved dragon on top.

What secret made her father hide a work of art so staggeringly beautiful away from the eyes of the world?

Bernadette's curiosity overrode any doubts. Her heart pounding, she lifted the lid carefully and peered inside.

It was full of neatly folded linen stationary!

What had she expected, the Crown Jewels? After all, he had mentioned letters.

Her hands trembled as she carefully unfolded each sheet. She felt like a child peeking through a forbidden keyhole as she anxiously began to read.

The letters cryptically spoke of matters from antiquity. Events that weren't familiar to her at that time, but she was instantly intrigued. She read them again and again, each time feeling more mystified than before. *What could this all mean?* The pages were embossed with unusual emblems and geometric symbols. She wished her father had said more about them, given her some clue to their meaning.

Fifteen years later, Bernadette was still pondering over those letters. She had spent years researching the symbols they contained and the incidents to which they teasingly alluded. In the process she had unearthed truths about historical events that had been purposely misrepresented to the masses. Truths many historians and theologians had known for years; that the Holy Grail was more than a chalice that Jesus drank from at the last supper - that it was a symbol which alluded to the feminine. More pointedly a specific woman. The wife of the man called Jesus, and the subsequent bloodline they produced together.

This staggeringly controversial information challenged the fundamental beliefs of Christianity, however, it was hardly a blip on the screen for Bernadette. No one in her family was particularly religious. It didn't matter to her if Jesus was married or not. *So why did her father feel the need to keep these letters hidden?*

Just the fact that he had possession of them was astonishing. He hadn't been known to be a secretive man, yet why had he never spoken of it to anyone in the family? It was all so strange, almost illusionary. Her father had been a simple, blue-collar worker all his life, his parents humble immigrants. The things in these letters referred to families of wealth and prestige. None of this made any sense.

The howling winds outside brought Bernadette back to the present. Her hand was still resting on the book in her lap. It dealt with similar issues. Samuel Sinclair had exposed the controversial information about Jesus' alleged marriage and subsequent bloodline to the general public, causing quite a stir around the globe. But Bernadette suspected the mystery went much deeper than the DaVinci code. Did the author of this book know more than he was telling?

Her eyes were drawn to the fire dying in the hearth. I can't give up. I have to do this for my father, she whispered. But her words were drowned by the echoing winds as they wailed and moaned out of the darkness of the night.

CHAPTER 1

Attired in a gray sports jacket and a white turtleneck, Samuel Sinclair tried not to look as self-conscious as he was feeling sitting behind a table in a popular Boston bookstore. Copies of his follow-up novel to his book about DaVinci's code surrounded him. A lull in the crowd had given him a moment to collect himself. He disliked this part of being a writer, however, his agent kept reminding him that these promotional outings were as necessary as the editing of the book.

His light blue eyes were drawn to the attractive woman approaching. There was something about her that caught his attention. Her hesitant stride as she moved towards him, as if someone was holding a gun to her head. *That was his fanciful writer's imagination again. Creating drama and tension out of the smallest details.* Sitting down in front of him with the apprehension of someone going into a confessional, her shoulders sagged as if burdened by the weight of a secret held for many years. She cleared her throat, yet said nothing, her dark, mysterious eyes studying his face with a gripping intensity.

Uneasy, Samuel ran his hand through his sandy blonde hair. He kept it short and perfectly groomed. His voice was tentative, "Would you like me to sign a copy of my book for you?"

Her smile was one of apology, yet her penetrating stare continued to hold his eyes magnetically. The color in her cheeks was accentuated by the deep cranberry shade of her coat. Without a word she pushed two short letters written on unusual stationary towards him, her hand quivering.

Samuel reached for them questioningly and their fingers touched, drawing his eyes uncomfortably back to hers.

After glancing through the letters, he returned her silent gaze.

"They were my father's. He died fifteen years ago." Again silence. "You're familiar with the symbols and subject matter in the letters."

Samuel nodded in reply.

Her next question stunned him. "Will you help me?"

With a shocked expression he lowered his voice, "I'm an author. I write mysteries. I don't solve them."

Ignoring his response, Bernadette continued, "Based on the accuracies in your last book, I know you're an avid researcher and clearly this subject is of interest to you."

"Researcher, yes. Author, yes, but detective, no," and his hand pulled further away from hers.

"To solve this riddle it would take someone who knew of such things."

"Look Ms.____?"

"Percival," she responded, "Bernadette Percival;" and she secretly enjoyed his reaction. Anyone who had studied the Holy Grail, as he had, would respond to that name. In the original Grail stories dating back to the twelfth century, Percival was the main protagonist. It wasn't until later versions that King Arthur became more prominent. However, even in the tales of Camelot, the Knight Percival held an exulted position. Sir Percival was the only knight to ever see the Grail.

Aware that a line was forming behind her, Bernadette anxiously handed him a slip of paper. "I know you're a busy man, but I flew all the way from California to see you. This is my hotel and room number. If you could just give me an hour of your time in the next few days, I would be most appreciative. Perhaps there's a clue I've overlooked in my research that you've uncovered in yours.

Samuel's voice was noncommittal. "I'll see what I can arrange."

The next morning Bernadette lazily watched the sun stream through the lace curtains of her hotel room. She had chosen this particular hotel because the brochure boasted it had been an inn since Colonial times. As she gazed down on the cobblestone alleyway lined with old-fashioned gaslights, she got a strong sense of the lifestyle of the early colonists. She visualized Paul Revere riding through, announcing the arrival of the British - the excitement, the fear that pulsated through his veins. *Such turbulent times.* And then a crazy idea popped into her mind – that she, too, had a mission – one of preparing the country for something to come. She laughed at her ludicrous thoughts, but the sense of mission remained, bringing with it the memory of her brief encounter the afternoon before with Samuel Sinclair. There was something about his mannerisms that seemed familiar. She stretched. *It's probably nothing, just my imagination,* and she headed towards the shower.

Above the sound of the running water, she heard the phone ring. *Oh good, it's Mr. Sinclair.* Grabbing a towel, she dashed to reach it, her damp feet leaving light footprints on the carpet.

"Leave Boston immediately," a deep male voice commanded. "It would be unwise to make any further contact with Samuel Sinclair," and the phone went dead before she could respond.

Bernadette froze. Then clutching the white bath towel that was around her torso, she pulled it tighter, as if it could shield her. Her head spinning, she sank to the bed. It had been fifteen years since she heard that voice on the phone, but she would never forget it. It had a hint of a foreign accent and an unusually deep resonance that was branded in her memory. She received a similar phone call after her father died, threatening her not to try to discover the identity or whereabouts of the persons who had written those mysterious letters to him.

"You and the girl will be safe if you leave this alone," the deep voice with the slight accent ordered fifteen years ago, "Otherwise, we can't promise to protect you."

She was stunned. Protect them from whom? Most shocking to Bernadette was that fifteen years later they had found her in an obscure hotel room in Boston. She lay unmoving, paralyzed, her eyes focused on the ceiling.

Don't go into panic mode. Stay calm. But her maternal instincts kicked in, and frantically she jumped up. *I need to warn Mallory.* Impulsively, she reached across the nightstand for the phone, then paused. Releasing a long sigh, she resisted the urge to dial. She knew how her daughter felt about all this. And what exactly would she warn her about. *Be careful! Of what? Mallory was an adult, college educated. It wasn't as if she needed to tell her not to take candy from strangers.*

Past experience had taught Bernadette that it was useless to bring in the police. She had tried to engage their help when she received that fateful phone call fifteen years ago, but the police merely shrugged it off as a crank call. She understood. There was nothing factual to go on besides a random phone call, now two, fifteen years apart. Hardly what one would define as a stalker. So once again she was on her own.

Reluctantly putting the phone down, Bernadette turned, instantly jumping in fear at the sight of an unexpected figure. Through her panic, it took a moment to recognize her own reflection in the wall mirror across the undersized room. The face staring back at her had wide eyes and was as white as the bath towel held tightly around her body.

What was happening here? She tried to calm herself, but her thoughts couldn't be put to rest. *How did that unidentified voice know she had spoken with Sinclair? And what difference did it make to anyone?* She was a nobody, a housewife turned writer who could never get published. Her writings weren't of a controversial nature. She considered them mystical love stories that offered hope. Yet, clearly, she was being threatened, her actions monitored by someone. But who – and more importantly, why?

CHAPTER 2

Montpellier is a short drive inland from the northwestern shores of the French Mediterranean, and because of its close proximity to Spain, its architecture reflected both countries. During the first century, it was on the trade route from Western Europe to the Middle East and consequently became a Mecca for the mystery schools. It was still renowned as a liberal cultural center, supporting a large and eclectic philosophical society that generated out from the hub of its bustling University. It wasn't unusual to hear lively debates sifting through the ancient walls and spilling out into its busy streets.

On the third floor of an office building that faced the sprawling Place de la Comedie, two men spoke in hushed tones. The man seated across the large antique desk was clearly agitated, his ample moustache moving erratically as he presented his concerns in clipped phrases. Philippe, his supervisor, was attempting to placate him. "I understand your concern, Francois. Clearly, we miscalculated Bernadette's persistence. I spoke with Paris twice today and they assured me they have the situation under control."

"To Paris only?"

"At this point, yes. It will have to be their decision to take this further."

Francois stared out the window for a long time before he ventured, "Perhaps it is time to go to the next step," and his compact, muscular frame grew tense as he moved restlessly in his chair.

"I had the same thought myself recently, based on what is happening in the United States. The current administration seems to be out of control." Then looking down, Philippe sighed almost to himself. "Humanity - will we never learn? If wars ended war, we would have been living in peace long ago."

Philippe's face showed resignation when he focused his attention back on the man across his desk. "As you know, the decision to take this further than Paris is not ours to make," and removing his wire-rimmed glasses, he began wiping the lenses clean to indicate the conversation was over.

Francois nodded, and his finger absent-mindedly stroked his moustache. "I suppose, as always, we must exercise patience and bow to the powers that be," he murmured, his sour expression reflecting his opinion on the matter.

Philippe smiled in silent agreement, his compassionate eyes accentuated by his full white eyebrows. He knew it wasn't easy following orders from unknown faces in unknown places. He too was getting weary, and his heart was no longer in it. Let humanity be damned. He was ready to take an early pension and retire. Let the young worry about the world at large. His life was in its final stages; he had no offspring to think about. If men didn't have enough sense to keep from blowing each other up, then so be it. Let them suffer the consequences of their own foolish acts.

Meanwhile in a remote corner of the planet: "Bring me my cape, Cassarra. I think the time has come."

Cassarra raised her eyebrows. She could feel her heart begin to accelerate in anticipation, but her training had taught her to maintain a quiet façade.

Lenzi responded to the unasked question. "I know the timing is off, but sometimes circumstances dictate schedules, rather than the other way around. At this point it might be more difficult to keep the status quo. I know everything is not in place for the next step, but we'll simply have to be more resourceful. Perhaps there are agendas more important than ours," and those incredible silver eyes looked upward.

Cassarra understood completely. Lenzi accepted the cape and affectionately patted the young woman's long chestnut tresses. Worn straight and shoulder length, they were unusually thick and lustrous. "Do not send me your worry thoughts, now. I have taught you better than that. If you can't send me positive energy, then pray for me. That is the most positive energy of all, *if* it comes from the heart and is unattached to anxiety."

"Remember the wisdom of Lord Tennyson," Lenzi reminded Cassarra by quoting a favorite passage from his writings: "More things are wrought by prayer than this world dreams of," and then, throwing a smile at the young woman, departed.

Cassarra smiled back in return. She had been with Lenzi since she was an infant, and she sent off daily prayers of gratitude for that privilege. She couldn't imagine being under the tutelage of a kinder, more intelligent person.

Cassarra was too young to remember the circumstances of their union, but Lenzi had described the scene so often it seemed to be part of her own memory. Lenzi had been traveling through war-torn Kosovo with a group of international relief workers when they came upon a small village that had been totally decimated by the bombing. Every house had either collapsed or been blown apart. Everywhere, boards and stones were piled high like pick-up-sticks, bodies strewn across the landscape in every imaginable condition.

Shocked by the horror of the devastation, Lenzi struggled to gather strength. Despite past experiences and a lifetime of training, there were still these moments that made one feel helpless. The dark spots that tested the human soul. No matter how many times one witnessed scenes such as this, it was always a challenge to overcome the horror.

Setting up camp, they began searching for survivors, but there didn't seem to be any.

It was late in the evening when a faint cry was heard. Lenzi called out, but the night was silent. *Did I imagine it? Perhaps it was only the forlorn sound of an animal in the distance.* But again, a faint whimper trickled through the darkness. This time there was no question. It was human. Calling to the others, they carefully began sifting through the debris until, miraculously, a soiled infant emerged - less than a year old, frail, a wisp of reddish hair matted to her head. At just that moment the moon moved from behind the clouds and lit up the little tear-stained face as she stretched her chubby arms towards them.

Lenzi liked to tell that after being turned away from two already overcrowded orphanages and having no luck finding family members at any of the refugee camps, that fate had made the decision for them. They had been together ever since. It was divine intervention, Lenzi repeated many times through the years. That always made Cassarra feel incredibly special, as if the angels had brought them together.

An ancient Roman archway, a relic from an empire lost, gracefully exposed an inner courtyard where the fragrance of jasmine and gardenias blended with the salt air, stirring the senses. Against the backdrop of the translucent turquoise of the sea, it created a setting that had inspired many an artist's paintbrush through the ages.

Cape flowing behind, Lenzi walked into Mari's office with an air of urgency. "I'm considering putting the next step into place. Would you like to go on a little trip?"

Mari's slender face froze. It was framed with a mane of unruly jet-black hair. *Just like that: "I'm putting the next step into place." It wasn't scheduled for another five years.*

"I'm going to France," Lenzi continued in a matter-of-fact tone, as if nothing out of the ordinary was about to happen. "I thought perhaps you would enjoy spending some time with your people. I could drop you in Biarritz and pick you up on the way home."

"When?" Mari asked, her face still ashen from the surprise Lenzi had dropped on her.

"I'll leave in six days. We should be able to arrange everything by then. If the world was created in six days, we should be able to complete this much simpler task in the same amount of time. In the meantime call an emergency meeting of the council to begin at noon today. They will have much to do to prepare Cassarra. You will also need to alert Montpellier and Paris that I'm coming."

Going to Montpellier and Paris! That should be quite an event. Neither of the French operations had ever met Lenzi, who was known only as Le Perfector to them. They will be in for a surprise, and Mari suppressed a chuckle. "After France you will return here?" And her almond-shaped eyes searched Lenzi's face. They were a rich hazel.

"For a short time. Long enough to be assured Cassarra is ready."

Mari sighed. "That I fear is the least of our worries. It's the American contingency that concerns me. We needed those five extra years to get them better positioned."

"Perhaps," Lenzi conceded. And then in a prophetic voice that was low, but commanding, "They will be ready, I feel it. I've been suspecting for some time now that events are unraveling at a faster pace than in the past. And we will be up to the challenge. It's what we've prepared for all our lives."

CHAPTER 3

Samuel Sinclair gazed out the window of his study towards the restful wooded landscape he so loved. He was first inspired to try his hand at fiction in this exact spot. What began as a hobby, something to take his mind off the daily pressures of teaching at a prestigious Boston college, had turned into an amazingly lucrative profession that ultimately allowed him to walk away from his professorship - a career that had spanned several decades, but which ultimately lost its luster. College students had changed. Their zest and thirst for knowledge had been replaced by their insatiable material desires, and college degrees had become nothing more than the means to satisfy those desires. It offered him few challenges to stand before a classroom of disinterested and hung-over students.

Samuel's talent for research along with his fascination for intrigue ultimately transformed him into a successful mystery writer. They were the same characteristics that propelled him to call Bernadette Percival the morning after she had unexpectedly walked into his life. He had to admit, when he rang her up, he was at first surprised and then disappointed she had changed her mind. Why would she fly all the way across the country to meet with him and then abort her plan? And when he pressed her on the phone, she sounded frightened. Now he *was* intrigued. Any other man might have been relieved from becoming involved, however, Samuel's inordinately curious mind was pulled into the unfolding drama. The letters she showed him that dealt with the same symbols he had unearthed on his own while researching the Holy Grail, and the coincidence of her last name were more than captivating. But he didn't want to overstep his bounds. Samuel's rationale told him it was best to drop the entire episode. It could be this Percival woman was simply an overzealous admirer of his books with a vivid imagination. Yet as the day progressed, he found he couldn't shake the incident from his mind.

Bernadette jumped at the sound of a firm knocking on her hotel room door. She had been addressing postcards at the small round table to keep herself distracted from thinking about that last phone call.

She stood apprehensively. *Who could it be?* Focusing on the bronze knob, she quietly approached the door. In one swift movement, an envelope was slipped underneath. Startled, she instinctively drew back, a feeling of panic rushing in. Staring at the stark white rectangle as if it were alive, tears began to roll down her cheeks. It was a long moment before she could summon the courage to reach down and retrieve it. There were no identifying marks on the outside. With trembling hands and a pounding heart she opened it cautiously and silently read, "Look for me at your church in Revere," and it was signed 'S'.

Samuel Sinclair?

She pondered over the note. *Was this really from Samuel Sinclair - or was it a trap set by the anonymous voice on the phone?* She tried to pull herself together. *Keep the emotion out of it. Use your analytical mind and focus on the facts.* She knew that Revere was just north of Boston. But what was 'her church', and there was no appointed time. Then, realizing it was Saturday, she deduced that, if it were a Catholic church, there would be a mass this evening. Her intuition was telling her that the note *was* from Samuel. If it were a trap, they wouldn't have left the time and place so vague. Clever of Samuel. He must have sensed the need for secrecy when she retracted her plea for assistance.

After lunch, she nervously waited until the hotel lobby was empty before she asked the young clerk at the front desk for a list of Catholic Churches in the area, then retreated to her room to study it. She was looking for possibly a St. Bernadette's, for obvious reasons, or a St. Sulpice, since it played a major role in the *Holy Blood Holy Grail* story. The story on which Samuel had based his best seller. When neither of those showed up, she began to go down the list hoping something would jump out at her. It did. Our Lady of Lourdes in Revere. Very clever she thought. His note had said meet me at your church in Revere. Saint Bernadette had made the city of Lourdes in France a famous pilgrimage site. A smile blossomed on her face. *He's good at this! I see why his books are so fascinating; he has a natural gift for intrigue.* Phoning the church, she found they had a 4:30 evening mass.

Bernadette's surprise when she drove up the coast to Our Lady of Lourdes Church was immediate. She expected a cathedral, not the small wooden church that sat on a barren corner, looking vulnerable and forlorn. Parking her rental car, she anxiously ascended the wide steps. Feeling like a sitting duck in her bright cranberry coat, she quickly scurried into the protection of the interior and sat in the last row of pews close to the aisle. She scanned the heads in front of her searching for Samuel's neatly cropped, sandy hair. No one resembling him was already seated.

As she waited, her attention was drawn to the beautiful stained glass windows that artfully portrayed scenes of the church's patron saint. The dim light of dusk filtered through the brilliant colors, and as they blended with the heavy, incense-laden air, a memory stirred. She had asked her mother many times why they had chosen her name, a French name closely associated with the Catholic religion. Her mother was never able to give her an answer. "I guess because we thought it was pretty" was the best she could come up with.

Bernadette felt herself stiffen as Samuel entered the church. He made eye contact but passed by and sat a few rows in front of her. She idly wondered if he was Catholic and what his connection to all this was.

She was raised in an unreligious family herself, in a neighborhood surrounded by an eclectic blend of Italian Catholics and German Jewish immigrants, all of whom were deeply steeped in their religious customs. It made for an interesting combination. As a young girl, she often went to church or synagogue with her friends and through this association, was introduced to the philosophies of both religions without having the dogma of either forced upon her. That exposure had allowed her to be open to many different and opposing thought systems from an early age, and she quickly realized that most religions essentially held the same basic ideals. It was simply how they put them into practice that varied and the rituals that surrounded them. She also saw how these practices and rituals built walls between the different sects. Walls that through the years had become thicker and higher. *Men have always sought religious tolerance, yet those who have sought it have often been the most reluctant to give it to others. What a crazy dichotomy!*

When mass was over, she waited for a sign from Samuel. It came as a quick motion of his hand to follow him. As she exited into the parking lot, she saw him heading towards a silver Jaguar. *I wonder if it came with the success of his DaVinci book?* And again there was a fleeting twinge of envy. *That should have been her book!*

Instinctively, she got in on the passenger side as he started the engine. He barely looked at her, but seemed very aware of his surroundings as he pulled onto the street. Only after they were several blocks away did he smile and make eye contact. "As you can see, your hook worked. I'll help you in any way I can."

Her smile was one of relief as she nestled into the luxurious leather seat. "You can't imagine how much that would alleviate my anxiety. Going this alone hasn't been easy," she exclaimed.

He nodded. "Now tell me your story."

It didn't take long. There wasn't much to tell. It was mostly conjecture. The only facts she had other than the letters were the two phone calls she received fifteen years apart. She noticed the look of apprehension on Samuel's face when she mentioned the phone calls.

"And you have no idea who would be threatening you?"

"None. I only know it has something to do with the letters. Yet, I don't understand how my family is connected to them. I've collected tons of research. Probably the same material you exposed in your book, but no matter how hard I try, I can't see how my ancestors could possibly fit into the riddle of the Holy Grail.

"What made you contact me instead of one of the author's of the many research books on the subject?"

Her expression was one of surprise. "I honestly don't know. I only know when I finished reading your book that the compulsion to contact you was so strong, I couldn't resist it."

Samuel's curious blue eyes studied her face as if to read her intentions.

"Are we going somewhere?" she asked.

"No, driving around seemed the safest thing to do. Do you think anyone followed you here?"

"I don't see how they could have. That's the one good thing about the congested Boston traffic."

"You seem to manage in it very well for a Californian."

"My brother went to school here. Well, Cambridge, but his fraternity was in Boston. My family lived in Connecticut at the time, so I came to visit him fairly often."

"So your brother's a Harvard man?"

"No, M.I.T." Samuel's reaction didn't escape her. Bernadette liked to drop that on people. It was amazing how much status she derived from her brother's accomplishments. People were so silly about those things.

"Is he involved in anyway?"

"Unfortunately, no. In the beginning I tried to solicit his help, but he wanted no part of it and waved it all off as the fantasy of an over-active imagination. He's a true scientist. You know, if it can't be proved, it doesn't exist."

Samuel knew the type. There were lots of them in the intellectual circles around Boston.

"You said your father was a simple man, uneducated, but there must have been something that connected him to all of this."

"Perhaps," and she drifted off into her memories. "Looking back, I realize he had some sort of gift of prophecy, although he never defined it that way. But everything he said *would* happen, did. I don't know why I didn't realize it when he was alive," she trailed off, almost to herself. And then, turning her attention back to Samuel, she uttered, "I've researched this subject for years, but never have been able to connect it to my family. However, what I *have* come to realize through all my research is that this is much bigger than the Holy Grail. I believe the Holy Grail is a very small piece to a very large puzzle, and the mistake we've made has been to analyze it as if it were the whole picture."

"An interesting observation. Do you have any of the other pieces?" The intrigue in his voice evident.

"I have a few possibilities."

"Any of them that would somehow connect your father or his family?" he asked.

"Possibly," she answered cryptically, her dark eyes holding his. They were framed with long, thick lashes. "There's something, but I hesitate to tell you."

Pulling into a busy shopping mall, he parked the car and turned towards her.

"I can't be of much help if you don't tell me everything," and their faces seemed very close in the confines of the car.

She smiled in a strange way and the tone of her voice changed perceptibly, commanding his attention even further.

"This is pretty far out, so don't over react," and she paused for what seemed to Samuel an eternity.

Summoning her courage, Bernadette took a deep breath.

"It's the Pleiades connection," she finally stammered.

CHAPTER 4

"The Pleiades connection! You're not suggesting what I think?" Samuel blurted out.

"I'm not suggesting anything. I'm only trying to convey the information as I know it," she responded softly, fully understanding his reaction.

"Try to keep an open mind," she implored. "I truly have no agenda. I'm simply trying to understand what's happening and how my daughter and I are involved in any of this."

He nodded. "You're right. Go ahead. I'll try to stay open."

She began slowly, trying to bring back memories from her past. "As a small girl, my father always showed me how to find the Seven Sisters in the sky. He often referred to it as 'our constellation', commenting that was why seven was our lucky number."

Smiling self consciously, she admitted, "At the time I didn't know that Pleiades and the Seven Sisters were one and the same. That was something I learned after my father died. Through the years I had read of the many supposedly mystical connections between Pleiades and the Earth, but I had no belief system either way. But when I found out it was another name for the Seven Sisters, that changed everything for me, and I began to study the facts and myths surrounding Pleiades with a different perspective."

She paused to gather her thoughts. "Then, several years after my father died, a most peculiar thing happened. I was awakened one evening by a voice in my head." She saw the expression on Samuel's face change, but she continued. "It told me to go upstairs and put the television on. Why I followed this command, I can't say. Still groggy, I went upstairs and turned on the television, hardly paying attention to it. I went into the kitchen to get a drink of water, but when I heard the word 'Pleiades' mentioned, I ran back into the living room just in time to hear it said that early Celts believed that on Halloween, when Pleiades hung directly overhead at midnight, there was a period of time when a door was opened between the spirit world and our world. That's how the custom of dressing up on Halloween got started. It was to scare off any bad spirits from entering one's home."

Then she made strong eye contact to emphasize her point. "The interesting thing is it was only a five-minute program that comes on Saturday nights between 11:55 and midnight on the Public Broadcasting System. So if I hadn't followed that voice in my head, I would have missed it."

Samuel's brow was furrowed. "I'm not quite seeing the connection here."

Bernadette was nervously fidgeting with her purse strap. "My mother was born on Halloween," she said in a hushed tone.

"That is rather strange," Samuel admitted.

She smiled knowingly, "Yes, one of those 'strange coincidences' that I couldn't dismiss. Particularly since it appears I was awakened that night specifically so I would have that information." Bernadette's eyes were wide "What are the odds of having a father who was fascinated with Pleiades, who just happens to marry a woman, my mother, who was born on Halloween, and my happening upon the fact that the early mystics believed there was a connection between the two?"

Seeing the skepticism stamped on Samuel's face, she continued cautiously, "Whether there's a correlation between my father's letters and any of that, I have no idea, but it seems it was important for me to have that information. *Why*, is something I still don't understand."

And then she fixed her attention on him with a look that penetrated his very being and said in an indescribably compelling voice that came from the very depths of her soul, "But I believe with all my heart that someday soon, I will have the answer, and my intuition is telling me that somehow there is a connection between Pleiades and the Grail."

CHAPTER 5

The door to Samuel's study was closed. He sat alone, staring into space, his thoughts consumed with Bernadette's story. It was more fascinating than any novel. Almost unbelievable, yet there was something about her that commanded his trust. He had seen how reluctant she was to bring up what she called "the Pleiades connection", and understandably so. It suggested things one did not want to consider, yet he knew he shouldn't dismiss it either. From his experience it was best to look at everything with a neutral eye. Often information taken out of context could be misconstrued and lead the observer in the wrong direction. Best not to speculate.

The threatening phone call to stay away from him was disturbing. *Who would be threatening them and why?* And again he had a fleeting thought that perhaps Bernadette was some neurotic woman looking for attention, but immediately dismissed it. His instincts told him otherwise, and she did have those letters.

It *was* possible that the phone call she received at her hotel was from some religious fanatic that overheard them talking at his book signing. He knew his book about the DaVinci code had stirred a great deal of animosity in Christian communities. At first he was shocked, and later appalled, at the amount of hate mail and the intensity behind it that was sent to him through his publisher. How could people who identified themselves as 'good Christians' threaten the things they had, and all because he had a different opinion than they?

As far as the phone call Bernadette received fifteen years ago, she could have been mistaken that it was the same voice. Fifteen years was a long time to remember a voice that only spoke a short sentence. He suspected her imagination connected the two calls and there was probably no correlation between them.

Samuel was definitely intrigued by the letters Bernadette had in her possession. Coupled with the added connection of her significant last name, her story was difficult to dismiss. His draw to the mystery of the Holy Grail happened quite accidentally when he picked up a book in a used bookstore. He had never given it a thought before, believing as most did that it was the cup from which Jesus drank at the last supper. But this book exposed a secret that had been kept hidden from the masses. The premise was that the Holy Grail was more than a cup, that it was symbolic of the womb. Specifically, the womb that perpetuated Jesus' bloodline. Immediately he was drawn into the mystery. *Jesus had been married and fathered a child!* His interest was heightened further when he found that his last name was connected to the recorded bloodline.

Now Bernadette was suggesting a completely new twist to the mystery, and her words kept coming back to him. *"This is much bigger than the Holy Grail. That's only a very small piece to a very large puzzle,"* and the tone of her voice combined with her expression had been daunting, almost mesmerizing.

Turning on his computer, Samuel began recording everything Bernadette told him. Then he checked it against what he had collected himself. Nothing jumped out at him. She seemed to have the same pieces as he, with the exception of Pleiades. He knew that there was a mystique that had grown around Pleiades in recent years and many scholars believed that myths often perpetuated truths that could not be passed down in any other way. He decided to surf the web and see what he could find out.

A soft knock on his study door interrupted him. His wife peeked in, her strawberry-blonde hair coiffed for a special occasion. "You haven't forgotten that we have a party to attend?" She smiled affectionately.

"No, I was just finishing up," and he put a bookmark on the website titled 'Pleiades, Myths and Facts' and shut down his computer.

As Bernadette pulled out of the church parking lot, she cautiously eyed her surroundings to make sure she wasn't followed. She hated all this cloak and dagger stuff, but it was difficult to overlook that threatening phone call.

Sighing, she remembered how surprised she was when Samuel announced that he needed to get back because he and his wife had plans to attend a cocktail party. For some reason she assumed he was single. She had to admit, there was a brief moment of disappointment. Samuel *was* a very attractive man *and* intellectually stimulating. The later being a priority for her and a trait that was hard to find. In retrospect, she was glad it turned out this way. The last thing she needed in her life right now was a romance.

Darkness had closed in by the time Bernadette reached the hotel's parking garage, and rather than go directly to her room, she stepped outside, moving away from the artificial lights and looking towards the beauty of the night sky. She was able to find Pleiades easily. Her father had taught her to identify it from the time she was a small girl. "That's our constellation," he said to her many times as she was growing up.

She had since come to learn that Pleiades wasn't a constellation at all, but a star cluster, which from Earth's perspective, appeared to be in the constellation Taurus. Was that significant? She had no idea. No one in her immediate family was born under the sign of Taurus, so she had ruled that out.

But what could daddy have possibly meant when he said that Pleiades was their constellation? There were many times in the last fifteen years when she wished she had asked him that question before his sudden death. Unfortunately, he had taken his knowledge to the grave with him. Except for the letters, she did have the letters. And clearly, based on those mysterious phone calls she received, somewhere out there someone else knew the letters held the answer – and they knew she had them and were tracking her moves.

CHAPTER 6

Mallory Percival's apartment complex was tucked into a creekside ravine of a quaint foothill town in northern California, not far from her mother's house. There was a small patio off the living room. The ad in the paper had called it a garden apartment, something she still joked about with her friends. Talk about a stretch. There was one straggly plant in the corner, which she immediately replaced with a bright pink geranium.

Mallory was still puzzling over her mother's last phone call. It came as a warning: "Be especially careful and aware of your surroundings," her mother's trembling voice cautioned. Yet when Mallory questioned her mother, the answer she received was ambiguous. Mallory sighed as she absentmindedly pulled her long, brunette tresses away from her face. She had been glad when her mother said she was going on a vacation to New England. Since divorcing her father, her mother had become way too involved in her life, showering her with attention that often bordered on smothering.

Recently, Mallory's restlessness had escalated into the pressing need to put some distance between she and her parents, and something inexplicable was drawing her to the Blue Ridge Mountains in Virginia. She often found herself entertaining the thought of applying for a job on the East Coast, for the sole reason of being near them.

Her friends thought she was crazy. "You'll hate the winters, they're cold and blustery, and the humidity in the summer is awful," they chanted.

"What about the autumns?" Mallory retorted.

"They're pretty, but short, and they won't make up for the difference in salary you can earn in California."

She knew they were right, but there was still that undeniable pull. She didn't understand it herself, it defied logic, yet instead of subsiding, it had actually become stronger in the past few months. She hadn't brought the subject up with her parents yet. Her mother had been acting so unpredictable lately that Mallory decided to put it off for a while.

Mallory worked for an environmental agency and loved what she did. As a young girl, her maternal grandfather had instilled a deep love for nature in her, and that connection had stayed with her as she matured. From an early age she had been taught that human beings were the stewards of this planet and it was their responsibility to care for it. It made her feel as if she was fulfilling her life's destiny in her chosen profession, until lately, when the current administration in Washington's attitude towards the environment began to cause her great concern. It was as if they had turned the clock back fifty years.

First she was shocked with Washington's actions, and then she became angry. Now the politicians were talking about drilling for oil in the Alaskan tundra. How dare they think about disturbing that pristine area, particularly when the facts were known that it would only produce eight months of oil and it would take ten years to get it to market! Even a sixth grade student could see that wasn't a sound investment. Can't those eggheads in Washington see that this is the only planet we've got? What they're doing is tantamount to taking a bulldozer to their own billion-dollar home. She absolutely didn't get it. It wasn't somebody else's home they were destroying, but their own. Were they so detached from the Earth that they couldn't make that simple connection? Or was their greed so great that it overrode their own well-being?

Mallory remembered a Cree Indian prophecy her grandfather had taught her when she was still in grammar school. Even as a young child she understood it's meaning. Now it came back to her as a grim prediction:

    Only after the last tree has been cut down.
    Only after the last river has been poisoned.
    Only after the last fish has been caught.
    Only then will you find that money cannot be eaten.

CHAPTER 7

Candles of various sizes and shapes flickered throughout the circular sanctuary, presenting a decidedly serene and mystical atmosphere. Its one large, airy room offered picturesque vistas of the surrounding sea. The focal point was a round table that sat directly in the middle. Made from an unusual metallic material that was impressed with geometric symbols, the pedestal on which it stood gave the appearance of graceful branches naturally entwined. Amethyst vases overflowing with gardenias and white lilies were artfully placed throughout, filling the air with their opulent fragrance.

The council filtered in and took their places. Six men and six women who sat in alternate chairs. Lenzi, whom they called Le Perfector, was the seventh member. They began with their usual prayer of gratitude and request for guidance.

"Mari told you why we have gathered today. I know there is some concern about the advanced scheduling, however, at this point I see no other alternative than to accelerate our time frame. I meditated yesterday, and the answer that came to me confirmed it. I have decided to go to France and speak with our units there in person. A trip to the United States may also be necessary. I will be leaving Cassarra in your hands for her final preparation. I think you all agree that she is very close. It would have been nice to have had the luxury of the additional five years for the added maturity of the younger ones, but I have the utmost confidence that, with the wisdom of the council behind them, everything will fall into place, perhaps not as smoothly as we had hoped, but with the same results. Now, I want everyone's views as to what we can each do to bring the desired goal to fruition.

Once over the initial shock of what was about to happen, Mari began to look forward to accompanying Lenzi for a trip home. She hadn't been with her people in a very long time. She came from a Basque village high in the Pyrenees Mountains. It would be very green this time of the year, with snow still on the higher peaks. Although, in truth, she would have preferred to accompany Lenzi to Montpellier and Paris, but she wasn't given that option. To read the faces of the French units at their first meeting with Lenzi would be something to see. Mari suspected they were in for quite a surprise. It promised to be a fascinating event to witness, but she would settle for a long overdue visit with her family instead.

Back in Montpellier, Philippe gathered his contingency at an unlikely hour, and the suspense had been building between the time they were first notified and the actual meeting. A similar meeting was taking place in Paris. When Philippe arrived, his members all noted, it was with a renewed energy. His slight frame, which through the years had become somewhat stooped, was pulled soldierly erect, making him look like a younger man. The man they use to know and in whom they had great confidence.

"As you may have guessed," he began, running his hand quickly over his tuft of white hair that had been smoothed into place earlier with pomade, "I have some exciting and rather unexpected news." He paused for affect. "Le Perfector will be coming in three days," and his deep baritone voice reverberated around the room while fervent glances were exchanged between the members seated at the large rectangular table. He expected as much. Until now, their only contact had been through coded exchanges by letter and email, often routed through Paris, which always gave them the feeling of being secondary. To meet Le Perfector in person was quite an honor. "We are all expected to be here at the appointed time and ready for another phase. That is all I know at this time. It was also suggested that we have our passports in order. Travel may be necessary."

Several questions immediately arose, but Philippe was quick to put them to rest. "I know it's human nature to be curious, but it's important, especially at this time, to remember all we have learned. Let us not waste our time indulging our intellects in speculation over what is to come, but put them to better use by taking the time to properly prepare. We will know all too soon what is on the agenda," and the gleam in his eyes belied his composure.

Several hours later when Philippe locked the door to his office and exited into the city streets, his eyes still glimmered from the anticipation of upcoming events. His step was light as he passed through the familiar surroundings. Montpellier was a city that came alive with the passing of the sun. Sidewalk cafés that had basked sleepily under its warm rays now bustled with activity as the sound of laughter mingled with the clinking of wine glasses, naughtily filling the air with romantic expectations.

Philippe flashed back to his younger days while a lieutenant in the French Foreign Legion. There had been many romantic liaisons on nights such as this. Although he had never allowed those relationships to interfere with his main objective. Beginning with his brief stint in the French Resistance as a young boy, through his later association with the foreign legion, his primary motivation had always been freedom and equality for all. It was a natural progression that his next step was to find an organization such as the one headed by Le Perfector.

It wasn't very long ago that Philippe had given up hope that he would ever see the efforts of his life's work become a reality, and he had tried to take comfort in the fact that he was instrumental in setting the stage for future generations. But a single sentence emailed to him last night changed all that. In that one short paragraph was the smallest of hints that he would see his dream come true after all.

CHAPTER 8

The sidewalk cafes that bordered the Place de la Comedie in the old part of Montpellier were sprinkled with patrons enjoying the almost too bright Mediterranean sun, its reflection off the marble fountain momentarily blinding Lenzi, who paid the taxi driver with an ample tip and pleasant smile before entering the office building that faced the square.

The well-groomed receptionist looked up. "Yes?"

"I'm here to see Philippe Boulier."

"I'm sorry, Mr. Boulier is in a meeting and can't be disturbed."

"I believe I'm to be a part of that meeting," Lenzi declared with a confident amiability.

The receptionist appeared confused. "May I tell Mr. Boulier who is here to see him?"

"Tell him it is the one for whom he is waiting." Lenzi was clearly enjoying this little charade.

The receptionist's finger moved to the intercom, and then hesitated. *It might be better to make this announcement in person, so she could whisper something to Philippe.*

"I'll be right back," she smiled at Lenzi and proceeded to open the door to the conference room, but before she could close it behind her, Lenzi strolled in on her heels, saying, *"Bonjour mes amies, je suis Le Perfector."*

The reaction of those gathered was unanimous shock.

"*Mon Dieu,*" Francois muttered under his breath. "Who would have thought?"

Lenzi stood before them, a sea of disbelieving faces staring back. It was a common reaction.

"I see by your faces that you did not expect a woman," she mused. "You have forgotten our code of expect the unexpected?"

An uncomfortable silence ensued as Philippe struggled to pull himself together, his grandiose welcoming speech lost in a paralyzed mind.

The confused receptionist continued to stand at the opened door.

Lenzi was not only a woman, but an older woman who looked like she could be anyone's grandmother. Hardly what any of them had pictured to be the head of this powerful organization. Small of stature, with gray hair that was braided and wrapped into a crown at the back of her head, there was little about her physical appearance that would convey authority. Her voice, however, although soft and feminine, had the self-assurance of one use to giving direction.

Smiling congenially, she motioned to the receptionist with her stunning metal cane. It was indigo in color and embossed with gold symbols, giving it an oriental appearance. "You may be excused," she said to the attractive young woman.

When the door was firmly shut, she addressed the stunned faces seated around the rectangular table, "Now that you're over your initial shock, let's get down to business, shall we?" and her expression turned serious.

"The council and I have decided that it is time to put the next step into place."

Intuitively scanning the shocked faces before her with her incredible silver eyes, she continued, "We are very aware of the obstacles ahead of us, but we feel the obstacles would be greater if we tried to maintain our original time frame. I think you can understand how we came to that decision based on what is happening worldwide. The political unrest throughout the planet is becoming more and more unpredictable, the present administration in Washington forces our hand daily as to their environmental policies and," she paused for effect. "Bernadette Percival has discovered the Sinclair family."

Lenzi took a drink of water. "Our plan is to let the two young ones in the Western Hemisphere meet on their own – with our guidance, naturally. I was hoping that two people from your unit would volunteer to coordinate that effort. Philippe, you've been with us a long time, how does a trip to the states appeal?"

Philippe's expression revealed his surprise, and he nervously ran his hand across his tuft of white hair. "I assumed you'd select someone from the Paris unit." And then quickly added before the offer was withdrawn, "Of course, I'd be pleased to go. I would consider it an honor," and his compassionate features exuded confidence.

"I think it would be wise to have someone accompany you. You may choose whomever you want to work with from your unit, and then the two of you should make yourselves ready to leave in the next few weeks. My assistant Mari will be your contact person, once there. Will there be a problem leaving that soon?"

"No," Philippe said, almost too quickly, the hint of a smile still hovering on his thin lips.

Later that day when Philippe crossed the plaza to his parked car, his usually hunched slender shoulders were drawn back, reminiscent of his time in the military. He had been a person who felt he was overlooked most of his life, and to have this appointment bestowed on him gave him great satisfaction. To be singled out by Le Perfector was an honor beyond description for this humble man, and he was determined to make this mission successful. Lenzi had wisely allowed him to choose his own teammate. He and Francois had been together many years. It was an easy choice.

Lenzi spent the next two days with Philippe and Francois going over possible courses of action and time frames. She saw immediately that the two men worked well as a team and that Philippe was more than capable of pulling the American contingency together. As she suspected, he had the dexterity of mind, coupled with the emotional stability that this mission required, and Francois appeared to be a loyal comrade. One who didn't mind being second in command. *Yes, this will be a good team,* Lenzi thought.

In private late one night after a few glasses of Philippe's best French cognac, the lively Mediterranean breezes refreshing the stale air of his office, Lenzi confided in him. "I want you to understand that you were chosen for several reasons," and the light shining from her incredible eyes held his in more than mild curiosity. "You were selected because of your commitment over the years, your ability to lead and," a smile settled on her face as she raised her glass in a silent toast, "your Basque heritage."

CHAPTER 9

Bernadette sat on the edge of the motel bed, the busy flowered pattern of the spread accentuating her petite figure, which was wrapped snuggly in a white terrycloth robe. Her loose short curls fell forward as she began massaging her forehead. The phone still lay next to her. What kind of a game was this? Another phone call from that mysterious voice. Only this time he was telling her to contact Samuel Sinclair. His exact words were: "We have reconsidered. Contact with Mr. Sinclair might be helpful at this time."

Confusion overtook her. What had changed? Was this some kind of trick? The thoughts swirling in her mind were giving her a blinding headache, and she fell into a deep sleep.

Hours later the ringing phone woke her with a start. She stared at the inexpensive print of a famous Monet painting that hung above the nightstand.

Where am I?

The fog lifted as the memory of the earlier phone call flooded in.

She groped for the phone. *Should she answer it?*

Pushing the button with uncertainty, she hesitated.

"Hello?"

It was Samuel. "I know we agreed not to make phone contact, but something out of the ordinary has happened."

"What is it?"

"I received a most unexpected email. It told me I should help you. I emailed back and asked: "Who are you and why should I help her."

Bernadette's curiosity spilled over into his sentence. "Did you receive an answer?"

"Of sorts. It said when the time is right you will know. Until then, understand we are here to help."

"Help us what?" Bernadette blurted out. "Do they mean find the meaning of the Holy Grail?"

"I suppose. Their message was pretty vague."

"Well, at least were on the same page," she replied in a more controlled tone. Then, she shared the message in her phone call. "What do you make of all this? I don't like all this flip-flopping around. What changed that made them go from 'you can't' - to 'it would be beneficial?' And why can't they tell us who they are and what this is all about? Wouldn't that be better than keeping us in the dark?" and her voice showed her irritation.

"I don't understand their motives either, but I have some ideas. If you could spend the day at our house, we'll have the computer to help us."

The Sinclair's home was an old colonial that had been refurbished with impeccable taste. It sat on several acres in a wooded rural area. Bernadette savored the drive out, realizing how much she missed the beauty of New England. It was the groves of white-barked birch and the vivid green of the rambling countryside that spoke to her the most. California was never bright green. Most of the time, it was brown. The Chamber of Commerce liked to call it gold, but the only gold left in California was in the pockets of the politicians and large corporations that fleeced it daily.

Samuel's den suited him perfectly. Except for the modern computer set-up, it looked like a room out of another time frame. Paneled in a deep, rich maple, two walls boasted bookcases that bulged with volumes whose worn covers reflected they were well-read. Bernadette saw immediately that their tastes for literature were the same, and she experienced another fleeting regret that Samuel was married. Dressed in a brown tweed jacket and tan shirt, he cut quite a handsome figure. His wife was nowhere to be seen.

Appearing uncomfortable, Samuel remained standing.

"I have some water on the stove, I'll get us some tea," he announced rather abruptly, and then disappeared down the long hallway, leaving Bernadette alone for what seemed a long time.

As the silence of the house closed in on her, a thought flashed across her mind.

I'm alone in an isolated house with a man I barely know!

Panic rushed in and began to suffocate her, as she realized her intrigue with her father's letters and Samuel's good looks had overshadowed her common sense. A deep dread hit in the pit of her stomach. *What was I thinking coming here by myself? What if it was Samuel who made that second phone call as a ploy to get me out here?*

Her immediate instinct was to bolt. *But where?*

Her eyes nervously scanned the room looking for another escape route when they were drawn to a half-opened drawer where something glimmering in the light captured her attention. Focusing her eyes, she was shocked to see it was the ornate handle of a long-barreled pistol. At the same time she heard Samuel's footsteps coming rapidly down the hall.

CHAPTER 10

The door banged against the wall as Samuel pushed it open with his foot, causing Bernadette to jump, her face etched with fear. He was carrying a tea tray, but the look on his face seemed anything but sociable when he placed it on a small table between them. He immediately began to pour, and in the process his hand glanced the creamer, spilling it onto the floor.

Bernadette instinctively grabbed some napkins to soak it up, but when she sat upright, her apprehension heightened. The drawer with the pistol had been closed. *Had Samuel purposely spilled the cream to divert her attention?*

She nervously searched his face. It seemed innocent enough, but if he had no ulterior motives, why would he hide the gun? She tried to keep her hand from shaking when she picked up her cup.

Samuel, seeing her uneasiness asked, "Is there something wrong?"

Should she tell him the truth or would that tip the scales. Perhaps she should humor him. Pretend she had to use the bathroom and slip out the door.

He took a step towards her, and she recoiled into the chair.

"Look, I'm feeling uncomfortable myself," he confessed. "I expected my wife to be home when I extended my invitation to you. I didn't realize she had a committee meeting scheduled for this afternoon. If it would make you feel better, we can do this another time?"

Bernadette stammered, "I saw . . . a gun in the drawer . . . you hid it . . . when . . . when I was bent down!"

Samuel opened the drawer, and as he pulled out the gun, he saw the alarm spread on her face.

"It's empty," he showed her. "And I doubt you can find ammunition for it anymore. It's a relic from the Civil War. My father was a gun collector, and since I'm a pacifist, I've never felt comfortable having weapons under my roof. I've been selling them off, and there was a gentleman here yesterday to look at it."

"Why did you close the drawer, when I wasn't looking?"

"I didn't even realize I closed it. According to my wife, I'm a neat freak. I suppose it was an automatic response to something out of order."

Bernadette studied his face. *He showed her there was no ammunition in the gun and now she could see it was a relic. But___!*

"Look, you're the one who flew across the country to seek me out. I didn't come to you," he said, irritated that she might think he was capable of something sinister.

She hesitated, searching the depths of his blue eyes. Conflicting thoughts flashed through her mind. *The threatening phone calls. Samuel's strange behavior today. Yet, he was a best-selling author, a college professor. Would a man of that status succumb to . . . ?*

He continued to stare, waiting for an answer.

She hesitated. Summoning her courage, she tried to be logical. *If he had other things on his mind, he certainly had a perfect opportunity when I was alone with him in his car.*

Her rationale kicked in. *He's right, I was the one who instigated this relationship, and if I left now, I'd probably never come back and get the answers I came here hoping to find.*

"I'm sorry, but these strange phone calls are making me paranoid," she finally relinquished.

"I understand," he said sympathetically. "Feel free to leave, and we'll do this sometime when Julia's home, and he stepped back motioning to the door.

Attempting to control her nerves, Bernadette pulled in a long, deep breath. "No, I'm okay, now. "If it's all right with you, I'd like to proceed with our original agenda," and her eyes were apologetic.

Samuel nodded, although he sat down somewhat reluctantly. He was having his own doubts about this collaboration.

"I have copies of all the letters my father entrusted to me in here," she said, handing him a folder, and despite her efforts, her hand quivered. "You've only seen two. Perhaps if you sift through these, something will jump out at you," and her manner remained cautious.

Samuel exchanged seats with her so she could browse through the research material on his computer. A half hour later, blurry eyed he asked, "What is this reference to the next step?"

Bernadette appeared confused, so Samuel stood and handed her a letter, pointing to a sentence.

Reacting to his close physical proximity, she became guarded. "I assumed they meant the next thing to do on their agenda."

"That's not how it struck me. They way they refer to it in more than one letter, it almost seems to have a specific meaning. Listen to this, and he read, "Soon it will be time to put the next step into place."

Bernadette reached for the letter, and as she read it to herself, her look turned incredulous, "I can't believe in all these years, I never noticed it before, but you're right," and the thought of a clandestine organization having an unknown agenda made her heart race as uncomfortable thoughts for her and Mallory's safety seeped in.

Sensing her apprehension, Samuel wished he had words of reassurance for her, but privately, he had the same concerns.

There was an uncomfortable moment of silence.

"Is it possible," Samuel ventured, "these letters are from the Priory of Sion?" Allegedly the Priory was the secret society that currently had possession of the documents that delineated Jesus' bloodline. They were referred to as the Sangreal Documents.

"Do you believe the Priory actually exists?" Bernadette asked with raised eyebrows. "There's been so much controversy about their legitimacy that I certainly have my doubts."

"It's hard to know for sure," Samuel conceded, "but I'm willing to bet if they don't, there's another secret organization that does, and it's so obscure that its name would be difficult to uncover. So for practical purposes, we can keep referring to it as the Priory. And if your father's letters are from the Priory or another secret society, the next step could mean releasing the Sangreal Documents, and perhaps even producing Jesus' assumed heir."

Bernadette shook her head, and a small frown formed between her eyes. "Although that conclusion seems probable, it stretches my comprehension of how any relationship between that kind of organization and my father could possibly have been established."

"Well, he did have the letters."

"Yes, and clearly he recognized their importance, since he passed them on to me as his dying words. I only wish he had given me some clue to their meaning. And now, all these strange phone calls." Bernadette's voice was strained. "What do you make of their recent about face saying it might be helpful if we established contact?"

"I don't know what to make of it," Samuel frowned, "It may be they're trying to gain our confidence to set us up. My instinct is not to trust them."

"I have an idea, though," he continued. "I have a friend who's a computer whiz. Maybe he can trace that email they sent to us."

"Do you think it's wise to pursue this without the help of the authorities?"

"Under the circumstances, I doubt they can do anything. Didn't you try that once before without any results?"

Her expression was solemn when she nodded.

"I think it's worth a try to trace their email. Although I suspect if we do find out anything, it's only because that's what they wanted."

"I have to admit," she confessed, "there's a part of me that doesn't want to know who they are. It's hard to trust those who choose to stay in the shadows. Why can't they just come out and tell us what's going on?"

"If it is a secret society," Samuel said, "My understanding is that's how they work. Their rationale is, if you haven't figured things out for yourself, the information doesn't have the same impact on you. When you're handed all the facts, you're suspicious of the conclusion. On the other hand, if you discover it yourself, it becomes a great revelation. That's why enlightenment must be an individual journey and can't be taught."

Bernadette moved over to a deep leather armchair, her dark curly hair bouncing youthfully as she moved. In her gray slacks and light pink sweater, she looked much younger than her fifty-one years. She had slipped off her shoes and folded her legs under her. "What initially sparked your interest in the Holy Grail, Samuel?"

"Oh I suppose initially it was just my writer's instincts looking for a good story. And then, when it turned out my surname had some connection, I became even more intrigued."

"Yes, Sinclair, Saint Claire, the purported Scottish branch of the Holy Grail bloodline. The branch that many believe brought the Grail to this continent."

"Isn't it strange, each of us having a name linked to the Grail. Mine from the Scottish bloodline and yours from the mystical French tales. Do you suppose your father's connection was through his name and French heritage?"

"But my father wasn't French, nor was my mother," she emphasized. "Percival is my married name, and my father's correspondence dates back to before I was married or even knew my ex-husband."

Bernadette's declaration truly surprised Samuel. It had never occurred to him that Percival wasn't her given name, although it should have. She'd mentioned her daughter more than once. He pondered, "That makes it even more coincidental that you happened to marry a man with that name, *after* your father had these letters."

"Exactly, one of the many coincidences that plague my life, yet seem to go nowhere. Although I must admit that more and more I'm beginning to see that these coincidences aren't coincidences at all. Somehow they're prearranged. Like we have the blueprint in our DNA, and then we're just drawn to certain people or things. That's why it's important to follow our intuition. That's what brought me to Massachusetts to contact you. When I first saw your picture on the back of your book cover, I felt an immediate connection and a strong compulsion that we needed to talk. Now, I'm suddenly realizing that, if we can stay out of the fear of this situation, the clues will continue to come, and ultimately lead us to the answers," and she looked at him with a steadfast gaze, pausing a long moment. "Pleiades, the Holy Grail, you and me - somehow we're all connected," she whispered, and again the conviction in her voice gripped Samuel, pulling him ever deeper into the mystery.

CHAPTER 11

Washington, D.C.:

Now don't get so riled up, boys. I'll have the president eating out of my hand again in no time," the vice president promised in his smooth southern drawl. "Truth is, it's a good thing that he's beginning to have that kind of confidence. I'll just make sure it's pointed in the right direction. No one can be controlled easier than a man who's full of himself. I think this might be a good time to start feeding him all those poll statistics that we've manipulated to make it look like he's way ahead of the opposition. He's a *great* front runner, have you noticed?" Snickering could be heard around the room.

"Whatever you do, Henry, do it quick. We can't have that idiot thinking he's really at the helm of this ship. Last week he had the audacity to question me in a cabinet meeting about that bill we pushed through Congress disguised as a tax break for the elderly. Keep him busy doodling around with insignificant issues. And, for God's sake, get his wife out in front of the cameras! She has that all-American housewife look that the public seems to love."

"That might be a little harder than dealing with the president. She can be a tough little cookie that one. Doesn't say much, but I can see the wheels turning."

"Well, get her under control and into the limelight. It might be interesting if you had them interviewed on television as the ideal American couple by one of the big three. Someone we're sure will ask the right questions. You know, the sweet little wife who's totally supportive of the take-charge husband angle. The conservative right will eat it up."

"I'll see what I can do," the vice president shrugged. "Word is that behind the cameras the sweet little wife is getting fed up with that expanding ego. Like I said, he's starting to believe he's a great and inspired leader. I hear tell he's getting pretty headstrong around the home front. Wouldn't want his constituents to pick up on that."

"We don't care what you do or how you do it Henry, but keep him busy until we get the Phoenix Project sewed up. We don't want him to get wind of that one."

Henry Connolly breathed a sigh of relief as he walked down the back steps of the historical brick building to where his car and driver were waiting. Exiting into the fresh air, he took some deep breaths, relishing the coolness before he slid into the back seat of his car. He didn't like the way things were lining up. Keeping track of the President was getting to be a full time job these days, and he was getting tired of being in charge of damage control. He had too many other things to take care of to be wasting his time babysitting that egotistical moron.

When Henry made the decision to come back into the political arena, he knew there'd be lots of pressure, but this had surpassed anything he imagined. He preferred the private sector where he could work without the omnipresent eye of the media cameras. He straightened his conservatively striped silk tie several times. It was a nervous habit he developed since the reporters began hounding him. It was important in this business to project the right image.

The cell phone in his car rang. *"Now what?"* he wondered. *Life in Washington was becoming one emergency after another.* His voice was abrupt when he answered.

Paris, France:

News traveled with uncanny speed since the ushering in of the age of sophisticated electronics. Paris had already received word from Montpellier that Le Perfector was an aging woman, giving them ample time to adjust before her arrival. What they didn't know until Le Perfector told them was that the Montpellier Unit would have a more active role than Paris in setting the stage in America. And that didn't sit well with some of them, particularly Alain DeBuine.

Alain was a handsome man with a regal bearing. Born into an aristocratic family that had long been associated with Lenzi's organization, Alain's membership had been his birthright more than a personal choice. Although Alain studied with them most of his adult life and believed in the information, he was generally lacking in application. His strong ego was resistant to accepting those he considered to be beneath his station as equals. Generally, he preferred to mingle only with others from his privileged class. As a consequence, he felt more than a little slighted by what he considered to be this monumental irregularity in protocol by Le Perfector. *Imagine someone from Montpellier being selected above him. Why let the lowly stepson handle what was the rightful job of the son? Leave it to a woman!*

Alain pondered for many days over what, in his eyes, was a major indiscretion. During that time he dragged himself through a labyrinth of negative thoughts that ultimately brought his heart to that dark place where reason can no longer exist. Under the circumstances, it was not surprising that his tormented ego ultimately sabotaged his finer instincts, and one morning, after a fretful night's sleep, his face drawn with contempt, he slipped into his silk robe and pulled the belt into a tight knot with an angry jerk. His stride was purposeful as he moved towards his designer phone, revenge stamped across his handsome features. Dialing the international operator, he requested a number in Washington D.C.

"Who did you say you are?" the voice on the other end was having difficulty with the accent and the crackling line.

"It's not who I am, but who I am associated with that is important to your government. There is a plot that has been put into place that will greatly affect the goals of the present administration. Mention the name Phoenix Project to the highest-ranking official that you have access to and then give them my phone number."

When Alain replaced the phone, he had a sardonic smile plastered on his face, giving his handsome features a fiercely sinister look.

CHAPTER 12

Samuel's offer came as a surprise. "My wife suggested that you consider moving into the small guest cottage on our property. It's far enough from the main house to give us all complete privacy. Why don't you give it a look, and see what you think?"

"That's very generous of your wife. You're sure I wouldn't be in the way?" Bernadette had yet to catch even a glimpse of the wife.

"Positive. The guesthouse is small, but pleasantly situated in the back of the garden. It's entirely self-sufficient, if you're inclined to prepare meals. It would save you a good deal of money and cut down on commute time for both of us. It would also give you the opportunity of getting acquainted with Julia. My wife worked with me on the research for my book and knows as much about the Holy Grail as we do. I consider her input invaluable, and I'm sure you will too. She often sees something I might miss or has a different slant that propels me in another direction."

Bernadette felt her face flush as an uncomfortable jealousy emerged upon hearing Samuel brag about his wife. It took all of her effort to subdue. "I'd like to meet your wife before I make a decision."

"I understand. She'll be home this afternoon. Come for lunch – let's say noon?"

Bernadette tried not to show her surprise when at last she came to meet Samuel's wife. She had visualized an attractive woman with a model-like figure, fashionably dressed in the latest style. Julia was nothing like she imagined. The best description Bernadette could come up with was plain. Julia's strawberry blonde hair lacked style, and her manner of dress was rather frumpy, which did little to enhance her rather plump figure. Bernadette couldn't help but think she would have been a perfect candidate for a makeover. All the possibilities were there, nice hair color, blue eyes that twinkled, features that were even.

Blessed with a perky personality, however, Julia instantly lit up the room with her delightful conversation and easy laughter, complimenting Samuel's more conservative style, and completely winning Bernadette's confidence. It was almost as if she and Julia were old friends, and with that immediate bond, Bernadette felt an instant abating of any sexual attraction towards Samuel.

After lunch they moved down the long hall where simply framed photographs of the New England countryside guided the way to Samuel's study. While the women were seating themselves, Samuel picked up a large book off his desk and flashed the title towards Bernadette.

Her eyes became wide as she read the title. *"UFO Contact From the Pleiades."*

"Julia picked it up at a used book store," he smiled, as if pleased to prove to Bernadette that his wife could be of assistance to them.

"Tell her what you found out," he prompted his wife.

Julia had a pleasant singsong voice and round blue eyes that twinkled. "The book is about a farmer in Switzerland named Billy Meier, who professes to have made contact with the Pleiadians. It's full of pictures that he's supposedly taken of their spacecraft. He's even had discussions with them about their planet and why they're here, which is supposedly to help us evolve. Naturally, this is all very controversial. The thing that struck me was he said the same thing that you did."

Bernadette's expression was one of shock. "And what was that?" She had seen a synopsis of Billy Meier's story on the Internet, and just brushed him off as some crackpot. Being compared to him wasn't exactly a compliment.

"He said he heard a voice in his head that told him to get his camera and drive to a specific place in order to take pictures of their spaceships," and she smiled somewhat triumphantly, her apple cheeks becoming more pronounced.

"Samuel said you had a similar experience where a voice woke you up and told you to turn on the T.V. When you did, there was a program being aired that gave you information on Pleiades."

Hearing it come from someone else's lips made Bernadette realize how bizarre her story sounded. *Would she have believed it if someone else told her? Probably not. Ha, who was she kidding, definitely not? So was she a crackpot as well!* She stared at the couple across from her.

Seeing Bernadette's distress, Julia added, "I thought it would please you to know that someone else had the same experience."

"It would have if the someone wasn't a little loony."

"This from the woman who told *me* to keep an open mind," Samuel accused in jest.

Bernadette blushed. "You're right, but you have to admit his story is out there."

"So is yours, and yet you *know* it happened. In fairness to this Billy Meier fellow, I checked him out on the Internet and found there are as many experts who support his experience - based on what they believe to be the authenticity of his pictures - as those who refute it."

"Also based on his pictures, which others claim have been tampered with," Bernadette quipped.

"Always a pro and a con," Samuel retaliated. "But to keep a perspective, we know that through the ages it hasn't been uncommon for men to be demonized or persecuted because they held a belief that was different from the accepted thought of the day. A classic example was Galileo who was tried for heresy and sentenced to life imprisonment because he claimed the Earth wasn't the center of the Universe. Even though his prison sentence was quickly converted to house arrest, many of his manuscripts were burned as the work of the devil. Who knows? Billy Meier might be the Galileo of this century!"

"Do you believe his story?" Bernadette asked incredulously.

Samuel shrugged. "Let's just say the jury's still out. However," and the word seemed to hang in the air, "I think it would be wise not to entirely discount it. And apparently there are many others out there who believe his story or who at the very least have great interest in it, because the owner of the used bookstore told Julia that his book is often requested and it's difficult to get copies of it. "

"What I thought was interesting," Julia interjected, "Was that the Pleiadians told Herr Meier that they send messages to many people, but most choose not to listen or give it any credence."

Bernadette laughed, and her curls moved seductively. "Can't imagine why people wouldn't listen to voices in their heads talking about spaceships!"

"You did." Samuel's voice was soft.

Bernadette became defensive. "Mine just said to go turn on the television. I didn't know what the subject matter was going to be. In fact, it was an astronomy program on the public broadcasting channel discussing facts about the heavens – not spaceships!" And then, realizing how angry her voice sounded, she flashed them a sheepish look of apology. "Guess I'm not as open-minded as I pretend to be."

Julia was full of information. "I'm sure you're aware that there is a lot of what they call channeling going on these days."

"I've heard the term, but I'm not exactly sure what's meant by it."

"It's purportedly a voice from another dimension speaking through someone in this dimension. It would probably be a good guess to say that some of them are not legitimate, however, I've read more than a few books that have been written through channeled sources, and I have to say the information seems to be valid."

"Define valid," Bernadette said, making an effort to keep the sarcastic tone out of her voice.

"As if it came from a higher source. One of the more widespread works is compiled under the title *A Course in Miracles*. Have you ever heard of it?"

"No, I haven't, but it sounds religious."

"I would define it more as spiritual than religious. It's information that was given to Helen Schucman, a professor of psychology at the Columbia Medical Center." Julia paused to make her point. "She received it the same way that you and Billy Meier did."

"A voice in her head?"

"That's right. In this case the voice was purportedly that of Jesus. This woman was a professor of psychology, hardly a charlatan."

Bernadette sat motionless, staring at the couple across from her in disbelief.

Samuel broke the silence. "I find it interesting that you were the one that brought up the Pleiades connection, and now you're the one who is backing away from it."

"You're right," Bernadette relented reluctantly, and with a slight grimace she extended her arm towards Samuel.

"Maybe I'd better read that book," and the moment she reached out for it, she had a flashback. She was seven or eight years old, bundled up in a red winter coat, her curls peeking out of the matching hat. Red had always been her father's favorite color on her. He had bought her the outfit for her birthday. It was a cold autumn night in Connecticut, but that hadn't kept them from their nightly ritual of stargazing. She could still hear her father's voice as he pointed towards the sky. "There's our constellation," he murmured poignantly, pointing to The Seven Sisters.

It was only after daddy died that she discovered that The Seven Sisters was another name for the Pleiades.

CHAPTER 13

"You're staying where?" Mallory asked incredulously. "Who are these people, Mom?"

In frustration, Mallory flopped onto the chair in her office cubicle, her long brunette tresses falling in waves around her shoulders. Nothing her mother was doing was making any sense. Moving onto the property of a couple she hardly knew and extending her trip indefinitely was completely impulsive and out of character. What was she thinking!

The situation wouldn't have been so disturbing if her mother hadn't mentioned that threatening phone call the last time they spoke. Yet, when Mallory brought it up today, her mother shrugged it off as if it was nothing. Again, out of character.

Leaving the parking garage of the downtown office building where she worked, Mallory maneuvered onto the freeway, checking her watch. It was the one her mother bought her for her birthday, and the memory of the occasion brought a smile. She hoped she was leaving Sacramento early enough to beat the commuter surge, but looking ahead, she could see the traffic already beginning to snarl. It depressed her to see the highways leading up to the foothills beginning to resemble the clogged freeways in the Bay Area. She remembered a time when it wasn't this way. *How long can this population explosion continue without disastrous results? It was already too taxing on the planet.*

Mallory added today's mail to the stack that was already sitting on the kitchen counter, and then as an afterthought, picked it up and sorted through it. Mostly bills and advertisements, but there was one envelope that looked interesting. Slipping off her shoes, she opened it while she clicked on the evening news. Halfway through the first paragraph, she muted the television and began reading it again. This time more slowly, so she could absorb every word.

It was from an environmental consulting firm in Virginia asking her to apply for an available position. She reread the letter several times, wondering how they had gotten her name. The letter said she had been recommended as a prospective candidate, but it didn't say by whom. The available position was as an environmental consultant working with the private sector. Exactly the kind of job she had always hoped for, something that would give her the opportunity of influencing private industries that truly wanted to better serve the environment. This was her dream, but in her wildest fantasies she hadn't expected it to happen this soon or even in the foreseeable future. It was as if a miracle had been unexpectedly dropped in her lap.

In her excitement she felt the sudden need to move. She wanted to tell someone or shout it to the skies. She began to dance through her apartment, her long tresses twirling around her like waves of chocolate satin. *Calm down, calm down. This is just a request to submit an application. You haven't gotten the job yet.*

Rereading the letter, her pounding heart felt as if it might explode. She wasn't familiar with the company, but she liked the name – The Trillium Group. Most noteworthy was the logo in the upper right hand corner of the letterhead - a fleur de lys. Her familiarity with the symbol went back to her grandfather's letters that her mother had shared with her when she reached her teenage years. Strange letters sent to such an ordinary man. She was only nine when he died, however, he had been a significant influence in her life. Grandfather had little formal education, but he was very wise in the cosmic sense. A visionary, who was a true citizen of the Universe. Interesting, the coincidence of the symbol.

Mallory's computer was old and sluggish. Investing in a new one hadn't been a priority. Her nimble fingers typed in *fleur de lys* and hit the search key.

She quickly moved from Website to Website, reading snippets of information from here and there. Often referred to as a controversial emblem, the fleur de lys was said to represent the lily, a flower that was claimed to have sprung from the tears of Eve as she left the Garden of Eden. Although from its earliest records it was also synonymous with purity. Originally associated with the Greek moon goddess Hera, it later became symbolic of the Virgin Mary. It also had a strong association with the Holy Trinity through history, yet was conversely associated with the Jewish custom of circumcision as well. *Hmm, didn't her mother mention something about that in the past? That the symbol tied Jesus' Jewish heritage to the Catholic faith?*

Mallory continued searching. Sometime around the tenth century, the fleur de lys became the emblem of the French royalty, which Mallory thought rather odd, since during that period it was common practice for the sovereignties of Europe to choose animals to portray their houses, usually those depicting great power such as the lion. *How strange that the French would have chosen the symbol of a humble flower – one that was strongly connected to feminine energy - when most were displaying emblems that represented a strong warrior image!*

Moving away from her computer, Mallory read the letter from the Trillium Group one more time, a big smile dominating her pretty features. The company was based in Richmond, Virginia. Was it a coincidence that the perfect job opportunity magically appeared out of nowhere, and it was close to those famed Blue Ridge Mountains that kept calling her?

Her fingers brushed across their logos. "Fleur de lys," she whispered. "Maybe Grandfather is helping me from the other side."

Everyone on the plane noticed the attractive young girl with the bright smile and the dark flashing eyes. Her wavy hair tumbled over her shoulders in a most becoming style, adding to her youthful appeal. She had an innocence reflected on her face that made her appear younger than her twenty-six years.

"You look very happy, my dear", the older woman in the seat next to her commented. "You have the look of someone going to meet their lover."

A spontaneous laugh rippled into the air. "No, not a lover, but the next best thing," Mallory confessed. "An interview for my dream job."

"Oh, how nice. I hope it works out for you."

"I don't know why, but something is telling me it will." And she settled back in her seat.

Mallory had been too excited to sleep the night before the trip. Asking the stewardess for a pillow, she quickly dozed off to the hum of the engines and the slight rocking motion in the cabin. Later, when the plane dropped suddenly, it woke her with a jolt, and she flashed on a dream she was having.

She was on a mountain ridge enjoying the solitude and beauty of the spectacular view, when a movement on the trail in the distance caught her attention. It was someone approaching on the footpath winding towards her. As the figure wove closer, she could see it was a young man about her age. He waved as if he knew her, and she returned the greeting. There was something familiar about him, yet she couldn't say what. He wasn't close enough for her to see his features clearly, except for his long blonde ponytail that tumbled down his back in a mass of tangled ringlets. That's when she was jarred out of her deep sleep by the turbulent motion of the plane.

"That was quite a bump," her seatmate said. "I'm glad I wasn't standing at the time."

Mallory smiled. Her dream had left her with a pleasant feeling, a promise of something to come. The scenes seemed so real. *Maybe it's something I'm going to experience while I'm back here,* and that thought pleased her as she adjusted her pillow and settled back in her seat.

Mallory graduated from college four years ago, and had since been working at a job in Sacramento, which was an hour commute from her home in the foothills of the Sierra Mountains. She began at an entry-level position, and in four years had worked her way an insignificant distance up the corporate ladder. The job she would be interviewing for in Richmond appeared to require a lot more responsibility, but she felt confident she could handle it.

It wasn't only her professional ambition that was pushing her, but her desire to have a positive impact on the environment that she so dearly loved. And moving to the Atlantic Coast was something she had been thinking about for some time. To find them both packaged in one opportunity was very exciting. *I never did ask them how they got my name.* And with that thought, their logo flashed in her mind. *The fleur de lys.* And again she was tantalized by the coincidence that the perfect job came with the symbol that was liberally sprinkled through those strange letters her grandfather had kept hidden? Letters that her mother seemed convinced had something to do with the Holy Grail.

CHAPTER 14

The atmosphere in the Vice President's office was frenzied as assistants scurried in and out in a frantic attempt to get a handle on the current situation. There seemed to be no end to the ringing phones. Two days ago a Frenchman called saying he had information regarding the Phoenix Project. The message took almost two full days to reach the Vice President because no one in the White House had ever heard of the Phoenix Project. Only a handful of people on the hill were privy to that information. So how the blazes did somebody in France get wind of it! In an act of frustration, Henry ran his fingers through his thinning salt and pepper hair. He thought *that* one was sewn up tight.

The circumstances had become all the more complicated by the fact that he couldn't tell anyone in his office why this situation was so urgent. That he was upset was a fact experienced by all. His usually smooth-as-silk southern accent had been replaced by a fire and brimstone intonation that could be heard echoing through the halls.

"I want you to find out everything, I mean everything on a Frenchman named Alain DeBuine. And I want it before noon today," and he slammed his fist against his massive oak desk, rattling the framed pictures of his family that sat off to the side.

Dashing out, his assistants shrugged. Who was this guy DeBuine, and why had he suddenly become top priority?

Alone in his office, Connolly slipped off his jacket, something he rarely did unless he was home alone. He went to great expense to have his suits tailored to make his slender shoulders look broader while at the same time hiding his pouching gut. He knew how important it was to present the right image in Washington. He wiped the sweat from his brow. Now he was left to face a serious dilemma. Should he inform the others in his tight little group about the current situation? His immediate reaction was 'No!' Why stir up the pot if it was nothing? But if it was something and he didn't tell them __!

Opening the prescription bottle in his drawer, Henry slipped a pill into his mouth and made an instant decision. He'd wait until he got some information on this Frenchman before he alerted the others. Two hours wouldn't make that much difference at this point, and it might save him a world of trouble. What disturbed him the most was this guy had dropped the name Phoenix Project. What were the odds that he was simply a crackpot who had inadvertently come up with the right name? Connolly's hand was visibly shaking when he unscrewed the cap of the prescription bottle for a second time and slipped another pill into his mouth.

Four hours later in France, four men in an unmarked sedan were speeding towards the German border. The driver's eyes were glued to the road, his face expressionless. The man in the passenger seat had a military haircut and eyes that squinted even though the sun was to the rear. Alain DeBuine was wedged in the back seat, noticeably uncomfortable in such close proximity to the large, muscular man next to him. There was no conversation.

When they reached the military base in Stuttgart, the driver showed his credentials to the guard posted at the gate, who after examining the papers and vehicle, saluted and waved them past, and Alain was whisked onto the military jet waiting for him. He was quite irritated with the Americans' treatment thus far, and he didn't bother to hide his disdain for them. His expectation had been one of hero, not the glorified prisoner status he felt he was receiving.

The muscular gentleman from the back seat of the car accompanied him onto the plane, shadowing his every move as if he was a dangerous criminal. *I suppose I should forgive them. They probably have no idea why I'm being escorted to their country. Lowly creatures that they are wouldn't be privy to that sort of classified information.*

The jet engines roared with thundering power as they lifted off the runway, the angle of their assent so steep that Alain's body was thrust into the back of his seat with a powerful force. He turned and looked disturbingly at the muscular buffoon next to him.

"Is this normal?"

"Military take-off," the expressionless face grunted over the plane's roar.

Back in Washington, Henry Connolly nervously paced his office, his eyes focused on the ticking clock. Before he dialed his cell phone, he checked to see that his office door was locked. His face looked desperate.

"What___!" The voice on the other end responded.

Henry mustered up a false confidence. "Don't worry, we already have the scoop on this guy. As we speak, he's being escorted onto a military jet headed for the States."

"Is he a double agent?"

"I don't think so, he appears to be clean. One of those European aristocrats; his family's French and Austrian."

"Who knows about this besides you?"

"No one. I didn't give the military any explanation as to why they're bringing him here. The biggest problem I see is keeping him under wraps until we can have a nice long chat. We can't keep him in Washington – and Camp David's out. It has to be somewhere close, otherwise we have the problem of secured transportation that's not highly visible. I thought you might know of a place."

"Maybe. Let me check with the others and call you back. And Henry," and the voice on the other end turned dark. "Don't let this situation get any further out of control or some extreme measures will have to be taken." Pause "You get my meaning?"

Henry froze in his chair, beads of perspiration glistening on is forehead. He knew *exactly* what that meant.

"Don't worry, one way or another I'll have this under control by tomorrow," he stated with a confidence he didn't feel.

CHAPTER 15

Located in an old Victorian structure that at one time housed the City Hall, the building in downtown Richmond, Virginia where The Trillium Group now maintained their office boasted a beautiful interior courtyard, reminding the two men of the architectural ambiance of their native city. Philippe had worked hard at losing his French accent and had Americanized his name to Philip Boule. Francois was now Frank, and although he had not been as successful in the accent department, his was at least acceptable.

"It is nice that Le Perfector selected a city not far from the water, or I would have found it difficult. The Mediterranean has been our backyard for so long, I would have succumbed to homesickness had we been too landlocked."

"Yes," Francois agreed, "and the climate here is similar to Montpellier's, but not the ambiance."

"No, but it is pleasant. The Americans have been quite welcoming, don't you agree?"

"Yes, but the name Frank! It's so harsh," he complained. "Francois rolls on the tongue. Frank sounds like an assault."

"It's only for a short time. You will become use to it."

"I hope not," was the disgusted reply.

Philippe smiled. He knew Francois' penchant towards pessimism was only surface. Underneath he was quite a good fellow. But he did love to complain.

"Well, I wanted to call you Francis, I knew that would be more pleasing to your ear, but they tell me that's not a name so popular for men any more. Frank is macho, like the bull!" Philippe knew what appealed to the younger man.

Francois' face lit up. "Maybe there will be a time for the bull to check out the marketplace, eh?" And his broad smile was accentuated by his distinct moustache. "This one we just interviewed – Mallory Percival. Oh la la! She's a beauty." And then seeing Philippe's stern gaze, he put both his hands up, "I know, I know, but it doesn't hurt for the eyes to appreciate God's masterful creations."

"Keep your appreciation from a distance, my friend," Philippe cautioned, and he punctuated his warning with a harsh stare over his wire-rimmed glasses. "Le Perfector has plans for this one, and it is much more serious than a fleeting romance with you. Now let's get down to business, shall we? We still have much to do."

"Where is that list of Congressmen?" Philippe asked, raising his pure-white eyebrows. "We are about to become great lobbyists."

"Do you think it will be that easy to persuade them to see our point of view?"

Philippe's smile had more than a hint of smugness. "Our persuasion will come in more than words," and he waved a checkbook in the air. "Le Perfector understands the ways of politicians, *non?*"

Locking their office, the two men headed towards their favorite lunchtime eatery. They had grown fond of the local Virginia-style ham sandwiches piled high with an assortment of fresh vegetables. The day was mild, so they ordered them to go and headed towards the James River to find a bench where the gentle breezes off the water could be enjoyed.

Since early childhood, Philippe had been drawn to the water's edge. As a youngster, his father often took him to the Mediterranean where they would swim or fish or sometimes do nothing more than watch the boats. The activities were always of a joyous nature to the young boy, and he came to equate water with happiness.

The James River flowed through the heart of Richmond, revitalizing the lifeblood of the city by economically connecting it to the Atlantic seaports, and just as importantly, providing its residents with many opportunities of connecting with nature. Today, the balmy temperatures and sunshine had enticed more than Philippe and Francois to its shores. Philippe took great pleasure in watching the assortment of colorful boats - kayaks, canoes, sailboats - drifting in and out of their view. He was especially fond of the large, white paddle wheeler that cruised up and down, its decks lined with tourists.

"Some day we must take a ride on her," he declared softly as his tuft of white hair moved with the gentle breezes.

Francois didn't bother to answer. *Boats, who cared about boats?* He was preoccupied with studying the pretty women passing who were wearing a pleasing array of short skirts and tight pants!

Philippe's thoughts drifted back to a conversation that had taken place with Lenzi before he left France. He had been surprised when she revealed to him that one of the reasons he had been chosen for this mission was his Basque heritage. His astonishment at the time had kept him from asking the obvious. *What possible difference would that make?*

Since then, Lenzi's revelation plagued him. He knew there where elitists who propagated the idea that the Basque people were genetically distinct and even superior to other races. The fact that the Basque language was unique, unlike any other language in existence was something that could not be denied. Linguists and historians had tried to discover its origins, hoping it would reveal the origins of the people as well, but to no avail. So a Basque claim to uniqueness was a legitimate one. However, Philippe knew it was a vast mistake to bridge that uniqueness into superiority. Didn't Hitler show us, without a doubt, the pitfalls of that kind of irrational thinking?

Philippe had been associated with Le Perfector and her organization for most of his adult life. It was a society based on the belief that humanity was on the cusp of a new way of thinking, and consequently, a new way of living. A kinder, gentler way in which all men live interconnected in peace and harmony with the earth and everything on it. It would be difficult to believe that someone who professed such loving thoughts and ideals could entertain the idea of a superior race. But what else could Le Perfector have possibly meant when she brought up his Basque heritage? He must remember to ask her.

CHAPTER 16

As a last minute thought, Mallory grabbed her sweatshirt, remembering how cool they kept the temperatures on planes, and draped it over her shoulders. Earlier she had brushed some blush on her cheeks in a vain attempt at perking up her appearance, but a quick glance in the mirror told her it hadn't helped much. She was exhausted from the emotional extremes she was experiencing worrying over her recent job interview. On the one hand she felt very confident about the way her meeting with the Trillium Group had gone, on the other hand a great deal of anxiety was attached to the outcome. One never knew about interviews, and she so badly wanted this job. Her worry was that her portfolio might not be as extensive as the other applicants. She had no way of knowing that there were no other applicants.

Finding her designated seat, she settled in for the flight to Boston. The plane appeared to be full to capacity and she immediately felt claustrophobic in the cramped cabin. Gratefully, it wouldn't be a long trip. As the 'fasten your seat belt' sign flashed, her mind rushed back to the dream she had on her last flight. *It hadn't been much of a dream, really. Nothing of importance happened, yet it left her with an overwhelming feeling of excitement. No, it was more than excitement, it was a wonderful expectation that something exhilarating was about to happen.*

She remembered vividly how genuinely pleased the young man in her dream was to see her, almost as if he had been expecting her to be there. The memory of the moment made her heart soar with anticipation.

Like many young women, Mallory tended to be a romantic and secretly held the hope that her knight in shining armor would one day appear. In her early teens, she was drawn to the romance and adventure of the Arthurian legends and stories of Camelot, all the more personal to her because of her last name. The knight Percival, through his innocence and purity of heart, was the only knight to ever see the Grail, which many believed was a sign of his chosen divinity.

She smiled. Perhaps the young man in her dream was her chosen knight who would turn out to be innocent and pure of heart. She liked that thought and dwelt on it during the boring flight. It helped keep her mind off the disappointment she felt at being compelled to make this trip to Boston to check on her mother's new adventure. She would have preferred to stay in Virginia to do some hiking through the Blue Ridge Mountains, especially after that dream. But the mountains – and her potential knight in shining armor – would have to wait for another day.

It was Saturday midday and the traffic going to Logan Airport was light. It seemed a long time ago that Bernadette flew into this same airport from California, so much had happened in those few short weeks. It was almost as if she had known the Sinclairs forever. They were like the family she lacked for so long – ever since Daddy died. He had been her only connection to family besides her daughter. Her mother and brother she shared moments with, but distance had become the great separator. In her mother's case the distance was not in miles, but in minds. There had never been an understanding between them, not even the smallest thread of common ground. When her parents separated later in life, Bernadette was relieved she could spend time alone with her father without having to deal with her mother's constant interference.

The excitement of seeing her daughter escalated as Bernadette entered the baggage claim area. A large group of passengers had already gathered around the carousal, their eyes fixed on the bags tumbling out. She waved to Mallory, who looked disheveled and sleepy. She was in jeans and a T-shirt, with her favorite navy sweatshirt slung carelessly over her shoulders. Mallory flashed her a smile, and the two hugged.

"How was the trip? You look tired."

"I didn't sleep well last night. I was too excited about the prospect of this new job," she admitted, stuffing her sweatshirt into her backpack.

"I'm keeping my fingers crossed for you, but you know I have mixed feelings."

"I know, Mom, but remember, it's only a four hour plane ride away."

Bernadette gave her daughter's hand a squeeze. "I know, honey."

The Sinclairs had offered one of their guest bedrooms to Mallory, but she declined, opting to stay on the hide-a-bed in the guest cottage with her mother. In many respects they were more like two close sisters, often sitting up half the night in their bedclothes, laughing and sharing their daily activities.

Bernadette handed her daughter a copy of Samuel's book about the DaVinci code. "Here read this. It's a quick read, and then you'll understand better why I made the decision to stay here."

Mallory looked questioningly at her mother.

"Read it, and then we'll talk. In the meantime, enjoy the country charm of the surroundings. Isn't it lovely?"

Mallory could easily see why her mother chose to stay here, knowing how much her mother's Libra personality related to beautiful and serene surroundings. It was a trait they shared. The cottage was decorated in various shades of green set off by white trim and accented with splashes of bright yellow prints. It looked like something out of a designer's magazine. Ample windows brought in views of the English-style garden that surrounded the cottage and seemed tempted to bloom, though it was still early spring.

"I'll bet it's gorgeous in the summer."

"Yes," her mother agreed, and then pointing to the surrounding woods where wild dogwoods were just beginning to bloom amongst the birch and maple trees. "This is what I miss the most – all the trees."

"They truly are inspiring. Remember how Grandfather talked about them - as being rooted in the earth, yet at the same time reaching up to the heavens?" She smiled at her mother. "He saw them as they are – as living, breathing things that are here to support us. Once he taught me how the Native American Indians purposely leaned against them to draw and renew their own energy. Maybe it's their energy you miss as well."

Mother and daughter smiled at one another, each remembering the man and his wisdom. "He brought us a great deal of knowledge, didn't he?"

"Yes, we were lucky to have him in our lives. I only wish, for me, it had been longer." Mallory's voice echoed with a deep sadness. Her unique bond with her grandfather made his presence a strong influence in her life for the nine short years they were together.

"Mom, there's something I didn't tell you about this job," Mallory blurted out with a smothered excitement, and the tone of her voice grabbed Bernadette's attention. She stopped fussing with her daughter's suitcase and made eye contact.

Mallory hadn't planned on telling her mother this, but when they started talking about Grandpa, it welled up inside and burst out. "Now don't make a big deal about this."

"Okay," was her mother's hesitant reply, however, her dark eyes shone with a deep curiosity.

"The company I had the interview with – the Trillium Group," and she paused for what seemed to Bernadette an exceptionally long time. "Their logo is the fleur de lys."

"How interesting," her mother replied, trying to keep the excitement she felt out of her voice. "What an inordinately strange coincidence."

Over the years, the subject of grandfather's letters had become a source of friction between mother and daughter. For the most part, Mallory felt her mother made too much of the matter, however, on the rare occasion such as today, she succumbed to her own natural curiosity about what they revealed. Bernadette had learned from past experience that the best strategy was to say as little as possible, only dropping a hint here or there and allowing her daughter to come to her own conclusions.

"I thought so too," was the only reply Mallory made, and the subject was dropped.

Bernadette could hardly wait to tell the Sinclairs. "Another strange coincidence," she said after sharing Mallory's disclosure with them. "My life seems to be full of them, yet they don't seem to take me anywhere."

"They brought you here," Julia said.

"That's true!"

Julia seated herself next to Bernadette on the sofa. "I've always believed that coincidences, if we pay attention to them, only bring us to the next place or confirm we're on the right track. They're not the answer in themselves, only little arrows or road signs pointing the way. The final destination is often years down the road. I know you're not happy about Mallory's accepting a position on this coast, however, the coincidence of the symbol may be telling you it would be in her best interest. The fact that she responded to it enough to tell you, says a lot to me."

Samuel smiled, adding playfully. "That's my little Hungarian fortune teller; she has great intuitive abilities."

Bernadette was staring, her mouth slightly ajar. "You're kidding, right?"

"Only partially," Julia waved her hand dismissively. "I am Hungarian, and that very fact seems to give my husband great leeway in making silly remarks about fortune tellers and clairvoyant powers. It's an ongoing family joke."

Bernadette was staring at them in the strangest of ways, her mouth agape.

"Is something wrong?" The couple asked.

"I'm Hungarian, too," Bernadette replied simply.

"Oh my," Julia gasped. "What an extraordinarily strange coincidence."

Her next question came as a whisper, "What was your maiden name?"

CHAPTER 17

Comprehending the implications behind the question, Bernadette shifted her weight on the burgundy sofa, her hand nervously fidgeting with the tufted buttons. She looked from husband to wife. "Racoszy," she finally answered in a voice that was trembling.

Julia's sigh was audible. "Well, that's not it. Apparently we aren't related – at least not on our fathers' sides. For a minute there __!"

"I know, that would have been *too* weird."

"However," Samuel rolled the word off his tongue. "That's not the end of the line. It might not be a bad idea for each of you to construct a family tree."

Julia leaned towards Bernadette and gave her a hug, her silky strawberry blonde hair brushing across Bernadette's cheek, "I'd love it if it turned out we are related, even if it is a distant connection. I've always wanted a sister."

Bernadette smiled. "Now wouldn't that be the all-time coincidence? But the truth is I have very little information on the history of my family. All my grandparents were immigrants, and I know little about their backgrounds. I wouldn't even know where to begin, and as far as I know, there's no one left to ask."

"I'm in the same boat, I'm afraid. But then, I've never really pursued it. Maybe if we both scratch around we'll come up with some distant relative, and if nothing else, we'll learn something about our family history to pass on to our children."

"You've never mentioned your children," Bernadette said. *Why did I think they were childless?*

"As a matter of fact, our son, Matt, might be stopping by for a quick visit later this week. He works in Baltimore and occasionally pops in on us when he's up here on a business. It would be nice if Mallory were still here when Matt arrives. I think they might enjoy each other," and although Julia's words were cheerful, there remained a tone of constraint in her voice that Bernadette was unable to decipher.

Later that evening, as dusk began to approach, Julia knocked on the cottage door.

"Could I entice you to go for a walk before it gets too cool," she asked Bernadette. Mallory was curled up on the couch, fully engrossed in Samuel's book about the DaVinci code.

They had only walked a few steps from the front door when Julia began nervously. "I want to explain to you about our boys."

"You have more than one?"

"Two. But Samuel has severed his relationship with the younger one. He refuses to speak to him or about him. It breaks my heart," she sobbed.

"Oh honey, I'm so sorry. It must be awful for you."

"You can't imagine the daily pain it brings me."

Bernadette entwined her arm through Julia's in a show of support as they continued down the path.

"Do you have contact yourself?"

"Some, but not on any regular basis. He's rather... dropped out of society."

"I'm so sorry," was all that Bernadette could think to say. *The drug problem has been such a blight on our culture,* she thought. *It has no boundaries. Young, old, rich and poor alike have all been affected.*

"I mustn't dwell on it," Julia said, trying to rally her own spirits, and she changed the subject abruptly. "I did have a thought, though, about why you may have ended up on our doorstep. Maybe it's one of the missing pieces."

"Really?"

"Could it be that Matt and Mallory were supposed to meet?"

Bernadette stopped. "Of course! Their both arriving at the same time is another one of those magical coincidences, isn't it? Maybe we *will* be related some day through our children," she speculated, and the idea pleased both women.

Mallory closed the book as her mother entered the cottage. "Did you have a good walk?"

Bernadette nodded. "Although it's turned chilly. I was wishing I had worn something heavier."

Mallory tapped the cover of Samuel's book. "Interesting stuff. I'm glad you gave it to me to read. Now I understand your affinity for the Sinclairs. Sounds as if you're on the same path."

"It does seem that way. It will be interesting to see where it takes us. I hope not down another dead-end alley." And then remembering, "Oh, and you'll never believe this one," she added, her face animated. "Julia is also Hungarian."

"Mother! There are hundreds of thousands of Hungarians in America," her tone implying that her mother was making something out of nothing as usual.

"How many have you ever met? I mean a full-blooded Hungarian?" Then realizing how testy her voice

83

sounded, Bernadette smiled at her daughter. "You're right, dear. I just thought it was rather unusual. I haven't met that many in my life, but I suppose there are more here on the East Coast," and seeing the look of resistance on Mallory's face, she changed the subject.

"The Sinclairs have a son, Matt, who'll be coming to town in a few days. Hopefully, before you leave. Julia and I thought you might enjoy each other."

Mallory's expression turned guarded. She knew her mother had hopes that she would settle down soon and start a family. She had dropped more than one hint that she was looking forward to grandchildren. "I hope you and Julia aren't plotting a romantic scenario, Mother."

"Not at all, dear, we just thought it would be more fun for both of you to be around someone your own age." And then in a more serious tone, "Would it be so terrible if you did meet someone who was interesting enough for you to want a relationship?"

Mallory's response was flat. "No, mother, it wouldn't be so terrible," and her thoughts immediately flashed on the young man in her dream. *But maybe I've already found him!*

CHAPTER 18

The dogwood trees were in full bloom, giving a magical quality to the surrounding countryside. Tucked in between the taller birch and maples, the delicate white blossoms looked like fairies floating in the shadows of the woods. Fairies that, as a small girl Bernadette remembered, seemed to be beckoning her to come and play. She often did.

Samuel's voice cut through her memories, jarring her sensibilities. It seemed unusually loud. "What did we do before the Internet was around?" he mused, knowing full well the answer. His expression was one of repressed excitement as he rolled his computer chair towards Bernadette and handed her the sheets of paper he had just ripped off the printer. "Wait until you see this!"

Julia leaned over Bernadette's shoulder to catch a glimpse just as Bernadette exclaimed, "The Royal Dragon Court of Hungary!"

"Isn't *that* interesting," he remarked as he studied her face. "Take a look at their logo, it's on the next page," and his blue eyes sparkled with anticipation.

When she turned the page, her reaction was immediate. "Oh my," she gasped, her complexion noticeably paling.

"Is it a match?"

"Exactly," she gulped, "Just like the dragon on the marble box my father left me." Her eyes were full of questions. "But what does all this mean?"

"I wish I knew. It seems the more information that comes our way, the more questions that arise," he admitted.

"So what your saying is we're nowhere," Bernadette concluded gloomily, and she thrust her head back into the leather armchair.

"Pretty much," he agreed.

"Don't be so pessimistic," Julia offered as she settled herself on the couch. Her strawberry blonde hair was pulled behind her ears, accentuating her plump, apple cheeks. "Let's go over what we know, and then Samuel can tell us how the Royal Dragon Court of Hungary fits into the picture."

Samuel pulled himself erect as his professor persona kicked in. "What we *believe* we know," he prefaced with a strange smirk, "is that there's been a mystique surrounding the Holy Grail since sometime around the twelfth century, which seems to have changed it from a pagan legend to one that is curiously Christian. And there is evidence that suggests among other things that it has to do with a bloodline. A bloodline that supposedly can be traced back to Jesus, who allegedly was married - probably to Mary Magdalene - and together they had children or at least one child."

He looked evenly at the women to make sure they were following him before continuing. "Beginning with the Knights Templar, there have been secret societies that were - by many accounts - organized to pass on this information as well as to protect and document Jesus' lineage. On the opposing side was the Roman Catholic Church who has been attempting to suppress the same information, fearing they might lose their control and power if the masses perceived Jesus as anything but divine. In fact, according to many historians, the church retaliated with the Inquisition."

"Is that what the Inquisition was all about?"

"Yes, it was the Vatican's strong fist, ruthlessly persecuting thousands and in the process destroying any documents that didn't support their own belief system. Then the Church maliciously tainted those they killed by accusing them of outrageous religious practices and referring to them as heretics. And since they destroyed all their documents, who could prove otherwise?"

The two woman stared at him before Bernadette exclaimed passionately, "And that's how men have perpetually re-written history through the years, by conquering and then burning all opposing evidence."

"And the Church wasn't the only one to have resorted to foul play," Samuel reminded them. "There seem to have been fringe elements on both sides that were far from above board, and many terrible crimes have been committed in order to eradicate the information about Jesus' suspected marriage - or protect it."

"It is interesting that the Roman Catholic Church isn't particularly interested in the Grail stories. If the Grail *was* the cup that Jesus drank from at the last supper, one would think the Church would be completely enamored with them, however, their interest has barely been lukewarm." Samuel stopped a moment to sip his tea.

"So how does the Royal Dragon Court of Hungary fit in to all this?" Bernadette asked.

"They're claiming their genealogy can be traced back to the Merovingians, which is the alleged bloodline of Jesus. And their claim may be as legitimate as the French and British claims, considering the penchant for royalty to intermarry."

"I wonder where the name Dragon Court came from? One doesn't usually associate dragons with Hungary," Bernadette questioned, her mind flashing on the day she found the marble box hidden in her father's wall safe, and the exquisitely carved dragon on the lid.

"I'm hardly an expert on the subject," Samuel admitted modestly, "but my recollection is that the Dragon

Kings originally came from Egypt through the Davidic House of Judah` to Europe."

Bernadette looked inquisitively at the others. "Do you see something important in all this that I don't?"

Julia shrugged and looked at Samuel.

Ignoring the women, Samuel walked over to the bookcase that lined the wall next to his computer and began searching for a book, his hand moving quickly down the volumes with familiarity. "Here it is," and he began flipping through the pages of a book whose spine showed many readings. "Yes, just as I thought. It's been said that King Arthur's father was Uther Pendragon." He looked up at them, explaining, "Pen equates to head, indicating Uther was the head Dragon King." And in his excitement he began talking faster.

"As you know, many believe there is a connection between King Arthur and Jesus. Certainly, all the tales of Camelot are entwined with the Grail. So one could make the implication that if Arthur was from the Dragon Court, Jesus was of the Dragon Court as well. Assuming that's true, it would explain the dragon as the symbol for the Hungarian connection to Jesus' bloodline."

A light bulb went off in Bernadette's head. "You know, I remember reading somewhere that St. Elizabeth of Hungary is credited with having a miracle-working goblet, which I didn't find unusual. There have been many claims throughout Europe of such goblets, many of them purported to be the one used at the last supper," and despite the placid tone of her voice, her dark eyes shown with excitement. "But the reason it stood out for me was that it was said that St. Elizabeth's father, King Andrew II of Hungary was the patron of the author of the Grail romance Parzifal."

"Hmmm, very interesting. It seems each new piece of the puzzle we unearth brings with it a set of possibilities that are circuitous to say the least."

"But where do we go from here? Bernadette asked in frustration.

Julia's face turned reflective. "I think it might be a good time for us to stop a minute and regroup," and her tone commanded the full attention of the others. "Aren't we forgetting something important?"

Samuel and Bernadette looked at her questioningly.

"When Bernadette first arrived, she voiced a very strong feeling that this puzzle was much bigger than the Holy Grail. And yet we've been focusing all of our attention in that area."

"A point well taken," her husband agreed. "Good time to broaden our quest. I'd like to suggest that since there are so many different turns in this maze, it might be in our best interest for each of us to focus on one subject and then report back to the others. Since I'm already enmeshed in the Holy Grail, I'd like to continue with that research if no one has any objections."

Julia volunteered, "I'm rather intrigued with the Hungarian connection. If it's alright with Bernadette, I'd like to pursue that end of it."

Bernadette smiled, "I guess that leaves me with Pleiades," and the instant she spoke the words, a memory of her father pointing to that beautiful cluster of stars in the night sky forced itself into her consciousness.

"That's our constellation," he had murmured mysteriously.

CHAPTER 19

The warmth of the sun's rays had enticed Bernadette and the Sinclairs to congregate on the flagstone patio. It was bordered by a perfectly manicured lush green lawn and beds of colorful perennials that spilled onto the stonework. A small patio fountain created out of a large blue ceramic pot was gurgling off to the side.

"I had a call this morning from my friend who volunteered to trace the email from the mysterious strangers who profess to be helping us," Samuel shared. "It was a surprise to me when he said he wasn't able to track it. I consider him an expert, having been involved with computers at a high level all his life. Even *he* was surprised by the elaborate and intricate system they had devised to protect themselves."

"But here's the shocker," he added. "I received another email from them this morning, telling us not to waste our time trying to find them. That even if we did, it wouldn't help us."

The frustration in Bernadette's voice burst like a balloon. "Help us what?" and the unexpected motion of her hand sent the two sparrows that were drinking from the nearby fountain, flying off.

"I suppose they meant finding out who they are and how we're involved in all this. The strange thing is how did they know it was us that was trying to trace their email? My friend was doing this from his computer."

Still visibly agitated, Bernadette moved her chair under the shade of the bright-blue patio umbrella. She flipped off her sandals. "Damned if I know. With all the new technology out there, I suppose anything's possible. I just wish I knew who these people were and what they want from us. I swear this whole situation kept me up half the night thinking about it."

"You're not alone," Samuel lamented.

There was a long silence as Julia poured everyone a glass of fresh ice tea.

"Here's something that's been rolling around in my mind for some time" Bernadette exclaimed, and her tone remained feisty. "Let's say Jesus *was* married and did have offspring, and a secret society was able to document his bloodline. So what? Would that make the great great great to the tenth power, or whatever, grandchildren of Jesus any different from anyone else? We've had many great leaders whose children weren't so great, not to mention an heir two thousand years later."

"That's always been a rather murky area for me, as well" Samuel confessed. "Clearly in the passage of two thousand years a family tree would have multiplied and spread any number of times. By now, it could literally be a forest. There could be any number of candidates who might qualify as the rightful heir, which is probably why squabbles have arisen between the handful of powerful aristocratic families who claim direct lineage."

Bernadette was looking off into space. The heat of the afternoon had tempered her irritability. "Why do I keep thinking there's something more here? Something important that we're overlooking."

"Like__?"

"I don't know, but my instinct is telling me it has to do with more than the bloodline. I think the connection runs much deeper. Like it has something to do specifically with the properties of the blood."

CHAPTER 20

The view of the Pyrenees from the train station was magnificent. Unlike the Alps that displayed an openness that welcomes the visitor with child-like innocence, the Pyrenees have the brooding, mysterious quality of secrets forever hidden within their steep crags and deep, verdant valleys. Lenzi was all too familiar with the checkered history of the region. She sighed heavily. *Men have not been kind to each other in their pursuit for individual happiness. I pray they are ready for a new way of being.*

Mari bustled into the station knowing she was late, her long peasant skirt rustling as she moved through the crowd with a determined gait. Her olive skin was slightly flushed from the unseasonable heat and the rushing. She had a thin, bony frame with just a hint of feminine curves and features that were bold, yet becoming. The week spent with her family high in the mountains had put a smile in her eyes. They were almond shaped, and at the moment, appeared more green than hazel. The two women embraced.

"*Bonjour, bonjour.* Let me look at you," and Lenzi held Mari at arms length. You have lost ten years. Things must be well with your family."

"The pure mountain air always refreshes. As for my family, things are the same, some good, some bad, but they were pleased to share both with a fresh set of ears. You know how it is, the telling of the good things magnifies them and the telling of the bad can be a great release," and she pushed her unruly raven hair away from her face.

"Yes, often humanity simply needs someone to listen. And you, my dear Mari, are a great listener," the older woman added affectionately. "I know Cassarra has found a good friend in you through the years."

"That one has been like a daughter to me. Her gentle soul is a great reminder to all of us that we can do better. I'm so proud of her. I will miss her when she's gone."

Mari looked squarely into Lenzi's eyes. "How soon?"

"Soon," the older woman proclaimed with a sad reluctance. And then seeing the great sorrow in the eyes of the other, offered. "But now that your obligation of raising that one is almost over, perhaps the Universe will send a replacement."

"Another child?"

Lenzi laughed spontaneously. "Perhaps a child inside, but in the body of a mature man," and her statement made Mari blush. *A romantic relationship!* But Lenzi offered nothing further, and the two women left the busy station.

Cassarra rushed into the arms of the returning women with honest enthusiasm. "I've missed you both."

Lenzi's arm was still around her waist. "We've missed you, too," and she pulled her closer. "Perhaps this was a good trial run for all of us." Then, with the great compassion that she felt in her heart. "You know you'll be leaving soon."

Cassarra's large chestnut eyes were filled with mixed emotion. Excited about the prospect of going into the world to have a new experience, she still felt the sadness of leaving the only home she could ever remember. She nodded at Lenzi. "I am ready," she said, her voice steady.

"I have been thinking that perhaps it would be wise to have Mari accompany you for the first few months. Until you feel comfortable in your new environment."

Both Mari and Cassarra broke out in wide grins. Mari reached for the younger ones hand and squeezed it. This was a welcomed and unexpected surprise. It had always been understood that they would say their goodbyes here.

"Now, let Mari and I get unpacked and settled in and we'll all go on a long walk and discuss a time frame. Shall we meet back here in an hour?"

"The lake is so lovely this time of the year, with all the plants and trees bursting into bloom." Mari picked up a small rock and skimmed it across the water as she had done many times in the past.

"...five, six, Cassarra counted as the rock skirted across the surface before disappearing into the calm waters. "Seven, my lucky number. You have always had a knack for skipping rocks, Mari. Mine rarely go that far."

"Perhaps it is her knack for the selection of the best rock, rather than her skill at skipping them that is superior," Lenzi contributed, and she smiled knowingly, causing the other two to smile with her.

"Always a lesson our Lenzi has for us, is that not right Cassarra?"

"Always," Cassarra agreed. "But offered in such a gentle manner."

"Tell me, Cassarra, are you not a little apprehensive about going out into the world?" Lenzi asked.

"A little, but excited as well. I'm anxious to test my own performance. You can train the warrior forever, but until he faces the battlefield, it's difficult to know how he will perform."

"This is true. But I know you won't forget that you have many on your side, and you know well how to tap into that energy. This I've seen many times."

Cassarra smiled. "Yes, the angels who guided me to find you. I feel them always."

Lenzi arranged for Cassarra and Mari to leave in three weeks, before the next full moon. The elders would spend time with them daily to keep them balanced and in remembrance of the power of divine love. They knew how the ways of the outer world would tempt them in other directions.

Cassarra, now twenty-one, had lived her life protected by the colony away from the narrow-minded ways of the world. The elders taught her daily by example, and encouraged her to think, rather than telling her what to think. She knew no other way than to walk in love. She had been introduced to the outer world by their newspapers and television news programs, so she could see how those that lived there remained trapped in strife and disharmony, the victims of their own emotional imbalances. She had been shown how those in control set the stage for that imbalance, so the masses could be held down. An ample work force of drones that was duped into believing they were free. Who were supplied with ample prescription drugs to keep them lethargic. Who were provided with televisions and Play Stations to keep their minds focused on trivialities while their spirits were being held prisoners from the world of nature.

Cassarra was not judgmental of this world. She understood and had compassion equally for both those who were down trodden and those who held the power. She understood that they were all victims of a misguided belief system. Her job was to help wake them from this terrible nightmare in which they had trapped themselves. The elders had given her great confidence and belief in herself. Not an arrogance, but a genuine confidence, a knowing that she was being guided by divine intelligence. Her path had been set early in life, and she walked it with a steady faith. And now that faith would be tested in the cruelest of ways - in a world that did not honor truth, nor those who spoke it.

CHAPTER 21

At a U.S. Military Base outside Washington D.C.:

Alain DeBuine's long legs were beginning to cramp from the lengthy flight across the Atlantic, making him tired and irritable.

"I'd like to walk and stretch my legs." He complained as he was quickly escorted from the plane to a waiting vehicle. The motor was already running.

"That's not an option," the muscular man uttered, holding the back door open.

The windows of the vehicle were heavily tinted. There was only the driver in front, the thick glass between them shut tight. The muscular man edged his way into the back seat next to Alain.

"How far are we going?" Alain asked, a complaining note in his voice.

"I don't know," was the only response.

Based on his treatment to this point, Alain was seriously regretting his hasty phone call to Washington, and his mind was busy calculating his options. Anything could happen to him here and who would suspect? He told no one that he had left the country. His wife and two children were on holiday in Switzerland when he left, and all he told his housekeeper was that he would be away for a few days. They wouldn't have a clue where to search if he didn't return. He began to realize that he had to reach someone back home to tell them where he was. His cell phone was in his briefcase. Perhaps he could feign the need for a restroom and call.

"I need to use the facilities."

"The what?"

"A restroom."

Flicking on the intercom, the bulky man addressed the driver. "My friend here needs to make a pit stop. How much further to go?"

"Another hour or so, but there's a Howard Johnson's not far."

Muscleman looked at Alain.

"I can't wait another hour."

"Driver, pull into Howard Johnson's," and he clicked off the intercom.

In the meantime Alain was trying to come up with a plan for slipping his phone into his pocket without drawing attention to his actions. He was sure he wouldn't be allowed to bring in his briefcase. Was there some way he could divert his ever-present shadow?

Philippe and Francois were returning from a reconnaissance tour of Washington D.C. Their purpose was to acquaint themselves with the layout of the city. The interstate to Richmond was direct, and if the rush hour was avoided, it was a round trip of only three hours. Philippe would have preferred to take the train, however, practicality dictated a car would serve them better once there, and Francois felt no hesitation in driving. His only complaint, which was offered regularly, was "Americans, phew! They drive too slow!"

They spent the day playing tourists, venturing into the nation's monuments, the Capitol and even the White House to get a feeling for the beat of the city. They had learned in their work that it was very important to wade in whenever possible. No jumping into waters that could be camouflaging something sharp and dangerous. They would take their time, learn to resonate with their new surroundings, which Philippe found to be quite impressive. Beauty, whether natural or manmade, always touched his heart. He was remembering the wonderful reflecting pond surrounded by the heavily blooming cherry trees leading up to – what monument was that?

It wouldn't be long before the young one would be sent over to be taken under their wings. Philippe was anxious to meet her. See if all the years of teaching had the profound effect that was hoped. He knew that current events had forced Le Perfector to act several years earlier than originally planned. Was the young one up to it? Five years of maturity could make a vast difference in someone that age.

"Let's stop and take a break, stretch our legs, use the restrooms, and get some of that wonderful American coffee," Philippe said in a mocking voice. He knew that would get a rise out of his companion. He had done nothing but complain about the coffee since he arrived in the U.S.

"You mean soup!" Francois replied disdainfully. "Weak soup. And there'll be nowhere decent on the road. Only those sterile places with the rubber food."

"Yes, but it would be nice to stretch our legs and maybe get a chocolate."

Francois sneered. "Chocolate – wax is more like it. That's why it doesn't melt in your hands. Barely melts in your mouth."

"Now you have to admit, we've found some excellent dining in Richmond."

"Yes, but not those rubber factories."

Francois was looking ahead. "There, see that orange roof. Pull in there. They have clean restrooms."

Alain DeBuine had been unsuccessful at any attempt to retrieve his cell phone from his briefcase, and his frustration and fear mounted as he considered the potentially perilous situation he had gotten himself into by making that one fateful phone call. As he and the laconic Neanderthal exited Howard Johnson's his mind was racing forward. *Was there anyway to get himself out of this mess?* Had he been wise, he would have made them come to him, on his soil, under his terms. After all, he had information they wanted. But his anger had misguided him, and he accepted their invitation believing he would be treated as an important ambassador to their cause - a confidant. It was on the long flight to the states where he began to realize he had jeopardized his personal safety by leaving his country without going through any customs checkpoints. There would be nothing to trace him to a military base in Germany or a voyage across the Atlantic.

Alain and his ham-fisted shadow were leaving the restaurant just as Philippe and Francois ascended the steps from the parking lot. Philippe knew Alain casually from their years of contact through the organization, but they were never friends. Alain had a pompous attitude that Philippe found condescending. He was shocked to see him here. Le Perfector hadn't told him that Alain would be involved in the American synchronization. Their eyes met, and Philippe was quick to assess that Alain's held the look of fear. With a quick motion of his head, Alain cautioned them from delivering a greeting, and they passed without any sign of recognition.

Philippe had good instincts. He waited a few moments and then in French directed Francois to follow him back to their car. Francois knew by Philippe's tone not to ask any questions. They had worked together as a team for a long time, and when there was urgency, they moved as one.

In the safety of their vehicle, Philippe commanded in curt tones. "Follow the black car that's pulling out of the parking lot, but not too closely."

The pursuit took them back onto the interstate heading south towards Richmond. Philippe took out a map and began tracing their route, taking care to write down the license number and the description of the car as well as a description of the thug wearing a designer suit with the large, bald head accompanying Alain.

The black car kept changing lanes, probably as a cautionary measure, but Francois was doing a good job of anticipating his moves, while carefully keeping enough distance to avoid detection. Fortunately the traffic was manageable. Within twenty minutes they left the interstate and pulled onto a less-traveled highway. Francois was careful to always have at least one car between them, while Philippe kept his binoculars focused on the vehicle transporting Alain, but the heavily tinted glass kept him from seeing inside.

It wasn't long before they turned onto a road that was taking them into farm country. Philippe checked his watch. He suspected they would turn onto an unmarked road. His intention was to time the distance to the turn. He wrote down the mileage on the car and the speed Francois was driving. His instincts were accurate. After thirty minutes, the black car turned left onto a dirt road that appeared to go back to a farm.

Philippe took a picture of both sides of the road and the surrounding landscape with his cell phone. They wouldn't be able to follow any further without drawing suspicion. Francois continued forward for a few miles before making a U-turn. It never hurt to be overly cautious.

"Well, that was an interesting little side trip," Philippe declared, and he smiled at Francois who knew better than to ask any questions. Philippe would share with him when he was ready.

CHAPTER 22

Lenzi's attention was drawn away from the window and the view of the placid sea back to the decoded message from Philippe. This was an unexpected development. She had been aware of Alain DeBuine's discontentment with her choice of Philippe for the American unit, but she didn't think his disgruntled ego would cross the line.

Her voice was even when she shared the news with Mari. "Alain DeBuine from the Paris organization appears to be collaborating with the Americans. Philippe has seen him outside of Washington."

Mari squinted her almond shaped eyes. *This could be a serious development.* "Is it possible," she offered, "that he was taken without his consent?"

"That's a possibility, but I suspect not," Lenzi responded, as she poured herself fresh water from the glass pitcher. There were slices of lemon floating on the top. "I knew that Alain was displeased with my choice of Philippe over him. I should have been more sensitive to what he may have perceived as rejection and spoken to him personally. But," she added reflectively, "that is water over the dam. Now, I must deal with the consequences. I suspect our plans have been compromised in some way, if not completely. First, we must contact Paris to see if they know anything that might help us. Ask them to check Alain's phone records, and see if his servants or his family know anything without alerting them there's a problem."

"I assume we need to change all our codes immediately and the routing of our email."

"Yes, it's best to assume the entire structure has been infiltrated. Oh, and find out exactly how much Alain knew about the Phoenix Project," Lenzi added, almost as an afterthought.

As she waited for the council to gather, Lenzi could hear her own words, spoken so often, ringing in her ears. *Expect the unexpected.* This was definitely the unexpected! But she was wise enough not to waste her time admonishing herself for not being more perceptive about the depth of Alain's dissatisfaction. She understood that mistakes were merely lessons to be learned. Once the error was fully comprehended, it was important to move forward. But more often than not, humans forgot the lesson and only brought forward the pain of the mistake, which kept them locked in the repetition of the same old patterns. Lenzi understood the importance of the present moment. The sacred "now" referred to in all the great books. The only time action was possible. To misuse it regretting dead yesterdays or worrying about unknown tomorrows only perpetuated problems by setting up a deeper negative vibration around the circumstance.

Lenzi was seated with the elders. Tapping her extraordinary cane on the travertine tile floor, she brought the meeting to order. "We must develop a fresh code as soon as possible, and a new way to route our email. I have spoken again with Paris. They have accessed Alain's phone records. This appears to have been instigated by Alain himself." Her gaze passed around the table. "We must remember to be compassionate with the spirit that has been sabotaged by the ego," she warned. "Alain has not made an uncommon error within the human framework, and perhaps this is not as bad as it may seem at first glance. The Universe may have inadvertently placed one of us within the tight circles of the present administration in Washington to act as a conduit of information. I believe we have the ability to turn this situation in our favor. It was not a coincidence that Philippe happened upon Alain in that most unlikely of places."

Her silver eyes held a challenge as her gaze moved from one to the other with uncanny focus. "Based on Philippe's interpretation of the incident, I suspect Alain will be very receptive to any help we can offer at this point. So, let us see this as an opportunity to improve our skills of mental telepathy and remote viewing."

CHAPTER 23

In an isolated farmhouse in Virginia, Alain DeBuine was escorted into a rustic bedroom that was sparsely, but not uncomfortably furnished. There were at least ten Americans ambling about. They all appeared to have guns under their jackets.

Alain realized the enormity of his mistake on the long flight to the North American Continent and had, since, been contemplating how he could best keep himself safe. He suspected if he told them everything, he would no longer be of service to them and his life could possibly be in danger. If he said nothing and refused to cooperate, they might use extreme measures to extract the information. Neither was a pleasant prospect.

The coincidence of running into Philippe from the Montpellier unit had not been a mere chance of fate. Alain had studied with the Mystery Schools for long time and knew that there were no accidents in life. Philippe would have contacted Le Perfector and they would conclude why he was here in America. When he first saw Philippe, his heart sank, now they would know he was a traitor. But thoughts for his own safety quickly overrode his guilt, and he immediately shifted his hopes to those he betrayed for help. Le Perfector preached only forgiveness. She would find it in her heart to look past his behavior and see how his present situation could be turned into a positive.

He had worked at keeping his mind in a meditative state on the drive to the farmhouse so he would be open to any telepathic ideas Le Perfector and her council could send him. First he asked the question: *How can I get myself out of this mess I created?* And then he waited for the answer. It came the next morning. *Tell them enough to temporarily satisfy them, feigning that's all the information you are privy to at this time. Then offer to act as a double agent. Brilliant!*

Alain jumped when the door to the small room burst open and a stout man whisked in with an air of authority. He promptly closed the door behind him.

"Mr. DeBuine, I understand you have some information you'd like to share with us."

Ignoring the remark, Alain asked bluntly, "Am I being held prisoner?"

"Not at all. We simply need to know what you know about the Phoenix Project. After that, you're free to go back to France." The man who spoke was older than the men outside, the fullness of his face revealing a lifetime of indulgences. His air of authority and the respectful manner in which the others addressed him when Alain arrived made it clear that he was in charge, leading Alain to believe that this was the one person at the farmhouse who knew about the Phoenix Project. He and Alain were alone in the small room. Music played on a stereo directly outside the door. Alain assumed by the volume that it was to keep anyone outside the room from overhearing their conversation.

"May I ask your connection to the present administration?" Alain ventured. He had wisely dropped his contemptuous tone.

The man smiled in a manner that suggested he was a friend. He maintained a good ole boy drawl that frankly was lost on the Frenchman. "Let's just say I'm directly involved. Now why don't we make this easy? I know you're tired and want to go home to your family. So let's get to the point. When you called the White House, you said there was a plot to undermine the success of the Phoenix Project. Let's start with your connections. I understand you're a member of the Rosicrucians, the Masons *and* a member of a fraternal organization that goes under the name of WE." The eyes in the debauched face pierced through Alain. "Are you also a member of the Priory of Sion?"

Alain tried to keep his composure. It came as a surprise to him that Mr. Interrogator even knew the name of the Priory.

"No, I know nothing about the Priory, although I do belong to the other three organizations. However, there is a fourth organization, and that is where I gained knowledge of the Phoenix Project."

"This is very interesting. What's the name of this fourth organization?"

"I'd rather not divulge that information. If I did, it would jeopardize my standing with them, and what I'm offering to your country is the opportunity to use me as a double agent."

"Hmm, that's a very interesting proposition. Why would a man of your means want to take on a dangerous job as a double agent?"

Well, they had done their homework. It seems they even knew his net worth. "The truth is most of the money is from my wife's family, and she holds a tight rein on the purse strings. Recently I've acquired some gambling debt and found myself in, shall we say, the undesirable position of being cash deficient."

The interrogator was rubbing his hands together. "I see, so you're up for a deal, eh?"

Alain found the man's mannerisms offensive, however, remembering all too well how his ego had gotten him into this situation, he made a serious effort to keep it in check.

"I would say that's an accurate assessment of my situation."

"This could possibly be very useful to both of us, depending on what information you actually have."

Alain cleared his throat. "I know the Phoenix Project is a screen to hide the fact that nuclear waste is scheduled to be shipped to Mars." And then he added in a low voice, "Without the knowledge of the American people, Congress or NASA."

The interrogator's face turned a deep red. "And your organization has plans to block this mission."

"Precisely."

"How?"

"We have our ways."

"Leaking it to the press?"

"With very important documents that would be difficult to refute."

"How many people in your group, besides you, know about this?"

"I would say a handful."

"Is this some sort of an environmentalist organization?"

"That would be a fair assessment."

The interrogator didn't like the way the Frenchman was sidestepping his questions. He didn't like the Frenchman period. He had an arrogance and femininity he found offensive. His long legs crossed like a woman and the way he held his cigarette. Clearly this guy never held a shovel in his hands.

"Do you know any of the specifics of the Phoenix Project?"

"I know the laboratory is hidden in Colorado and you plan on sending the rocket into space towards the end of this year. I also know that others will follow."

"How the hell did you get that information?"

Alain knew it would be useless to explain remote viewing to this man. "Someone from within your circles passed on the information to us."

"I'd like the name of that son-of-a bitch."

"Unfortunately I don't have that information."

"Would you be able to get it?"

"I believe I would. *If* the price is right."

"And what might that be?"

Alain hoped his hand wasn't shaking as he lit another cigarette. Exhaling helped him relax. "I was thinking in terms of a million euros." He had no idea if that was too much or too little. When his interrogator didn't flinch at the sum, he had to admit there was a part of him that was beginning to enjoy this little charade. Mental competition had always been his specialty. When he mentioned someone from their side had been an informant, he could feel the energy in the room shift to him. It gave him the confidence he needed. "Fly me back home, and I'll guarantee that within a week I will have that name for you. I will then expect to have the cash delivered to my home in Paris within forty-eight hours," and he released a long exhale of smoke from his cigarette being careful not to send it in the direction of his interrogator. He wasn't feeling that confident.

"We'd better hear from you within a week," the lined face replied. "It just so happens we know exactly where your family is vacationing in Switzerland. I would hate for there to be a little accident of some kind," his expression leaving no doubt in Alain's mind that this man was capable of anything.

CHAPTER 24

As Henry Connelly waited alone in the elaborate study, he reflected on the oil painting of James Monroe that hung, rather obtrusively he thought, over the ornately carved fireplace mantel. The owner proclaimed a distant relationship to Monroe on his mother's side. Henry vaguely wondered how the thin, almost gaunt-faced Monroe could have possibly come out of the same gene pool as the face with the heavy jowls and rotund body who claimed kinship.

The owner of the portrait often boasted about his famous ancestor and his authorship of the Monroe Doctrine. "Yep, my ancestors had the balls to tell them sons of a bitches over in Europe that this hemisphere was off limits to them." and it was expressed in a tone that suggested it was a policy that should extent to modern-day practices, totally misinterpreting the context of the times in which the document was proclaimed."

Not that Henry was altruistic. His personal politics were based solely on the bottom line. If it brought him money, he was for it, otherwise, he didn't give a damn. Republican and Democrat were merely labels to him, he voted with the dollar signs. Henry knew that James Monroe was considered to be one of the great visionaries of his time, believing the world was bound to move in a democratic direction – and look where it got him. When he left the Presidency, he was virtually bankrupt after spending a lifetime in public service. Henry was going to make sure that never happened to him. He made it a point to always look out for number one first, because he knew no one else would.

The owner of the mansion burst into the room, clumsily closing the French doors behind him.

"Well Henry, we have quite a dilemma on our hands. More than we bargained for with this Frenchman."

"What do you think, is he on the up-and-up?" Henry Connolly asked, his southern drawl barely masking his frustration.

The portly gentleman shrugged. "We'll have our answer in a week. The bottom line is he *did* know about the Phoenix Project, so we have the problem of a serious leak somewhere."

Henry's face showed his exasperation. "Do you have any ideas who it could be?"

"No, I was going to ask you the same question. I've gone over every name in our group a dozen times, but I don't have a clue. There has to be a reason for someone to sell out. The Frenchman sold out to us because he needed the money, or so he says. We need to check that one out. But everyone in our little group is slated to make a bundle on this project. I can't imagine why they would jeopardize that amount of money. The only reason I can think of is someone is pissed off at another member, and they're willing to jeopardize everything to get even. Frankly, I haven't seen any of that. We've been working together a long time. I think one of us would have noticed an incident of the magnitude that would make someone a turncoat."

"I'm with you. I can't believe it's from within. It's got to be someone on the outside who got wind of this. One of the boys from NASA or one of the security guards at the site." Henry ran his hand nervously through his thinning hair. "Who the hell is this Frenchman connected with, do we know?"

"We know he's associated with the Rosicrucians and Masons and a member of some fraternal organization; but he claims it's his membership with another group, one he wouldn't name, where he got the information."

"He wouldn't give you the name? I don't like this," and Henry leaned on the arm of his chair to catch more of the breeze from the ceiling fan.

"I don't like it either, but what other options do we have? If we zap him, then we don't know who else out there knows. At least this way we have someone on the inside siphoning information back to us, which hopefully leads us to our leak. The one big plus on our side is that he has a wife and two kids. I saw the look in his eyes when I mentioned them. He knew exactly what I meant, and he knew I read his reaction."

"What's our next move?" Connolly asked.

"We sit and wait to see what he brings us."

"How long?"

"We gave him a week."

As Henry walked out of the room and through the highly-polished, marble foyer, he loosened his necktie with a quick jerk. Lately it was beginning to feel like a tight noose around his neck.

CHAPTER 25

The sun was hazy and still low in the morning sky as Bernadette slipped on her Bermuda shorts and bright colored matching top. Her daughter often admonished her for her habit of perfectly matching everything, calling her over coordinated.

Moving with a measure of excitement, Bernadette quickly ran a brush through her short curly hair before leaving the cottage and following the winding flagstone path that led to the main house. She felt like Dorothy in the Wizard of Oz, skipping along the yellow brick path. She chuckled. The information she uncovered last night definitely suggested they weren't in Kansas anymore.

Entering the Sinclair's kitchen through the back door, her voice resounded through the quiet of the early morning hour. "Wait until you hear this!" she announced excitedly.

Samuel and Julia were having their first cup of coffee.

"This must be a good one," Samuel joked, "Usually you at least knock."

"Oops, sorry." Bernadette adopted a sheepish expression. "But this is pretty exciting."

"Okay, let's hear it." Samuel said, as he walked around the granite counter top that separated the kitchen from the cozy breakfast nook to refill his oversized coffee mug.

Bernadette slid next to Julia on the deep cushioned seat of the banquet, her vivacious personality brimming with enthusiasm. "I began my research of Pleiades yesterday and was literally shocked at the overwhelming number of traditions among indigenous peoples throughout our planet who say they come from the stars - many of them specifying the Pleiades," and her voice bubbled with excitement.

Julia cocked her head to the side. "Really?"

"Yes, in our country alone, early Dakota and Hopi stories speak of the Pleiades as the home of their ancestors, and it turns out the Mayans and Incas considered themselves direct descendents from the Pleiades as well."

"That *is* interesting," Julia agreed. "And we all know what they say about myths - that they often have their basis in real facts."

"And like all truths, they can't be hidden forever, often surfacing at the most crucial times," Bernadette added.

"Is this a crucial time?" Julia's voice was inquisitive.

"It might be in our country's history. With the present administrations 'no tree left standing' attack on Mother Earth, this planet's life may be in serious jeopardy.

"So are you saying that our planet is in trouble, perhaps even more seriously than most of us realize, and our ancestors from outer space are making themselves known at this time to possibly offer help?"

"Just a thought," Bernadette admitted.

"And although it's far out, it's one we shouldn't dismiss," Samuel suggested as he slid into the banquet next to his wife. "Particularly since UFO sightings have been increasing exponentially in the last few decades."

"True, and there are many who feel the increase began with the advent of nuclear weapons. Some ufologists have even suggested that when we began detonating the atomic bomb, it sent a signal to outer space that we were headed in the wrong direction. Naturally scientists and politicians scoff at the idea, and since there's no factual proof, we're all left to our own beliefs."

"But there *is* proof that most of the ancient cultures deeply identified with the stars," Samuel stated flatly. "Especially Pleiades. Their temples and pyramids have proved that fact. A significant number of them are aligned to Pleiades. Add to that during the Dorian era of Greece, the calendar was regulated by the position of Pleiades," he added, coolly, "says to me that Pleiades held an important position in their culture."

"I agree with you," Julia commented. "Although our scientists would argue that only proves the ancients were excellent astronomers."

"I don't know about you two," Bernadette said, "but I feel that in some way these Native American beliefs about their ancestral connections to Pleiadians ties some of it together. Isn't it rather strange that the Egyptians built grand pyramids aligned to Pleiades and indigenous people half way around the world have a legend that their ancestors came from the very same star system?"

"It is to me," Julia agreed.

Bernadette's voice remained animated. "And this is just the beginning of my research. I suspect as I probe deeper, I'll unearth more compelling evidence about Pleiades," and she smiled broadly, as one who had just scored a bull's eye.

A crystal hanging in the window behind them had just caught the morning sun and splashed a rainbow across the table between them. Opening her palm, Julia moved her hand so the band of color fell directly across it, and she playfully attempted to catch it.

"Not to outdo you," Samuel remarked, ignoring his wife who seemed endlessly fascinated by the rainbow, "but I had a rather rewarding week myself. I unearthed an interesting story about the Merovingians. Again a myth, but hard facts are difficult to come by when you're going back that far in history. I discovered an old French tradition that claimed Merovee, who was one of the earliest ancestors of the Merovingian family, was born of two fathers. The legend goes on to say that Merovee's mother, who was already pregnant by her husband King Clodio, went swimming in the ocean one day where she was supposedly seduced by a beast of Neptune. When Merovee was born, it was said he had a commingling of both the blood of his Earth father and that of the mysterious aquatic creature.

Julia looked up from the rainbow, a huge smile on her face. "Maybe Father Neptune has a deeper meaning than we thought!"

"Wait there's more. Think about it. That legend might explain the origin of the Merovingian name. Merovingian breaks down into syllables we can easily recognize: mer and vin, or the sea and the vine. Broken down this way one might say that it alludes to the vine that comes from the sea," and then in a more dramatic voice. "Or the bloodline that comes from the sea."

"Wow, this is really getting interesting!" Bernadette's voice burst with excitement. "Because that corroborates something else I turned up this week. I found that many people who supposedly channel the Pleiadians claim the Pleiadians are related to the dolphins. "And," she emphasized, "there's a tribe in South Africa called the Dogon who insist their ancestors came from the star Sirius, and they claim these extraterrestrials were also amphibious."

"Where did you get that information?" Samuel questioned.

"There're several books written about it. The one I read was by Robert Temple, a Royal Archaeological Fellow, called *The Sirius Mystery*. Apparently this Dogon Tribe had information about the Sirius star system *before* modern-day astronomers. Information they claim was given to their ancestors by these amphibious extraterrestrials."

"Wait a minute," Julia said. "The two of you are going too fast for me. Let me see if I have this straight. The Merovingian bloodline has a legend connected with it that claims that its ancestor was sired by a human as well as an amphibious creature, which could possibly explain the *mer* and *vin* in their name. And there are indigenous people around the world who have oral traditions saying they came from extraterrestrials who were amphibious. And since Jesus is purported to be of the Merovingian bloodline are you saying that ___," and she stopped short as the magnitude of her question closed in on her.

Neither Samuel nor Bernadette answered the unspoken question.

Julia's voice was very soft when she asked. "Do any of us know when and why Jesus became associated with the symbol of the fish?"

CHAPTER 26

Bernadette and Samuel stared at Julia, scarcely believing where her compelling question was steering them.

Within moments Samuel was in front of his computer with the phrase 'Jesus - fish symbol' highlighted on his search screen.

The women watched anxiously as he scrolled down, quickly scanning the material.

"Well, this makes no sense," he announced brashly. "The first explanation is purportedly because Jesus said that he wanted to be the fisher of men, not fish. It would seem if that were the case the pentagram, which is the symbol for man, would be the symbol for Jesus."

"I agree," Julia confirmed. "If he said 'not fish', then why would they use the fish?"

Samuel continued scrolling. "Here, this makes more sense." And he looked towards the women. "Because Jesus was born and came to be recognized as a prophet in the Age of Pisces, and as we know, the symbol for the astrological sign of Pisces is the fish."

Samuel became animated. "That's right, I remember one of the things I discovered in the research for my DaVinci book was that many believed the Sangreal Documents were scheduled to be released to the world at the end of the Age of Pisces, but the millennium came and went without incident."

"Maybe it's because the millennium wasn't the end of the Age of Pisces," Bernadette shot back. "There seems to be differences of opinion about when the next age, which is that of Aquarius, begins. Theories go from as early as 1997 to as late as the year 2100. Still, others claim it will begin in December 2012, which is the date the Mayan calendar ends."

"How can there be that much discrepancy in the timeframe?" Julia asked.

"Apparently, each age is approximately 2,160 years long, which is the time it takes a constellation to march across the sky so it's no longer the one rising on the vernal equinox. But there's much dispute about the starting point, which has left the exact moment we enter the next age open to conjecture."

"Another possibility for the millennium coming and going without incident could be that there aren't any Sangreal Documents. It might all simply be a big hoax, as many have been suspecting right along," Samuel reminded them.

"That's true," Bernadette agreed reluctantly. "But I think we're getting off track here. Let's get back to Jesus' association with the fish symbol. Is there anything else?"

Samuel focused back on the screen. "Here's an interesting one. It refers to the Greek initials for the phrase 'Jesus Christ, Son of God, Savior'. In Greek the initials spell out the word ICHTHYS, which translates to fish. Since the early Christians were being openly persecuted, it's suggested that they used the sign of the fish as a code to identify themselves to each other."

Then Samuel's expression turned mischievous. "Or, it could be that Jesus or his ancestors came from the star system of Pleiades or Sirius, which are allegedly inhabited by amphibious beings. Add to that the legend that one of the earliest Merovingian kings was said to be born of two fathers – one of which was a strange aquatic creature – and we could have a direct hit!"

Samuel raised his eyebrows for emphasis before he added, "Perhaps that strange aquatic creature was from another planet."

CHAPTER 27

Inside their newly established apartment, the aroma of fresh herbs filled the kitchen as Mari busied herself over a simmering pot. Her coarse hair was pulled back into a loose knot. Cooking had always been great therapy for her, although she didn't like this electric stove. She much preferred to cook on gas. All the good chefs did.

Unlike Cassarra, Mari was having trouble finding a comfort zone in their new surroundings. But why? She had traveled to many other countries in her lifetime, and she spoke fluent English. Then a realization hit her. *It wasn't the country – it was the mission!* Cassarra had been the child she never had, and now as a young woman, Mari would have to let her go out into a world that might not be ready for her chosen purpose. Dropping her head, Mari tried to release the fear she had buried so deep that she hadn't recognized it until this moment.

She was grateful Philippe was available as a support system; he had the same gentle leadership qualities as Lenzi. Francois – he was another matter. At first Mari found him brash, and she ignored him whenever possible. But more recently, their relationship had slipped into a friendly bantering laced with sexual overtones. She had to admit she was beginning to have hopes that it wouldn't stop at the conversational level when something Lenzi said last month popped into her mind. *Now that your obligation of raising Cassarra is almost over, perhaps the Universe will send a replacement."*

"Another child?" Mari had asked, surprised.

"Perhaps a child inside, but in the body of a mature man."

So this was why Lenzi had allowed her to come to America! Suddenly life seemed a great deal brighter.

Claiming Cassarra was his niece, Philippe had gently twisted the arm of a Senator whom he already had in his pocket to find her a job. The dual citizenship Lenzi had established for her years ago, along with the council's insistence on her mastery of English, made the job as a White House tour guide an easy fit.

Meanwhile, Philippe had been very effective in convincing a few of the Congressmen to change their votes on some of the environmental bills before Congress. Lenzi's checkbook had been the great persuader. Everything appeared to be falling into place nicely. Mallory and Cassarra met recently, and as anticipated, they became fast friends. There was only the young man who hadn't arrived on the scene. Mari was anxious for that part of the puzzle to come together, as it was the most unpredictable piece. Then, it was merely a matter of time before they made their move.

The plan Lenzi devised to have Alain DeBuine volunteer to act as a double agent had masterfully turned around that unpleasant situation and turned it into a plus. The council spent many hours sending him the message telepathically. How it would all end with Alain, it was difficult to say. He put himself in a precarious position and now he would have to reap what he, himself, had sown. Lenzi could only do so much, and she knew better than try to play God.

In the meantime, they were acutely aware that the political atmosphere around Washington was becoming tense. The American people were tired of the ongoing war in the Middle East. Troops that were sent more than six years ago for what was sold to the American public as 'a quick easy war' were still there and there seemed no end in sight, and the American taxpayers were becoming alarmed at the financial black hole the war was creating. Even the President's most loyal supporters couldn't help but question his connection to reality after his recent speech. It seemed he and his speechwriters had become victims of their own propaganda machine.

CHAPTER 28

What was it about the Blue Ridge Mountains that kept drawing Mallory back to them? They were beautiful, but certainly didn't have the spectacular height or dramatic views offered by the Sierras that were right outside her back door in California. Was it simply the pull of that dream she had on the plane and the young man that waved to her? None of it made any sense, and yet in some strange way she had a deep-seeded belief that someday she would meet him in those mountains. Since moving to Richmond, she was often drawn to trekking across their rounded peaks, each time secretly hoping the young man would magically appear on the other side, then trying not to be disappointed when he didn't. *How silly I'm being. It was only a dream,* she chided herself. But she couldn't shake the memory.

She knew her mother and the Sinclairs were hoping that something would come of her relationship with Matt, the Sinclair's son. He was very nice and quite handsome, but – how could she explain it? There were no fireworks, he was just another guy. She had seen Matt several times since she moved to Virginia, but she didn't see it turning into anything serious. Maybe if she could get this young man in her dream out of her head, Matt would look differently.

Mallory had been tempted to talk to Cassarra about her dream several times, but always held back. The timing never seemed right.

A knock on her apartment door interrupted her thoughts. She checked the clock that hung on the wall in her galley-style kitchen. She wasn't expecting anyone. Fluffing up her hair, she peeked through the view hole before opening the door.

"I was just thinking about you," she smiled at Cassarra.

Cassarra leaned over and hugged Mallory, her long chestnut hair draping over them. It was thick and silky, its lustrous shine tempting you to run your fingers through it. She was wearing a cropped top and tight jeans that accentuated her long legs and natural gracefulness as she moved.

"I was in the neighborhood and thought I'd stop by. Why were you thinking about me?"

Should she tell her?

Cassarra's large round chestnut eyes searched her friend's face. "I had the feeling we needed to chat," she confessed as they moved into the calm ambiance of the living area where Mallory had accented the neutral beige palate with small splashes of purple and violet. Just the right amount to give it some punch, without being overwhelming.

The two girls had become fast friends since meeting, almost like sisters. Cassarra seemed so wise to Mallory and particularly grounded. So why was Mallory reluctant to share this dream?

It was muggy outside, so Cassarra gladly accepted the fresh squeezed orange juice Mallory handed her and took a long drink. Then she waited for Mallory to open up.

"Cassarra, do you believe dreams can be prophetic?"

Cassarra didn't answer immediately. "Sometimes. But more often I think they're our higher consciousness speaking to us at the only time it can get through, when our ego is asleep."

"Oh." That wasn't the answer Mallory was hoping to get.

"Why? Did you have an interesting dream?"

Mallory blushed. *This was so silly, why couldn't she let it go?* "It was nothing, really."

Cassarra reached for her friend's hand. "No, I think it *is* important," and her compelling sincerity invited Mallory's confidence. She turned directly towards her, holding her gaze.

"It was such a short dream, but it seemed so real," Mallory confessed, "that there's a part of me that believes it will happen," and she searched her new friend's face for approval before continuing. "The dream took place in what looked like the Blue Ridge Mountains. I had been hiking, and while I stopped to rest, I was mesmerized by a figure hiking up the trail towards me. As it came closer, I saw it was a young man. He waved as if he knew me, and there was something about him that was familiar. I couldn't see his features really well, but I remembered his long blonde hair that was a mass of curls pulled into a ponytail. That's when the plane suddenly dropped and I woke up." Holding Cassarra's gaze, she exclaimed, "I feel very silly putting so much importance on this."

Cassarra became animated. "When something grips you with this much intensity, it's wise to pay attention. Why don't you get your trail map and show me where you've been hiking."

As Cassarra studied the map, Mallory noticed her uncanny ability to focus, almost as if she were looking past the physical.

When at last the chestnut-haired beauty looked up, she said with eyes that were clear, but in a voice that was far away and dreamy, "I think you might want to try this trail."

"Any particular reason?"

Cassarra's perfectly even teeth glistened with a unique brightness when she smiled. "It just spoke to me."

CHAPTER 29

Mallory's long chocolate tresses fell in loose waves around her pretty face as her finger purposely traced the embossed fleur de lys on the blank sheet of letterhead lying on her desk. She and Philip were alone in their offices.

"Philip, there's something I've wondered about," and she smiled at the older man who reminded her so much of her grandfather.

Philip stopped what he was doing and gave her his undivided attention.

"It's been curious to me how the fleur de lys became associated with the French Royalty. Since it's our business logo as well, I thought you might be familiar with the history behind it."

Philip's smile was one of pride. *Yes, this one is a thinker. She will do well.* Removing his glasses, he leaned comfortably back in his chair. "It goes back to an old legend that took place when Clovis was king of the Franks. Up until that time, the Franks were considered pagans, however, Clovis changed all that during his reign by converting to Christianity. The story goes that during his baptism, the heavens opened up and an angel appeared with a golden lily, which was handed to him. Since the lily was often symbolized by the fleur de lys, Clovis adopted the symbol as his new coat of arms."

Philip paused, deciding if he should divulge anything further. When he continued, Mallory noted his voice took on a strange quality. "The lily had also been associated with the Virgin Mary for many centuries, and Clovis believed that by using it as his coat of arms, he and his kingdom would be granted divine protection by the Blessed Virgin. Since that time, it has traditionally been used to represent French royalty." And then he added casually, "Clovis was of the Merovingian dynasty."

"Very interesting. Do you know why the Trillium Group choose to use it as their logo?"

"I'm not sure," he finally said, "Possibly because of the reference to three in the name and the fact that the flower has always been represented by three petals." But the look in his eyes told her that he had more information, but chose not to share it with her.

Pulling her hair back, Mallory secured it with a clip before self-consciously glancing at her image in the mirror. Seeing her own reflection made her heart skip a beat. She had chosen to wear the same outfit she was wearing in that special dream she had on the plane – khaki pants and a light blue tee shirt with hummingbirds splashed across the front. Pushing away any thoughts of foolishness, she checked to make sure she had the trail map that Cassarra marked before she slung her backpack over her shoulder. *Follow your intuition, Cassarra had said with heartfelt enthusiasm, and it will lead you to destiny's door.*

It was exactly the encouragement Mallory needed as she guided her car in the direction of the mountains. She had brought enough food and clothes for the weekend. Two days alone in the wilderness. *Or maybe not alone!* Either way, she knew she would enjoy the break. Mallory always felt at home in nature where every tree was a trusted friend; every squirrel and chipmunk a loyal companion. Her sojourns into the wilderness always seemed to get her back in touch with her spirit.

Days on the trail tended to begin early, the dank morning chill prodding the camper into moving quickly.

Today was Mallory's second day in the Blue Ridge Mountains, and her plan was to continue following the trail Cassarra had marked.

She began her hike with high hopes, but as the hours slowly slipped away, it became increasingly more difficult to ignore her disappointment. She tried to distract herself by focusing on the beauty of the surroundings - the frequent creeks and waterfalls, the lush dense blanket of wildflowers that thrived so well in the humidity of the south. When she reached the summit, she found a flat rock where she could eat her lunch and enjoy the views. They were spectacular in every direction. Soon, the sound of nature's lullaby as it gently drifted through the trees brought with it a feeling of drowsiness, and she let herself slip into a peaceful reverie.

She woke with a start. She must have been dreaming, but it felt as if someone had touched her lightly on the shoulder. Looking around, a peculiar feeling washed over her, and she became aware of a perceptible change in the atmosphere. The air had become alive as if it had taken on the properties of liquid, appearing so dense that she could observe its movement. In this unusual state, where time seemed to have stopped, her focus was drawn magnetically towards the east where the steam rising from the land created the misty atmosphere that gives the distinctive blue haze to the mountains, and she quietly realized the scene was the same as in the lucid dream she had on the plane. In a very detached way she watched the trail as waves of passing images came and went, until as if magically, her young man appeared in the distance.

At first she wasn't sure if she was dreaming or awake, but she savored the moment as she watched him move towards her in a slow rhythmic motion. An eternity passed as he wove back and forth on the switchbacks before he looked up to where she was seated. He smiled amicably and waved as if he knew her – just as in the dream - and she returned the gesture. As he drew nearer, she could see his features more clearly. He was slender of build, yet he carried his hefty pack with the ease of someone who did it often. When he reached the ridge trail, she looked at him expectantly, but said nothing.

His face broke into a wide grin, "I'm glad you waited for me," he said, and his eyes held hers in a bond of friendship. "I don't often see another human face this early in the season," and his large blue eyes smiled in a face that was heavily tanned.

Her words flowed easily, "You say that as if you hike this trail often."

"I do. I started at the beginning and now I'm heading back. It's quite spectacular, isn't it?"

"Yes it is," and she held out her hand. "I'm Mallory."

His manner was almost courtly as he reached for it. "Hello Mallory, I'm so pleased to meet you." Yet he made no offer of his name, but continued to hold her hand, their eyes locked.

Her voice was breathless, "And who are you?"

"I'm nobody," he answered, but with no apparent sarcasm, causing Mallory to laugh spontaneously.

"My favorite movie when I was growing up was *A Man Called Nobody*," she explained.

"Mine too, and I've always wanted to say that. I don't know why I did today," and through their shared interest they began an intimate conversation about their childhoods.

They spoke for hours as if old friends reuniting, until Mallory realized by the angle of the sun that it was getting late. "I need to start down the trail or I won't make it back to my car before dark," and although she spoke of departure, she continued to linger, not wanting to leave his presence. When she finally stood, he helped her with her backpack.

"Will I ever see you again?" she asked, her anxious gaze searching his face.

He stood silent, looking deep into her eyes.

She held her breath, sensing he was making a life-altering decision as his quiet blue eyes studied her for the longest time. "Can you come next Friday?"

She nodded, her heart beating so fast she could hardly breathe. "How will I find you?"

"Here give me your trail map." He pointed to a campsite further north. "Here," he said as he marked the spot with an 'X'. I'll wait until you arrive."

CHAPTER 30

Mallory checked her speedometer and then made a conscious effort to slow down. There was no rational reason to be rushing. She had taken the afternoon off, so she would reach the mountains long before sundown. Philip playfully teased her all week, as if in some way he knew she had met someone special. He had even made a passing reference to her knight in shining armor. *Strange he had chosen those words.*

As she pulled into the campground parking lot, she felt her heart flutter as a myriad of doubts flooded her mind. *Would he be here, waiting? If not, how would she find him?* After she left him last Sunday, she realized he hadn't even told her his name. Nobody is what he called himself.

She quickly brushed her hair and touched up her lipstick. Then, leaving her gear in the car, she anxiously headed off towards the ranger's station where there was always a bulletin board for messages. She was practically running, her eyes fervently searching the landscape for his figure.

He was sitting on a rock next to the bulletin board. His smile big. It took all of her composure not to run into his arms.

"I was afraid you wouldn't come," he said standing.

"I was afraid you wouldn't be here," she responded, and their eyes held tight in the embrace they both longed for.

Later that night, the glow of their campfire reduced to a few burning embers, their sleeping bags placed side by side, they focused on the star filled sky, the only canvas on this moonless night. His voice pierced the darkness as though from another time, quoting:

"Many a night I saw the Pleiades, rising thro the mellow shade,
Glitter like a swarm of fireflies, tangled in a silver braid."

Mallory shifted to her side so she could see his face. "Lord Tennyson," she whispered.

His smile was one of surprise. "Not many people know that."

"I fell in love with his writing when I was in high school where I was first introduced to his works through the *Idylls of the King*. And ____," she hesitated.

"And?"

Should she tell him?

"My mother has always taken an interest in the Pleiades, so she has quoted that same stanza many times over the years."

"Yes, what is it about the Pleiades?" he murmured and they fell asleep under a blanket of starlight.

CHAPTER 31

Bernadette was standing by the answering machine, her finger still on the play button, a stunned expression dominating her features. *Well, that came out of the blue.*

A knock on the cottage door interrupted her thoughts.

It was Julia and Samuel. "It was such a pleasant evening, we thought you might want to join us for a walk."

Bernadette stood staring at them, her eyes glazed.

"Is something wrong," Julia asked.

Bernadette dropped onto the wicker loveseat, knocking one of the yellow print pillows askew. "Could you come in for a minute? I just listened to a very strange phone message from my daughter."

"Is she all right?"

"Yes, but__!"

"What is it?" The couple asked.

"She said that she just met the man she's going to marry. Can you believe that?"

"My, that is a surprise." Julia said, masking her disappointment. She had so hoped that their son Matt and Mallory would become a romantic pair. She knew they had exchanged phone numbers when they met at their home recently, and Matt had mentioned in his last email to them that he and Mallory had gone out to dinner several times since then.

"What's really strange about it is she said his name is Brit, and what's so disturbing about that is. . ." She stopped mid-sentence seeing the reaction of the Sinclair's. A quiet cloud seemed to shroud them.

Bernadette sensed she had stumbled onto something sensitive, but couldn't discern what. The couple continued to stare at her in the strangest of ways.

Shaken by their reaction, Bernadette waited for an explanation.

It came from Julia. "That's our youngest son's name."

"Oh my!" Bernadette gasped. "You have a son named Brit? This is all too strange," and her hand went up to her mouth as they silently stared at one another. *This couldn't possibly be their son! And that name – I had received something about it years ago. Should I tell them?*

Bernadette turned a ghostly white. "There's something I haven't told you," she confessed in a quiet tone, her pallor accentuated by the bright colors of the cottage's motif. "Only because until now, it seemed insignificant, and frankly, I had quite forgotten about it." She took a deep breath. *Where to start?* The faces staring at her prompted her memory.

"Many years ago, I was woken during the night and was given information about the name Brit. I was actually pressed to get up and get a pencil and paper and write it down. I didn't understand any of it, but I did as I was told. Years later, I showed it to a friend who had studied metaphysics. She told me what I had written was a form of numerology. Periodically I would take it out, trying to understand what it could possibly mean to me, but could never see a connection – until tonight."

"Do you still have the information," Julia asked in a voice that was constricted, while Samuel assumed a reserved, almost cold manner.

Remembering that Julia previously confided to her that Samuel had virtually disowned his youngest boy, Bernadette proceeded with caution. "What I was given was all numbers, and I clearly remember the sequence because I studied it for so long." Finding a piece of paper, she wrote:

```
BRIT          22
2992          11 11
11 11         2992
22            BRIT
```

"I was shown the name Brit, and then under each letter they wrote the first set of numbers, making it clear to me that the numbers made a triangle both going up and going down. I was then told that Brit was a perfectly balanced name."

Julia began to cry softly.

Samuel's eyes turned cobalt blue. "I think I'll go for that walk by myself," he said in a voice that was gruff, and he left abruptly, leaving the two women alone.

Julia was sobbing openly now. "Did Mallory tell you this young man's last name?"

"No. The only thing she said was she met him hiking in the Blue Ridge Mountains and that she had dreamt about him beforehand."

In between sobs Julia managed to say, "I haven't heard from Brit in almost six months, but it's very possible he's in that area. He was hiking the Appalachian Trail from one end to the other."

"Then he's not a ___," Bernadette stopped herself. *Should she say the dreaded words? Drug addict!*

Julia searched her face.

"When you said he had dropped out of society, I thought you were telling me the problem was drug related."

"Oh no, not at all. It's just that – well, he's never found a place to fit into this world. And Samuel's been so hard on him by constantly comparing him to his older brother, who in contrast, has always done the expected thing. Life was always easy for Matt, who's been successful by society's definition of success. He went to the right college, graduated cum laude, and then, immediately landed a high paying job in a top firm. Needless to say, he and Samuel see eye to eye on most things."

Her eyes were woeful as she continued between sobs, "Conversely, Brit struggled in school and eventually became a truant problem. After high school he refused to go on to college and worked at menial jobs here and there, but never found a fit. He and his father had terrible fights about almost everything, including the way Brit dressed, which was always bent towards the hippie look. Naturally, Matt's success always hung over Brit's head. When Brit announced he was dropping out of society to walk the Appalachian Trail, that was the straw that broke the camel's back for Samuel. He literally disowned him and forbid me to ever speak his name to him again."

"How does Brit support himself?"

"He has a very small trust left to him by his grandparents. It's not much, but apparently he doesn't need much. It seems he can live on berries and nuts."

Bernadette handed Julia a tissue.

"It's so hard to understand. I've tried not to worry, but it hangs so heavy on my heart. It would make it much easier if Samuel hadn't taken such a hard-nose position. But he won't budge an inch." And then in total desperation Julia pleaded, "Perhaps if you spoke to Samuel . . .?"

Bernadette was hesitant. She didn't want to become enmeshed in a family squabble. Right now her relationship with the couple was perfect, but if she started taking sides, it could turn ugly. *Her* goal was to stay focused on the hidden meaning behind her father's letters, yet if there was some way to help without interfering!

"Samuel seems so easy going. I can't imagine him being this uptight about it."

"It's all perspective. In Samuel's mind, having a son who's had all the opportunities handed to him and then doesn't do anything with them is lazy."

"It sounds to me as if Brit is a naturalist, not lazy. Walking the Appalachian Trail through all kinds of weather sounds like hard work."

"I've tried to get Samuel to see it that way. I've even compared Brit to Thoreau, one of Samuel's idols, but that didn't work. I guess it's one thing to idolize in the abstract and quite another to face it in reality."

Julia reached for Bernadette's hand, her eyes turning hopeful. "Maybe Mallory is going to bring Brit back into our lives!"

"That would be wonderful, Julia. I hope it turns out that way, but remember, we don't even know if this is your son."

"It is," Julia said with conviction, "I know it is, I can feel it in my heart. It makes complete sense as to why you came to us in the first place."

The next morning there was a knock so light on the cottage door that Bernadette almost ignored it. It came a second time.

It was Samuel and his face showed the anguish he had suffered through the night. "I assume Julia told you about our youngest boy?"

Bernadette nodded.

"It would settle matters between my wife and I if we knew this was him."

"I know. As soon as Julia left, I put a call in to Mallory, but I wasn't able to reach her. I left a message for her to call as soon as possible."

"Would you mind explaining to me again what you were told about the name?"

The paper with the numbers she jotted down the night before was still sitting on the end table. Bernadette handed it to him.

"I don't understand how these numbers relate to Brit's name," Samuel confessed.

"This is how it was explained to me. Every letter in the alphabet has a number equivalent from one to nine. For example A is one, B is two, etc until you get to nine and than you start all over with one. Following that example B would be a 2, I and R are both 9's and T is also a 2. Then you add all the numbers together. The number equivalent for Brit's name is 2,9,9,2, which adds up to twenty-two. However, there are certain numbers you don't add together, and not having studied numerology, I really don't have a fine grasp on all this. I only know what I was shown. The 2 and 9 were added together and the 11 was brought down on the next line; and the same thing was done with the 9 and 2, bringing the 11 down on the next line. Somehow that was significant, perhaps again to show the balance. Then they added the 11's together, coming up with 22. The only thing I was told was it was a perfectly balanced name.

My friend who was familiar with numerology informed me that twenty-two is a master number, meaning that the person it relates to has selected a pivotal role in society for their life's purpose."

Samuel stared at the numbers, his jaw tight, his mouth set in a straight line.

Bernadette continued, "I looked into numerology a little, enough to know it's a lot more complicated than just your first name. It also takes into account the date of one's birth and nicknames. I never investigated it any further, because I never understood what the name Brit had to do with me."

"Has this voice that speaks to you ever identified itself?"

"No. And frankly it never occurred to me to ask."

"Was it the same voice that told you to go up and turn on the television?"

"I couldn't say for sure. Keep in mind these two incidents were probably ten years apart, but it was my perception that it was the same voice."

"Is it male or female?"

"The voice I hear is male and sounds neither young nor old. But I must tell you, there have been other times when I don't even hear a voice. It's as if the thoughts are put in my mind."

"Like mental telepathy."

"Exactly, and at those times I perceive the source as male and plural."

"You never mentioned that this has happened to you more than the one time. I assumed when you were told to turn on the television that was your only experience with The Voice."

"It's the only one I mentioned because the other times didn't seem pertinent."

"What else have you been told?"

Bernadette looked off into the distance. "The two things that immediately come to mind are that I was suppose to study the Holy Grail and that I needed the Percival name to write. That's when I found out that the name Percival was entwined in the Grail stories."

"Hmm, anything else?" Samuel probed.

"Nothing I can remember off hand, but usually it's things like giving me the name Brit, which at the time makes no sense to me." It didn't escape Bernadette's attention that Samuel flinched each time she voiced his son's name.

"I find it hard to believe that everyone named Brit is some sort of a master."

Bernadette kept her voice neutral. "I understand. I'm only conveying the message. I truly know little about the subject. However, my friend who did have some knowledge explained to me that every number has a positive and negative expression."

"Meaning?"

"Meaning a person with a master number could be a master philosopher – or they could be a very good con artist."

Samuel stood abruptly. "I see. So they could excel at doing well or they could excel at doing badly. Well, let us know when you hear from Mallory, will you?" And crumbling the slip of paper with the numbers on it, he slipped it into his pocket and withdrew without saying another word.

Bernadette stared at the phone as if the very action would make it ring, her mind replaying the message her daughter left the previous night. None of the pieces made any sense, yet they were all beginning to fit together in the most unexpected of ways.

Bernadette could hardly grasp the situation. *Her daughter was talking about marriage to someone she had just met!* That was totally out of character for Mallory. She had never even had a serious relationship. Oh sure, she had many casual boyfriends in high school and college, even steady relationships, but none that ever approached anything close to marriage. Bernadette considered that a blessing while Mallory was in school. Better to get her degree first, then think about marriage and a family later. However, after Mallory graduated and got established in a job, Bernadette became concerned with her daughter's lack of interest in a permanent relationship. Yet, whenever she approached the subject, Mallory became irritated saying, "Would it be so terrible if I didn't get married?" So Bernadette backed off and left the topic alone.

And now this phone call, coming out of the blue. *Mom, I've met the man I'm going to marry!* So unlike her Mallory! Then, for this young man to have the very name The Voice had given Bernadette many years ago, was extraordinary to say the least, but to have it also be the name of the Sinclair's son was almost too much to fathom. Talk about strange twists and turns. But where were they all leading?

CHAPTER 32

As Lenzi's taxi pulled through the ornate iron gates of the Chateau de Bois and up the sweeping circular driveway lined with immaculately manicured rosebushes, she had but one thought. *How could a man who had so much be jealous of a simple man like Philippe Boulier?* The dramatic height of the trees stretching beyond the chateau outlined its turrets, which stood as sentries guarding the well-maintained gardens from the wildness of the forest.

Appearing to have just come from the stables, Alain greeted her at the door dressed in expensive riding attire. His usual pompous air was greatly subdued. At Lenzi's suggestion he had given the servants the day off to assure their conversation would be completely private. His family, she knew, was still vacationing in Switzerland.

"*Bonjour.* I hope your trip was pleasant."

"Without incident."

Alain showed her into the sitting room where his wife had recently engaged an international designer to create a soothing atmosphere of rich cream tones to complement their collection of Louis XIV antique furniture. Lush embroidered silk drapes were pulled back with elaborate ornate tassels and framed huge windows that looked onto the garden, while a marble topped table off to the side displayed an over-sized urn overflowing with fresh flowers. To the left of the velvet covered divan where Lenzi seated herself was a massive wall painting of a mythological scene.

Lenzi smiled inwardly. *Yes, Louis XIV – the flamboyant Sun King – would have felt right at home with the grandeur and opulence of this room.*

"Something to drink?"

"A port would be nice," she replied, leaning her unusual cane against the sofa, its magnificent shade of indigo magnified by the neutral tones in the room.

Pouring their drinks from expensive cut-crystal decanters, Alain broke into apologetic rhetoric as he handed Lenzi her glass.

"Le Perfector, I can't tell you how much I appreciate your coming. I know this is an inconvenience, and I do apologize – for everything," he added with meaning.

Lenzi's extraordinary silver eyes radiated compassion. "We all make errors that need correction. I think you've already seen the results of your mistake – and you will have to suffer the consequences of your own misdoing. As I promised, I will do everything in my power to turn this into a plus for both of us. Forgiveness is my business, but I can only do so much," and her smile was genuine.

"It's not myself I fear for, it's – well my family."

"We will do everything we can to help in that area as well, but you must let go of the fear. It will only draw more negative into your life. You've studied with us a long time. You know that fear not released must manifest itself as an experience."

"Yes, but I have also found it is one thing to say and quite another to do, especially when one is looking down the barrel of a loaded gun."

"We will help in every way we can, but you must take charge of your thoughts and not allow them to lead you. Can you see that is what brought you to this place? You allowed your angry and jealous thoughts to grow into a power of their own. Soon they were whipping you around and controlling your actions. It's important that you take responsibility and not allow that to happen again. Since we can only experience our own thought patterns, it's necessary for each of us to monitor our thoughts continuously so that we manifest only peace and harmony in our lives."

Alain lowered his head in shame.

In an act of kindness Lenzi reached over and patted his knee. "I'm only telling you this as a reminder, not to place guilt in your direction. Guilt is merely a lesson not learned, and I believe with all my heart that you have learned this lesson. I only remind you that the mind allowed to run rampant is the ego's tool."

"Now, the council and I have spent much time devising a plan that will be workable and put you in the least amount of jeopardy. Naturally, your input is extremely valuable, since you've had first hand experience with the adversary and know best what your own capabilities are."

Alain's voice was troubled. "They gave me only one week to give them the name of my informant. What can I tell them?"

"Perhaps we can turn this creature of no morals upon itself. We'll use a code name that points in several directions and wait to see what happens. As they put each of their own under a microscope, we will create suspicion within, which may cause their tight little group to crumble. The dragon biting its own tail has little time to bite others."

CHAPTER 33

Footsteps echoed through the long wide corridors of the White House announcing the President's arrival, the ever-present secret service only paces behind. The President's mood was cheerful as he nodded confidently to those he passed. The vice president had told him that the polls were swinging back in his favor. He knew they would.

He flashed a particularly bright smile at the attractive chestnut-haired guide who had been hired recently. She had the sort of quiet beauty that appealed to him, the clean-scrubbed, wholesome type. She smiled back as she did every morning. It was an open, genuine smile. It always made him feel special.

He and Henry had a brief meeting scheduled in a few minutes, something about foreign policy. *Damn those foreigners, why don't they mind their own business and leave us to ours!*

The vice president was right on time. The President liked that; it showed respect.

"Good morning, Mr. President."

"Good morning, Henry."

"The Cabinet members wanted me to advise you that a trip to Europe was imminent."

"Now Henry, you know I don't like traveling over there."

"I know sir, but it's very important at this time to assure our allies that we're with them on the world climate control issues."

"Are we?"

"Not exactly. All the more reason to assure them we are."

"I don't like this Henry. My wife and I aren't comfortable socializing with those people."

"I know sir, but your wife does it well, and it makes good press - something you need right now."

"I thought you said the polls were swinging in my favor?"

"They are, but this could boost them even further."

The President's voice was resigned. "How soon?"

"Next month, but you won't have to stay long. We'll try to keep it under two weeks. That should be manageable for you."

A few hours later Henry Connolly entered a private residence over the state line in Maryland where he was quickly ushered through the highly-polished, marble tiled foyer into a den where two men were waiting for him.

"How did it go with the Prez?"

"Fine, he tried to dig in his heels, but I didn't give him a choice. You know he's not comfortable when he's out of the country."

"Hell, he's not comfortable when he has to leave his home state," and the three laughed.

"Anything new from the Frenchman?" Connolly asked.

"Not yet."

"I don't know about you boys," the owner of the manor said in a gruff voice, "but I'm getting a little impatient with that son of a bitch. I say bring him back over here and squeeze him until he talks." He stood abruptly and walked over to the bar where he added a splash of bourbon to his glass.

"What if he doesn't know anything? Then all we've accomplished is to blow our only contact."

"He knows the name of his organization and its members. How about that for starters."

"And then what?"

"Round them all up."

Henry's hand automatically went to his tie, which he nervously straightened. *This was getting out of hand.* "We can't eliminate everyone in the organization."

"We can take care of the top ducks."

"Do we really want to get Interpol involved in this?" Henry asked with raised eyebrows.

"Do you have a better idea?"

Henry hesitated. He knew he had to do something to disperse the anxiety. "Look, while the President's on that European tour and out of my hair for a while, I'll be able to concentrate on the problem of the Frenchman. Let's see what I can come up with before we do anything radical. I ran a few possibilities by NASA earlier this week to feel them out and see if they could move up the date of the Phoenix Project."

"What good would that do?"

"If we could get the Phoenix Project off the ground – let's say three or four months in advance, without any notice, we'd have everything up in the air before anybody got wind of it. Once that rocket's up in the air loaded with the nuclear waste, we're home free. Then we just deny and shift focus."

"Was NASA receptive?"

"At first they balked, but I think I convinced them it would be in their best interest to crank it up. Gave them some political jargon about it would make Congress happy and more apt to appropriate additional funds to their endeavors."

"You're assuming, of course, that whoever's passing information on to the Frenchman's organization isn't associated with NASA," the bulbous face spurted, as he slammed his fist on the end table nearly knocking over his drink. "No, we have to find out who the mole is first and eliminate the bastard. I say let's wait to hear from the Frenchman. He has two more days to contact us."

"And if he doesn't?"

"We bring him back over here and see how tough he is. My guess is he would break in the first minute."

CHAPTER 34

It was dusk. Brit and Mallory were standing, his arms enveloping her petite body as he held her in a close embrace. The sun had just disappeared behind the mountaintops, taking its warm rays with it. They snuggled closer. This was their third such meeting, and each time the separation became more torturous. When Mallory pulled away, she held both of his hands in hers. Her gaze was steadfast, her voice even.

"I've made up my mind, I'm not leaving you again." She took a deep breath, knowing what a huge decision she was making. "I want you to come home with me."

He said nothing, his bright blue eyes uncertain.

"You can't stay out here forever, can you? Sooner or later you have to come back into society."

Brit tilted his head to the side. "I don't think I can try to fit into that world one more time."

She reacted to his pain by folding herself back into his arms. "Then I'm staying out here with you."

He gently pushed her away so he could see her face. "You can't do that."

"Why not? You're doing it."

"It would be different for a woman."

"So, it turns out you're a male chauvinist," she chided, bringing a smile to his face.

"No, but I can't let you give up everything. I had nothing to give up. I was a failure, a nobody. But you've found the perfect job, something you feel passionate about. You have a supportive family and friends."

"And you have me," she said firmly, "And with me comes that supportive family and friends." Her eyes were pleading. "Come stay with me for one month. I promise, if you still feel the same way, I'll bring you right back here to go on your way."

He started to say something, then refrained.

"Brit, I just can't let you go. Don't you see, you're part of my dream. Without you, it would all be meaningless," she confessed, and she slipped back into his arms.

They entered Mallory's apartment as the phone was ringing. Mallory ran to catch it, almost tripping over the small area rug in the entryway.

"Hi honey, it's mom."

"Hi."

"You know me well enough to know I've been dying of curiosity ever since you left that last message on my answering machine."

Mallory laughed, "Yes, but I can't talk about it now."

"Is he there?"

"This just isn't a good time. I promise I'll call you tomorrow."

"Okay, but before you hang up, can you at least tell me his last name. You see the Sinclairs have a son who's estranged from them whose name is Brit."

A small frown formed between Mallory's eyes. "That's an interesting coincidence."

"Yes, and it's very important to them to know if he and your young man are one and the same."

"Actually, I don't have that information, but when I find out, I'll let you know. I promise I'll call tomorrow. Love you." And then knowing how persistent her mother could be, Mallory quickly hung up.

Bernadette was left listening to a dead line. She began to pace. *Mallory didn't know the last name of the man she believed she was destined to marry. This wasn't making any sense. Did her daughter know it was the Sinclair's son and not want to tell her! No, Mallory was never a game player. She was honest to a fault.*

When Mallory hung up, she looked at Brit in the strangest of ways.

"Is something wrong?"

"No, only my mother. But I just realized I don't even know your last name."

He smiled. "Pretty risky business inviting a man to your apartment not even knowing his last name," he kidded. "On the other hand I don't know yours either, so we're both skating on pretty thin ice."

"Mine's Percival," she volunteered.

He had the broadest smile. "As in Sir Percival who was chaste and pure of heart?"

"The very same."

"No wonder you were so interested in Lord Tennyson's *Idylls of the King*. One of your namesakes was an important character. Do you know what 'Percival' means?"

"Yes, I looked it up once. 'Piercing the valley' or the 'vale'. I decided that's why I liked to hike so much, it was my birthright."

"Maybe so," and then in a more serious tone he added, "But it could also mean to 'pierce the veil', and he spelled the word 'veil' out for her. Perhaps your birthright is more than taking pleasure in trouncing through hills and valleys," and his voice became mysterious. "Perhaps it's the ability to penetrate the most illusive veil of all - the illusion of life."

The next morning Mallory realized Brit had never shared his last name with her. *Was that an oversight, or was he reluctant to divulge that much information?* She decided it was best not to press the issue. It was a big enough concession for him to be here, she didn't want to push too hard. She guessed by little things he already shared that he had been living in the woods by himself for some time, with only an occasional hiker for company. Staying here was going to be an adjustment, not so much physical, but social. He truly believed he didn't fit into society, a lone wolf he called himself, and Mallory could relate. She had often felt the same way, like a fish out of water. That's probably why they connected so quickly.

"I usually don't get home from work until six o'clock. Will you be all right until then?"

He kissed her forehead. "I've already been eyeing your books. That was what I missed the most in the wilderness. Occasionally, I would find a camper who had brought one they were willing to relinquish, but few people, it seems, bring books on camping trips." His eyes were scanning her bookshelves. "I already see several choices that are tempting me. I'm sure I won't get bored."

"I left my work number on the kitchen table if you need to call, and there's plenty of food in the fridge, so help yourself," she said as she closed the front door, stepping out into the cool early morning air. Its refreshing effect, however, was obliterated by the memory of her mother's last words. *The Sinclairs have a son who's estranged from them whose name is Brit, and they're anxious to know if this could be him.*

CHAPTER 35

Brit hardly knew what to say. His first instinct was to run, but run where? He was trapped in a city apartment.

Mallory read his face. "Take a deep breath, I know how you feel. It was just as shocking to me, and definitely not my first choice of circumstances.

"Your mother is living on my parents property? And you've meet them and you've *dated* my brother?"

"Your brother and I just had dinner a few times, and it was *very* casual."

"How did this happen?"

She wanted to say fate, but her instincts cautioned her otherwise.

She was facing him on the undersized sofa. "I thought about this for a whole day and night before I said anything to you, so I've had a head start in the processing. It's a lot to digest, I know. But I believe we can work around these circumstances."

Her eyes held his in a challenge. "What would happen if, for the moment, we put our families aside? They're up in Boston, we're down here. They only need to know as much as we agree to tell them, and as far as I'm concerned, they don't need to know anything," she said defiantly, her fingers moving restlessly against the soft chenille throw pillow.

"You would agree to that?"

She took his hand. "I would agree to anything that would make it right for you, because I believe with all my heart we were meant to be together."

His face softened. "This is all very confusing."

"I know. Give it some time, maybe it won't seem so bizarre in a few days."

"Actually, It would please me for my mother's sake for her to know that I'm okay. I know how hurtful this has been for her, being caught between my dad and me all these years. I wanted to call her more often, but . . ."

"I understand. I remember what it was like when my parents went through their divorce. Conflict is never fun. But whatever is happening up in Boston doesn't have to affect us down here – unless we let it."

"I've never been good at making life work. I've always resolved things by . . ."

She finished his sentence. "By getting out of Dodge?"

"My dad would say I'm a quitter, but the truth is I tried very hard in every way I knew how to make my life work, but it never did. Eventually I had to face the fact that I was a failure, a person who didn't fit in."

"Well, you know what they say: 'it's not over until it's over'. You're still here, and you're still young. It may be you haven't come into your productive time yet, or found your niche. There might be a reason that will reveal itself later in your life why you had to experience what you've judged as failure. Maybe you've signed up for a crash course in understanding why we shouldn't judge each other. Remember one of the mottos of the Grail Knights: Durch Mitleid wissen - Through Compassion to Self-Knowledge. What you've been through has made you a very compassionate and understanding person, consequently a much wiser person. Those are qualities that are hard to come by these days."

"But are they qualities this world appreciates or respects? Be honest, if you told your mother about me and how we feel towards each other, would she be pleased, or would she be wishing you were more attracted to my brother?"

He saw the answer on her face.

Standing abruptly, he clinched his fists in frustration. "I shouldn't have come here. I was wrong to encroach on your life. In the end it will only bring you misery. Even Camelot couldn't withstand the passions of the human heart. I wanted to believe we could make it work," he said with emotion. "I really did, but in less than a week I can already see the dragon raising it's ugly head. I'm tired of fighting dragons. I need to go back where I'm at peace."

Tears welled up in Mallory's eyes. *Damn her mother, damn the Sinclairs and damn the world for taking this sensitive, intelligent young man and making him think he was worthless.* "Then I'm coming with you," she said firmly.

"No. It would just be a matter of time until you realized you made a mistake, and we'd be exactly where we are now."

A long silence ensued while Mallory wrestled with her own doubts. Brit's last statement struck a chord. Suddenly, all of society's programming smothered her hopes. *What did she know about him? The truth was not much, except he had willingly chosen to live outside of traditional society. Realistically, where could she expect a relationship with someone like that to go?*

Finding herself trapped between her cherished dreams and harsh social realities, tears began to well up in her eyes when, suddenly, a vivid memory of the dream where she first saw him popped into her mind.

No, I'm not going to give him up without a fight!

Holding back her tears, she looked deep into his eyes and challenged, "You promised me a month, and I'm holding you to it. I assume you're a man of your word?" she asked with mock defiance. Before he could object, she continued, "It's just a month, not a lifetime. Please hear me out. I have an idea that could work. I know you don't totally believe this, but I really do know how you feel. All my life I never fit in. I was better at playing the phony game than you were, but in my heart I was hurting just as much. Then, I found The Trillium Group, or more accurately they found me. And it was a perfect fit right from the beginning. The people, the goals of the company, they were the same as mine – and the same as yours." She took his hand. "What if you could work for them as well? I know I could arrange an interview."

He hesitated. "You have a college degree, I have nothing to offer them."

"I disagree. Your attitude towards the environment and your love for the wilderness are exactly what they're looking for in an employee." Her eyes were imploring. "What do you have to lose?"

Mallory was trying to read Philip's face.

"So, he'd be willing to work for free for say a month, to show us his determination?"

"Yes, a trial run, since he has no credentials or references in this line of work. But trust me, he's extremely intelligent and knows a great deal about environmental issues. His knowledge of politics and history are also pretty impressive."

"You seem to have a very high regard for this young man."

Mallory blushed and hated herself for it.

Philip smiled at the pretty face across the desk. "Well, I've never been foolish enough to turn down free help. Bring him in with you tomorrow, I'm sure we'll find something of value he can do."

As soon as Mallory left Philip's office, he winked at Francois. "Well, it seems our young man has arrived right on schedule. We must notify Lenzi."

CHAPTER 36

Inside the White House the vice president absent-mindedly rubbed his protruding jaw as he stared out the window at the light falling rain. A siren could be heard in the distance. Something about that Frenchman's story didn't ring true. He wished he had the opportunity to see him in person. Look directly into his eyes. They showed him a videotape made at the farmhouse with hidden surveillance cameras, but that wasn't the same as seeing him in person.

The Frenchman had presented them with two major problems. Somewhere in their ranks was a traitor and somewhere out there was an organization that knew about the Phoenix Project and wanted to stop it. Damn it, they should have forced that aristocratic pimp to give up the information when they had him in their grips.

Henry walked back to his desk. Opening the prescription bottle in the top drawer, he shoved a few pills into his mouth. His eyes drifted to a picture of his wife taken many years ago. She was beautiful then, although, even now, she would be considered attractive. She rarely came to Washington anymore, preferring her home in the Atlanta suburbs. Their preference of being apart was mutual, although she understood her presence in Washington was occasionally required, and she fulfilled her obligation pleasantly, when necessary.

It took a lot of money to keep two expensive households running smoothly, and Henry was counting on the money from the Phoenix Project to allow him the luxury of complete financial freedom. His tight little group was going to make millions, maybe even billions off this project.

They had formed a corporation whose main business was to dispose of nuclear waste, something that had become a major problem for American industries. An environmentally sound method of dealing with the substance had yet to be developed, causing a major headache for the industry. The underground vaults they hoped would contain the problem were all leaking, resulting in soaring cancer rates amongst the population contiguous to the sites. Of course, the government continued to deny any knowledge that the medical problems were related to the waste sites, but the truth was getting out, and it was becoming increasingly difficult to find dumpsites and companies who were willing to tackle the issue. That's when Henry came up with the ingenious plan to load tons of nuclear waste onto a rocket and send it off to Mars. Naturally, everyone would assume that their government-sanctioned company was using ecologically accepted methods for the disposal of the highly contaminated material.

The contract they had been granted was for an astronomical amount, so it didn't make sense that anyone within their group would be the informant. No, it had to be someone at the site in Colorado that got wind of it, or someone at NASA. Yes, that was it. But how to find the son of a bitch became another matter.

At that moment his phone rang.

"Henry," the gruff voice announced, "We have the code name. How soon can you get over here?"

CHAPTER 37

Henry Connolly's silhouette moved quickly from the car into the stately home. He was anxious to hear what the Frenchman had to say. Informants often selected code names that had meaning to them. It could be a clue to his identity.

He was escorted directly into the den where the smell of fine cigar smoke instantly engulfed him. Like most reformed smokers, he found it offensive. With a wave of his hand he declined the brandy offered. Best to keep a clear head. He would have a drink later in his Washington townhouse where he could relax and let down his defenses.

"Well?"

"He calls himself 'The Rock'. Does that ring any bells for you?"

Henry didn't respond immediately. He stared at the floor, digesting the information, his fingers tapping absentmindedly on the arm of the oversized wing-backed chair.

"Well, the first thing that comes to mind is the Rock of Gibraltar. Didn't Michael's family make their money in the insurance business?"

"Yes, but what the hell does that have to do with anything?"

"One of the big insurance companies uses that as their insignia – as a sign of stability."

"Interesting observation."

"The other possibility," he drawled, "Is the more obvious one. Pete has strong connections to Spain via his wife's family, and of course that's where the Rock of Gibraltar is located."

"Two possibilities. So how do we determine if one of them is our boy?" the other man croaked impatiently, his eyes never leaving the vice president's face. His own face was shrouded in cigar smoke.

"What if we gave both Michael and Pete each a different piece of 'confidential' information? Something explosive. Something that an environmental group would pay lots of money to have. And then we wait and see what happens."

The owner of the mansion bristled. "Michael and Pete have been friends and business associates of mine for a long time. Our families are close. It's hard for me to believe that either of them would do something like this," and his hand moved restlessly on the arm of the chair. "And I don't like all this waiting around while the clock keeps ticking away."

"I know, neither do I. And I feel the same way about Michael and Pete, but I think it's necessary to check out every lead, no matter how small and improbable. What are the other options?"

"I already told you. Bring me the Frenchman. I'll make that arrogant weasel talk."

Henry wanted to squeeze the Frenchman as much as anyone, but the thought of getting Interpol involved made him more prudent. It wasn't like this guy was a nobody who could just disappear without notice. He came from an aristocratic family - a wealthy aristocratic family - that had the means and connections to demand and get answers.

"Let's give it one more week and see what happens after we give Pete and Michael that phony information. In the meantime, I've got the FBI checking on all the security guards at the Colorado site. I still think it's someone on the outside. It makes more sense."

"You've got one week," the other man said, and he bit the end off his cigar and spit it into the ashtray.

CHAPTER 38

"Philip presented me with an offer today that was quite interesting." Brit's blue eyes danced with excitement, as he sipped his herbal ice tea. He loved the way Mallory prepared it with natural mint and a slice of orange. "He asked if I'd be interested in making speeches about the environment at college campuses."

"And that interests you?" Mallory had joined him on the small balcony of her apartment. She was seeing new facets of Brit's personality daily.

"I know this sounds strange," Brit confided, "But sometimes I feel as if Philip can read my mind; and not just my mind, but my past. He seems to intuitively know everything about me."

"I know, I've felt the same thing," Mallory shared. "And yet it's not an uncomfortable relationship."

"No, not at all. In fact it's refreshing to be around someone who seems to understand you completely," he said, slipping on his sunglasses. The sun had just moved beyond the large birch tree in front of their apartment complex and was glaring off the windshields of the parked cars.

"And accepts you for who you are."

"Exactly." His voice then softened into the hazy tone of memory as he confided, "When I was in high school, I took a speech class. Not because I was particularly interested in public speaking, but it turned out to be the only elective that fit into my schedule besides things like band or choir, for which I had no talent. The end result was that I surprised everyone, including myself, at how well I did with writing and delivering speeches. I actually won a few trophies."

"Really?" Mallory stopped slathering lotion on her tanned legs and looked directly at him. "If you liked it and were good at it, why didn't you pursue it?"

"My parents became too caught up with it. As soon as they saw I had some ability, they began pushing me until it wasn't fun any more. Dad wanted to be involved in writing my speeches, and then they both wanted me to practice in front of them, so they could critique my presentation. Frankly, it became intolerable. I never could handle it when my parents became controlling." He looked at her sheepishly. "I know they were trying to help, but it didn't translate that way for me. Anyhow, I never continued with it, but I always knew that it was a skill I would use someday."

Mallory reached over and hugged him. "I knew it would be a perfect fit between you and the Trillium Group," and although her words were of encouragement, an inexplicable trepidation rose in her breast at the thought of Brit giving speeches.

CHAPTER 39

Mallory's right foot moved restlessly on the wood plank floor of the large auditorium where she sat in the front row. She nervously glanced at her watch, hardly aware of the movement and sounds around her. This would be Brit's first speech.

They were at a private college tucked into the rolling hills of the Virginia countryside, its buildings a strange mix of stately old southern and ultra modern architecture, making them a visual conduit between the past and the future. Philip had chosen this particular campus because of the extensive environmental programs it offered. It was exactly the kind of crowd the Trillium Group wanted to draw from for Brit's first performance, students who were well informed.

When at last Brit walked onto the stage, a surge of pride swelled in Mallory's breast. He looked very handsome in his light blue oxford shirt. It accentuated his blue eyes and tanned complexion.

She held her breath as Brit hesitated. Giving a speech to a large crowd such as this was very different from practicing at the kitchen table with her as his only audience. Could he do it?

His eyes found her in the crowd. He smiled with such love that she melted, releasing everything except the love she felt in return. There was only the two of them. The room, the crowd, they all disappeared.

Brit's first words came slow, calculated, but soon he slipped into a familiar pattern that felt comfortable, and with this cushion of comfort came a wave of confidence that filled his being and overflowed into the auditorium, gripping the audience. With eyes that turned magnetic, his presence on stage loomed larger, and he very quickly commanded every ounce of their attention.

"Even though the most respected environmental scientists have persistently and clearly sounded an urgent alarm about global warming," he declared, "Washington continues to pretend that what's happening is the result of normal cycles. They know the truth, yet they go to great lengths to keep the general public misinformed. Why? So the facts about the deteriorating condition of our planet will remain convoluted. It's no wonder we are just beginning to understand the gravity of the situation. Because the gross polluters, in alliance with our politicians, have made us the targets of a campaign of deception and misinformation. For what purpose? To keep us confused so they can continue with their irresponsible practices without legal or financial repercussions."

He smiled sadly. "Big corporations are trying to convince us that the environmentalists are fighting to preserve our ancient forests for the sake of a spotted owl. I am here to tell you that is not true. Trees are vital to *our* health. Here are the facts. An average size tree produces enough oxygen to keep a family of four breathing for one year. One acre of trees is capable of removing 13 tons of dust and pollutants from the atmosphere. Trees reduce noise pollution. Trees serve as windbreakers, slowing the force of the wind. Trees moderate local climate by lowering air temperature. Every time you cut down a tree you increase land temperature." He paused and seemed to make eye contact with each one of them. "We are fighting to save the trees for us, to improve and enrich *our* quality of life. And yes, we are saving the trees for the spotted owl as well, and all the other creatures for whom they provide a natural habitat and who have no voice. We must be their voice."

Brit paused. "Can you picture a planet without trees? Without the wildlife for which the trees provide protection and nourishment? I don't even want to try to imagine a world as bleak as that. Do you? I'm reminded of what our beloved American naturalist Henry David Thoreau once said: 'What is the use of a house if you haven't got a tolerable planet to put it on?'"

The audience hung spellbound as Brit's speech built in emotional intensity while he continued to present them with fact after fact in his logical and clear-cut style. At the conclusion, he paused, and with the expertise of an experienced master of rhetoric, he riveted their attention even further. His next words were spoken with electrifying clarity.

"Now it is time for the people of America to recognize the truth. Our current administration has not only ignored, but purposely undermined what is best for the public's interests. Instead they have chosen to increase the profits of corporations – as well as fill their own pockets very generously - at the expense of the environment."

"And now the last bell has rung," he said in a tone that vibrated with the prophesy of higher realms. "We have no more time. There has already been irreparable damage to our planet. We cannot allow this to continue. It is time for us to step forward, one by one, and take back our planet, making it safe for ourselves and for every generation to follow. And the first step in that process is the recognition that we can no longer trust the politicians to make our choices for us, because their poor choices are what got us here. It's our job to speak the truth to those in power and spark outrage at their unconscionable practices. Then, we must continue by monitoring what is happening in Washington, because those in power have learned they can say the right thing and then do something else. But if we become the constant watchdogs of our government, politicians will soon realize that in order to stay in power they must truly serve their constituents, not their own wallets. Only then will our planet become a safe haven. A pristine Shangri-la that supports us, because we have supported it."

Brit's voice adopted a more intimate tone, as one friend speaking to another. "I want to leave you with a reminder of a Cree Indian prophecy. The Native American Indians were a nation of people who understood more fully than we their connection to the earth. They understood that men are the caretakers of this planet, not the owners."

The passion in his voice when he quoted the Cree prophecy that Mallory's grandfather had taught her rebounded through the building.

"Only after the last tree has been cut down.
Only after the last river has been poisoned.
Only after the last fish has been caught.
Only then will you find that money cannot be eaten," and he stared into the crowd.

The silence that first filled the auditorium was staggering, as the impact behind the meaning of his last words touched the crowd at their very core. But very quickly, thundering applause broke through the silence. Standing as if they were one, the audience had heard the call and they were ready to respond.

The applause still ringing in the air, Mallory looked at Philip who was seated beside her, "Where did *that* come from?" she asked amazed. Never in her wildest dreams could she have imagined Brit taking such command of an audience. He was such a gentle spirit.

Philip winked precociously. "It came from the union of the masculine and the feminine."

Mallory stared at him in disbelief. *Was he speaking of her relationship with Brit? How would that make a difference?*

As if reading her mind, Philip explained, "Your feminine attitudes when blended with his masculinity helped him to crystallize his ideas, and your unwavering belief in him rendered the necessary confidence." He paused, making direct eye contact. "That was why it was important for the two of you to come together."

Mallory flashed on the dream she had before she met Brit. *So was their relationship meant to be? Sanctioned by the gods? That was too bizarre an idea to even entertain! Yet, how could she forget that she had seen him first in a dream at the very spot where they later met?*

CHAPTER 40

Winding its way for eighty miles before reaching the Boston harbor where hotels and restaurants tightly hug its shores in a celebration of life, the Charles River creates a natural boundary between Boston and Cambridge. In contrast to the serene park stretching along its banks, a busy thoroughfare runs parallel, taunting the passing drivers with a taste of tranquility and reminding them there's more to life than the mad dash in which humanity seemed to be endlessly engaged.

In the middle of the dense traffic, a silver Jaguar pressed forward with a determined purpose. The mood in the car was strained as Samuel maneuvered through the maze of vehicles. Julia in her nervousness was chattering about inconsequential things, adding to the tension already felt by Samuel and Bernadette.

They were on their way to hear Brit speak at a college campus in Cambridge. This would be their first face-to-face contact with the young couple since the two met in the wilderness. Although they had been closely following Brit's meteoric rise to fame through the news media and exchanging quick emails with Mallory, she had cleverly avoided mentioning anything personal.

To say they were anxious about this first meeting was an understatement. For Bernadette there was a daunting curiosity. *What made this young man so special that Mallory began entertaining thoughts of marriage on their first meeting? A young man who dropped out of society and lived the life of a recluse, definitely not her first choice for a mate for her daughter.*

In the case of the Sinclairs the matter was more complicated. This was the son Samuel had literally disowned and, based on the disruptive nature of their past relationship, Julia was understandably nervous about how this meeting would go. She knew Samuel had finally let go of his fierce judgment of his youngest son's chosen path, but she also knew that when strong patterns were set in human relationships, it wasn't always easy to shift established behavior at a moment's notice.

When the silver Jaguar reached the stone bridge spanning the river, the pleasant scene of colorful sailboats charting the waters hardly registered with the tense occupants of the car. They were very close to their destination.

Mallory was easy to spot sitting in the front row wearing a bright yellow sweater that accentuated her dark eyes. Her hair was worn loose, hugging her slender shoulders. Greetings between the women were joyous. They all noticed, but chose to ignore, Samuel's standoffish behavior.

Fifteen minutes later, when Brit walked onto the stage, Mallory immediately noticed his step was slow almost halting, and when he reached the podium, she saw his eyes dart straight to his father. She held her breath. Was it her imagination or could she could literally see the confidence being sucked out of Brit. They had talked about this beforehand. At the time Brit seemed unconcerned that his father would be there, feeling he was past all that. *But ... what was happening here?*

Mallory watched in horror as Brit stumbled over his opening statements, his hands nervously shuffling through his notes. *This definitely wasn't the same person who gave the previous speeches.*

Bernadette's eyes were also glued to Brit. *So this was the young man who had captured her daughter's heart.* She studied his face. Brit was nice looking, with long honey-blond hair that was pulled neatly back at the nape of his neck. He had his father's curious blue eyes and determined chin, but she could see his mother's pronounced cheekbones and gentleness of manner.

As Brit continued to plod through his sentences with a lack of poise, Julia instinctively realized her husband's presence was the reason for Brit's poor performance. In frustration she reached over and gripped Bernadette's hand.

At the same time Mallory realized Brit needed her help to gain his composure. She forced herself to remember the advice Philip had given her.

You must stay centered in love and confidence, otherwise, Brit will pick up on your fear and feed off of it.

Mallory closed her eyes, sending Brit assurance and unconditional love. She released the anxiety hovering in the corners of her mind and visualized him in his previous presentations, when he easily captivated the crowd. She held that vision until she heard the tempo in his voice begin to change. *Yes, this was better.* Opening her eyes, she flashed him a brilliant smile as he settled into a rhythm that showcased his natural speaking abilities.

Once again Brit's compassionate tone began to ooze out into the crowd, mesmerizing them as he had in the past. His voice changed timbre as it adopted a wisdom that spanned the centuries, and the audience leaned forward hanging onto his every word.

"Here are the facts," he declared bluntly. "After thoroughly examining the evidence available on global warming, every major independent scientific group has come to the same conclusion. Our planet is getting hotter – man is to blame – and it's going to get worse - **unless** we make some major changes in our lifestyles - and soon." He paused, waiting for them to absorb his last statement.

When he spoke again, his voice boomed out. "Are we going to lay down and accept this as inevitable? Or our we going to organize and do something about it?" Shouts of encouragement emerged from the crowd.

"Right this minute, as we sit here, Artic glaciers have begun melting and racing with unprecedented speed towards our seas and oceans, causing them to rise twice as fast as in the past. At the same time, many of the areas that depend on mountain snows for their water supplies are running short as less snow falls. Hurricanes and cyclones are becoming stronger and occurring with more regularity, devastating our coastal cities in the process. But none of these facts have made an impact on our present administration. They keep tap dancing around the issues, ignoring the blizzard of data that is now available and conclusive."

"There is an old Sioux proverb that comes to mind," and he smiled at the audience, radiating his warmth and charm. "Even the frog is wise enough not to drink up the pond in which he lives." Then in a softer voice. "Apparently our politicians lack this basic wisdom. Time and time again they have demonstrated their willingness to deplete our natural resources and destroy our environment solely for the material gains of corporations who, then, return the favor with large contributions to their campaign funds and lavish gifts to them personally. It's a sad and vicious circle that crosses all party lines." Pause. "We must acknowledge that these people lack conscience. And we must take it upon ourselves to be their conscience. How? By closely monitoring their actions and by voting for candidates who are true leaders. A true leader is not governed by opinion polls. A true leader has a sense of integrity and vision that guide him and his country towards nobler purposes. These men exist, and we must seek them out and encourage them to run for public offices."

"Make no mistake about it, folks. This is our last chance to get it right. We have run out of second chances. Our planet desperately needs our help, and it needs it now."

Pausing, Brit leaned forward on the podium. "In closing I would like to remind you of the words of the great mystic poet, John Donne," and his voice boomed out to the expectant faces. "Do not send to know for whom the bell tolls, it tolls for thee."

The crowd instantly understood what Brit was telling them as the room exploded with an electrical charge that quickly swept across the nation on the wings of the news media. Brit Sinclair, with an unassuming humility coupled with a dynamic presence, had invited them to make the fate of their nation a personal quest. Fearlessly stating the facts, he had called them to a common purpose – the goal to save their planet, the only home they could ever remember.

CHAPTER 41

Great stress when applied to the human psyche can cause severe neurosis or, in the rare instance, manifests as a finely developed extrasensory ability. In Lenzi's case, it was the latter. She was barely two when her poverty-stricken parents were forced to sell her twin brother, Gabor, in a desperate attempt to avoid starvation for the rest of the family, leaving Lenzi with a void that no one could fill. It was as if her arm had been amputated. Inconsolable for months, she cried day and night until one ordinary night something quite extraordinary happened. As she lay whimpering in her bed, missing the warm body that had been next to her from birth, a bright light came down and took her up to a place where Gabor was waiting for her.

It became a nightly ritual for the twins to meet in the upper ethers were they romped and played as they strengthened their bond. By the time they were ready to attend school, they came to realize that what happened to them was out of the ordinary and to speak of it made most adults uncomfortable, particularly in Gabor's case, as he was in America where such ideas were thought of as Satanic.

Lenzi's family on the other hand, like most uneducated Europeans, was still wise in the ways of mysticism. Angels and fairies were more than tales to put their children to sleep at night, they were realities of other dimensions that they knew in their hearts existed. At first Lenzi's parents dismissed her chattering about Gabor as a young child's imagination, and they were pleased their little girl was at last able to let go of the terrible pain of her loss. But as she grew and could communicate with more skill, they realized something special was happening. But what to do?

Wisely, they turned to the young child and asked her.

"Take me to the Pyrenees Mountains in France she told them." So they packed up their family and their sparse belongings and followed the wisdom of the child. There she was bathed daily in the water at Lourdes until finally her connection with the Mother Goddess was complete. In those mystical waters the wisdom of self-enlightenment was passed on to the young girl, and as she grew, this wisdom also grew. And always, she shared everything she learned with her twin brother.

CHAPTER 42

Inside the refurbished colonial in rural Massachusetts three people sat in front of the expertly crafted oak entertainment center that housed the television with an air of anticipation. No one spoke, their eyes were glued to the screen.

Forty-five minutes later an active debate took place.

"Well that connects a few dots," Samuel declared rather triumphantly. "As far as I'm concerned that dispels any doubts about the existence of UFO's. When that many high-ranking retired military personnel are willing to come forward and substantiate sightings that they personally have experienced, one has to pay attention."

"How has the American government kept this under raps for so long – and why?" Bernadette blurted out, and she moved restlessly on the burgundy couch.

"The *how* is easy, they've controlled the press for some time now. The idea of a free press in America is an illusion that the restricted press keeps perpetuating so that we'll think we have freedom of the press." Samuel's face showed its disgust. "The *why* is another matter. Frankly, I don't understand it. And other governments don't understand it either. That's one of the reasons this tape is being distributed - to break the embargo the United States Government has had on UFO sightings."

"Every once in a while one has slipped through," Bernadette recalled. "I can remember in the early 90's the Russian scientists showed pictures of a cigar-shaped spaceship taken by their astronauts. There was a quick bleep on one of our national television channels, and then it disappeared never to be seen again. Then sometime in 2004 the Mexican air force distributed pictures of UFO's that were taken with sophisticated equipment. Again there was a quick airing. The next day the press turned it into a joke, saying things like: What's funnier, the fact that there are UFO's or the fact that Mexico has an air force?"

"It makes me so angry when Americans take the attitude that we're more advanced and therefore better than everyone else. It's an arrogance that's been perpetuated by the present administration, the 'we're number one' mentality. In the meantime the statistics show the truth. The United States' educational system doesn't even rank in the top thirty among the industrial nations."

"Just think," Samuel announced. "This video could verify what we've already been suspecting, and it actually ties in with everything we know about the Grail Romances."

"In what way?" Bernadette questioned.

"Remember, the original Grail Romances dealt with a mystery of lineage. Part of the oath of being a Grail Knight was they were forbidden to disclose their history or identity. It was taken so far that in some of the tales if someone even asked a Grail Knight a question about his heritage, he had to leave."

"The authors of the research book *Holy Blood Holy Grail* presented the hypothesis that this was because their lineage could be traced back to Jesus, and at that time, one wasn't allowed to speculate that Jesus could possible have been married and sired children, because they feared repercussions from the Church."

He looked at the two women, his blue eyes wide, "But what if the direction our research is pointing to is right? What if Jesus was an E.T., which would have made his offspring part E.T. and that's what they weren't supposed to divulge?"

"That would explain the stories about the Merovingian rulers who had magical healing powers and abilities to communicate with animals," he concluded, adding more wine to his glass.

Julia speculated, "But if he was divine, wouldn't he also have had those powers?"

Samuel barely nodded his head in agreement.

"You are determined to make Jesus an extraterrestrial," Bernadette teased.

"No, I just don't want to leave that piece out of the possibilities." Then, his blue eyes looked directly at Bernadette holding her attention.

"Why do *you* think your father kept telling you that Pleiades was your constellation?"

CHAPTER 43

Bernadette faltered. Her face scarlet.

"I confess," she stammered, "That my father's words have haunted me for years. Yet the logical part of me has rejected the obvious conclusion as ridiculous," and then she heaved a huge sigh and looked rather sheepishly before admitting, "Although in all honesty, there's another part of me that feels entirely comfortable with the idea. And the more I've researched the subject, the more my rational mind is beginning to recognize there is a chance that's it's a plausible hypothesis, particularly after watching this video."

She looked from one to the other. "I have to admit that when I originally discovered the Parthenon in Greece and the Egyptian pyramids were astronomically oriented to either Pleiades or Sirius, as well as the pyramids in Mexico, I kept telling myself that was only because the ancients were fascinated with astronomy, but as I found one after another ancient culture oriented their most sacred temples to receive the beams of light from these two star systems into their inner sanctums or onto their altars precisely on the equinoxes, it did raise a lot of questions for me. A big 'why' kept flashing in my mind. There are billions of stars out there. Why these two star systems? Certainly there's something here that needs to be looked at further."

Bernadette's slender hands moved nervously as her speech came faster. "But even more difficult for me than the extraterrestrial connection is the idea that our ancestors were aquatic." She paused. "Until this week," and she arched her eyebrows, as a glimmer of an exciting secret skipped across her face.

"I decided it might be helpful to learn more about dragons, since the dragon is the logo of the Royal Dragon Court of Hungary and was also carved on my father's marble box. What I found was that the original dragons were depicted as amphibious. So, then I started studying cultures where the dragon symbol was still prevalent, and I discovered that more than just the indigenous people of this planet have the belief that their ancestors were sea creatures. In India, the Hindus god Vishnu is half man and half fish, and the Chinese maintain their civilization was founded by amphibious beings."

"Actually, so do current-day American scientists," Samuel announced, the look on his face somewhat gloating at the surprise on theirs. "Don't scientists believe that we originally evolved from the sea as simple organisms?"

"My goodness, I never thought of it that way, but you're right!" Julia exclaimed.

Bernadette continued on. "I must admit that after I found out dragons were originally amphibious a million things started to pop into my mind. Like why are we baptized in water? Some ministers even say the words 'Born again in Water' while they're baptizing the person, but so far, no one has been able to tell me why. And why do we say 'I feel like a fish out of water?' Why don't we say 'I feel like a monkey out of a tree' or 'a bird out of the air?' Not to mention all the fables about mermaids who were always involved with the seduction of sailors. Then, of course, there was the legend that you brought to our attention Samuel about the Merovingian's descendent who it was claimed had two fathers, one of which was a strange aquatic being."

Bernadette searched the faces in front of her. "And since the Merovingian bloodline claims a connection to Jesus, is it possible Samuel is right? As much as I hate to admit it, the arrows do seem to be pointing to the possibility that Jesus or his ancestors could have been from another planet. A planet where the beings were amphibious, which would explain why he was represented by the symbol of the fish." And then she laughed nervously. "Just saying that out loud makes me feel ridiculous," and, at that moment, her eyes were drawn to the celestial globe that sat predominantly on a shelf of the Sinclair's entertainment center. Was it her imagination or did Pleiades seem to twinkle at her as in the night sky?

She shook the thought from her head and shifted gears. "Oh, and by the way Julia, when I was doing my research, I ran across some things of interest tying the Sumerian language to the Hungarian language. I thought you might want to investigate it a little further and see where that leads."

"I have to confess," Julia admitted, "I only have a dim recollection of studying the Sumerians in school."

"Yes, it's one of the many historical facts that's barely touched upon in most of our school systems, and it's unfortunate, because the land called Sumer was a sophisticated culture. It existed some 6,000 years ago in the area that is now southeastern Iraq and was similar to the Egyptian culture in that it appeared out of nowhere literally in tact with language, laws and artisans with highly developed skills. Their language, which has been reconstructed through the many tablets found by archaeologists, bears no relationship to any of the ancient languages in the area. So where *did* it come from?" Bernadette shrugged her shoulders.

"The fact that stood out to me is that, based on its grammatical structure, their language is the closest to the Hungarian language, which geographically speaking seems rather odd. Although the Turks invaded Hungary fairly early on in their history and could have brought it with them, it is interesting that the Turkish language doesn't have the same distinct similarities to the Sumerian language as the Hungarian language does."

Then a wide smirk beamed across her face. "And surprise, surprise. The Sumerians also depicted their gods as half man and half fish, which again brings the Hungarian connection into the picture from a different direction."

"Another case of the circles connecting, yet bringing us no closer to a conclusion," Samuel complained.

"But they keep connecting. And that's important. At least we're not running into dead ends," Julia's voice was encouraging.

"So where do we go from here?"

"I think we should keep going forward with our research until we run out of ideas." And then Samuel looked directly at Bernadette, "Since The Voice originally pointed you in the direction of the Holy Grail, why don't you try to initiate contact and ask it what we should be studying. It might be our best source of information, and possibly, it's just waiting to hear from you."

Bernadette scowled. "I doubt it," she muttered, wishing she had never told Samuel about The Voice.

Julia patted her hand, her voice solicitous, "Isn't there an old esoteric saying that goes something like: 'When the student is ready, the teacher appears.' Perhaps The Voice is quietly waiting for you to give some sign that you're ready."

"But am I?" Bernadette asked pointedly, and the anxious look on her face revealed her answer.

CHAPTER 44

"It can't be," the vice president bellowed into the phone, his southern accent sounding more like the roar of a canon than a drawl.

"You better get over here as soon as you can," the voice on the other end ordered.

Henry hadn't had a cigarette in years, but right now he would do anything for one long drag. He began to pace, his hand held at his abdomen where that troublesome burning sensation was beginning to flare. Out the window he could see the evening commute traffic stalled on Pennsylvania Avenue.

How could this have happened? The Frenchman gave them both sets of the phony 'confidential' information they had passed on to Michael and Pete individually, hoping it would help to identify if one of them was siphoning information about the Phoenix Project to the Frenchman's organization. Was it possible that Michael and Pete were working together leaking information, or had one confided in the other not realizing he was a turncoat?

On top of that the President was causing havoc over in Europe, offending heads of state right and left with his cocky isolationist attitude. Oh yes, and the third problem. Out of the blue comes some hippie kid going around the country stirring up trouble with speeches about the increase of pollution in the environment and making a direct connection to the policies of their administration. At first Henry dismissed the kid as inconsequential, but his following was beginning to gather momentum like a small, dark cloud. This might be the beginning of yet another storm.

Henry threw up his hands in frustration. Too much was happening at once. Best to work on the most important problem first. The Phoenix Project was his priority; it had been his baby right from the beginning. Henry had always played with the big boys of finance, but this project boosted him up to the elite. Each of his little group stood to make fifty million a piece on the Phoenix Project. Not a bad little haul for one contract. And if this went well, there would be more behind it. It didn't make sense that one of their select group would do something to jeopardize that much easy money. He decided it might be wise to have a long lunch with Michael and Pete separately to feel them out. Henry's southern charm had always been his greatest asset. That, and his good instincts. Yes, a nice long chat with each of these guys might tell him plenty.

Next problem – the president. That guy was so dumb he didn't have the good sense to keep his mouth shut. Walking over to his desk with long strides, Henry put in a call to the personal advisor he had hand picked to travel with the President. They were in Rome.

"Larry, what's going on over there?"

The vice president could hear the frustration in the voice on the other end. "We give him a speech, and then he goes and elaborates and gets himself into trouble."

"I understand, I'll speak to him directly. But listen, it's your job to see that the foreign press gets the message straight. Do you get my meaning? I'll take care of the press over here.

Henry felt exhausted. He wished he could take a nap, but there was work to be done. The loose ends were beginning to unravel fast, and he knew if he didn't tie them up quickly, something major was going to break open.

What to do about that kid, what was his name, Bret, or Brad, or something like that. Oh yeah, Brit, Brit Sinclair. They didn't need him stirring up folks right now about environmental issues, just when the Phoenix Project was winding up. Henry pushed his chair back as he dialed the phone. That young man just might have to have a little car accident.

CHAPTER 45

Although the night air was temperate, the Neanderthal looking thug methodically put on a pair of leather gloves before he lodged his bulky frame behind the wheel of the SUV. His gristly face was devoid of any emotion. He drove for forty-five minutes until he reached the auditorium on the college campus where he slowly cruised the parking lot looking for a specific license plate, his beefy baldhead shinning through the windshield in the light of the full moon. He appeared to have the element of time on his side.

It was an hour later when Brit walked out of the auditorium into the mild night air. He took a deep breath savoring the freshness. Cassarra and Mallory were already waiting by the car.

"Look at that beautiful full moon," Mallory exclaimed, as the other two shifted their gazes upwards.

"It's actually a blue moon," Cassarra mused. "It's quite a rarity," and the moonlight danced off her lush chestnut hair and lit up her beautiful face. It was a face that reflected an inner peace.

Brit and Mallory turned to see if she was jesting.

"A blue moon," she went on to explain "is when there are two full moons in the same astrological sign. On those rare occasions, the second moon is called a blue moon."

"Why?" the other two asked in unison, and then laughed at their synchronization.

"It goes back to an old Hindu tradition relating to the God Krishna, who has been portrayed as half-man, half-fish, and whose skin color was said to be blue." Her eyes held an element of mystery when she looked back at them. "It's believed when a blue moon occurs it's a potent time when communion with the gods is very powerful. More miracles occur during the presence of a blue moon," she finished softly, her eyes now looking off into the distance as if focusing on something in the future.

"So more miracles happen every time there are two moons in the same month?" Mallory questioned.

"Not the same month," Cassarra corrected. "The same astrological sign. Unfortunately the calendar we use to mark time doesn't relate accurately to natural cycles. It's an artificial configuration established by the early Christian popes that was devised to distance humanity from the Pagan calendars, which were in tune with nature. Our present calendar keeps us off balance with the natural rhythms of the Universe, thereby abusing our sensibilities."

"Wow," Brit exclaimed, "I never thought of it that way, but now I see it makes perfect sense. It's one more way they've kept us locked in their matrix."

Cassarra flashed a knowing smile at him. "That's why you had to keep retreating into nature to balance yourself. Can you see that now?"

"Yes, very clearly."

"With this understanding," she continued, "comes the ability to connect without having to physically remove yourself," and they drove off into the night each lost in their own thoughts.

The moonlight filtering through the trees cast shadows that loomed dramatically against the dark night sky as Mallory's white Volkswagen Jetta cut silently through the lonely Pennsylvania woodlands. They had been on the deserted two-lane highway long enough for the miles to become a blur when she offered, "If you get tired, let me know; I'm wide awake, and wouldn't mind driving."

Brit patted her thigh affectionately. "I'm okay for now. After my speeches I'm usually wound up and driving is a good way to relax."

They were headed towards Philadelphia where Brit was scheduled to make his next speech the following afternoon. It was still a few hours a way.

There was little traffic on the two lane highway, so when Mallory noticed Brit repeatedly checking his rear and side mirrors, she thought it strange. She could feel the car decelerate.

"What's up?"

"Oh, there's an SUV riding my bumper, and I'm trying to let him pass; but when I slow down, so does he."

"Maybe if I pull off the road, he'll pass," he said as he maneuvered the car onto the shoulder, almost slowing to a stop.

"He's following me. I wonder if he needs help?"

Both the girls turned to look out the rear window, the bright lights from the SUV instantly blinding them.

"Speed up," Cassarra's voice commanded with an unusual authority.

"Why?"

"Do as I say," and although her voice was low and even, it was compelling.

Brit pressed down on the accelerator, as Mallory turned to study Cassarra's face. "What's wrong?" she asked, her tone apprehensive.

"I can't explain," Cassarra confided. "It's only a feeling, but it's very strong. Whatever you do, don't stop."

Without any further questioning, Brit pulled back onto the highway, as the SUV continued to follow right on their bumper.

"Maintain your normal speed," Cassarra cautioned as she could feel their vehicle begin to speed down the highway.

Brit found it difficult to stay within the speed limit with the SUV right on his tail. He nervously kept checking his mirrors. As they approached a wide turn, the SUV accelerated and began to pass, but half way into the turn, instead of continuing forward, it began to edge towards them, forcing Brit back onto the shoulder in order to keep from being sideswiped. The rough pavement made it difficult for him to keep the car under control. In his peripheral vision he could see Mallory trying to brace herself from being jostled around.

His hands had a fierce grip on the steering wheel.

"Hold your ground!" Cassarra exclaimed and her voice sounded a million miles away.

"But he'll hit us!"

"Stay your course," she repeated evenly.

Brit fought desperately to keep control of the car on the uneven shoulder, all too aware of the SUV that continued to stay neck and neck with them in the right lane, until without warning it began to swerve towards them again. There was nowhere else for them to go except down.

Fighting his instincts, Brit followed Cassarra's direction and held his ground.

Mallory braced for impact.

"Brake now!" Cassarra cried out, her voice cutting through the terror of the moment."

Brit slammed on his brakes just as the SUV dramatically made a hard swerve towards them.

Screeching sounds penetrated the darkness, followed by Mallory's scream.

The SUV narrowly missed their front bumper as they fishtailed onto the highway.

With white knuckles grasping the wheel, Brit struggled to keep control.

As they skidded to a halt, they watched in horror as the SUV sped off the embankment with a devastating force head on into a tree.

Brit was shaking as he dropped his head onto the steering wheel.

Mallory slumped into the seat, sobbing uncontrollably. "Why did that man try to kill us!" she blurted between sobs.

Brit put his arm around her. "I don't really think it was directed at us personally. It was probably just a random road-rage thing. But, thanks to Cassarra's instincts, we were able to get out of it without getting hurt."

Through Mallory's sobs, Cassarra's mellow response came as a whisper as it drifted over the front seat. "It was a miracle of the blue moon," she murmured, as if to herself.

Bewildered by Cassarra's calm response, the emotionally fraught couple automatically turned towards her hypnotic voice. They were surprised to see dreamy eyes looking off into the distance and smiling - as if at the face of an old friend.

CHAPTER 46

Philippe was listening to Cassarra with a poised intensity. When she finished, he looked over his wire-rimmed glasses and smiled with amusement. His thick white eyebrows and matching shock of white hair, giving him the appearance of a character out of a Charles Dickens novel. "I didn't think we would be rattling their cages this quickly, but I have to admit, Brit's popularity has grown more swiftly than we anticipated. Perhaps we are closer to critical mass than we thought."

He patted her hand, affectionately. "Your intuition to travel with them that evening has, as always, proven to be accurate. The time may come soon when we must reveal more of their purpose to them."

She nodded in agreement. "We should convey this incident to Lenzi as soon as possible, don't you think?"

"Yes," Philippe agreed. "I will send word immediately. In the meantime, as a precautionary measure, it might be wise for you to travel with them whenever possible."

Washington D.C. was still quiet in the early morning hours, as the vice president's footsteps echoed through the wide, deserted halls. It wasn't unusual for him to start his day before his staff arrived. He was a man who liked to stay on top of things. When he answered the phone, he immediately recognized the voice on the other end. It delivered its message in a brief monotone.

"Mission aborted. Our man is dead."

"He's dead?" Henry repeated, his voice incredulous. "How?"

"Lost control of his vehicle and hit a tree. He was DOA when the paramedics arrived."

Henry slammed down the receiver and stared out the window. *How could so many things be going wrong?*

Hours later, he made what proved to be an unfortunate decision. Without identifying himself to the voice on the other end of the phone he blurted, "I think you're right, it's time to bring in the Frenchman, see what he really knows." Then, he pushed the intercom button. "Have my car ready immediately," he drawled, "and I don't need a driver," giving no further explanation to his secretary.

As he walked out of the White House, he nodded to the president who was chatting with the pretty tour guide with the lush chestnut hair. It wasn't the first time he had seen the president hanging around her desk. *I'd better get my assistants on that one and make sure there's nothing to it. Last thing we need right now is a sex scandal.*

CHAPTER 47

The sound of the summer rain through the screen door was invigorating, reminding Bernadette how much she missed the seasons. The predictable weather in California was monotonous in comparison. Mesmerized, she watched the large raindrops bounce off the patio, enhancing the rich colors of the flagstones with their dance. The only other sound in the room was the slow rhythmic beat of Samuel's pencil tapping against the desk, simulating the plink plunk of the rain against the metal downspout.

"Okay, what great thoughts are rolling around in that mind?" Julia finally asked as she joined them from the kitchen with a large pot of homemade soup.

Samuel didn't answer immediately. His blue eyes looking far away. "I was thinking about that numerology information Bernadette showed us on Brit's name."

Bernadette looked at him out of the corner of her eyes, surprised that he brought the subject up without sarcasm.

Samuel spoke slowly as he formulated his thoughts. "It made a triangle going up and another going down, right?"

"That's right."

Do you remember in my DaVinci book, I showed the ancient astronomical symbols for male / \ and female \ /?"

The women both nodded, wondering where this was going.

"And if you overlapped them, how they made a hexagon – the perfect union of male and female. I assume that's what The Voice was telling you, that the name Brit, because of its numerological components, is a perfect balance of the masculine and feminine. But last night I realized if you used them as the original symbols for male and female, and then put them point to point - you have the figure 'X'."

"And___?"

"Well, many of the secret societies repudiated the cross as the symbol for Jesus, because it was a despicable instrument used for torture. Instead they used the 'X', which was the symbol of light, or enlightenment."

Bernadette's eyes lit up. "Is that why we use Xmas as the abbreviation for Christmas? I always wondered about that because it made no sense. In fact, it always seemed somewhat sacrilegious since one normally thinks of the 'X' as the designation for someone illiterate who can't write their name."

"Exactly! Think about it." Samuel prompted. "With the very high-profile exception of Xmas, the letter 'X' is commonly used in negative connotations in our culture, so I began to check historically why that was. It turns out it was an attempt, and a successful one I might add, by the Church fathers to negate something positive. So now, instead of thinking of the 'X' as enlightenment, we use it to mark answers wrong on tests and to rate movies of undesirable content."

Bernadette shook her head. "Of course, 'X-rated' movies!"

"In the meantime," Samuel went on, "they've kept our attention focused on the cross and the crucifixion and away from the resurrection."

"Bernadette's expression was one of disgust. "It's amazing how those in power are able to shape history by how they have us focus our attention. So the Church took a symbol of torture and have us revering it, and conversely, they took a symbol of hope and turned it into a negative?" and she scrunched up her face in disgust.

Julia nodded sadly. "Yes, unfortunately as Napoleon once said, 'History is nothing more than agreed upon lies."

"Yes," Samuel agreed, "it seems the more I research, the more I realize that what we've been taught is a mere fragment of the truth. I suppose that's why secret societies were organized to bring the truth forward, and they often had to do it in unusual ways to avoid being persecuted. Da Vinci was only one of many artists who left clues using symbolism in his paintings. There was also Botticelli and della Francesca to name just a few. Then, of course, there were the troubadours, and bards who kept it alive in their poetry and songs. Society is finally beginning to see that even our fairy tales are clever ways to bring forth messages of truth."

"And where is this all taking us?" Bernadette asked.

"I don't have a clue," he admitted.

Julia turned pensive. When she spoke it was with hesitation. "Well, Brit's speeches are enlightening our country about environmental issues that, until now, have been pushed under the rug. And, all of this happened for him after he met Mallory."

Ignoring the dubious expressions across from her, she continued. "It could be this is all about them. The yin and the yang coming together," and she drew a long breath before continuing.

"Let go of your skepticism for a minute, and let's look at the facts surrounding Mallory and Brit. First, we have their backgrounds. They both have a name connected to the Grail, they're both half Hungarian, and they're both unusually passionate about the environment. Then, we have the circumstances leading up to their meeting and the meeting itself. He had been walking that trail for over two years, and it's two thousand plus miles long. What are the odds of him being at the exact place where she happened to be hiking for the day? Add to that the fact that she dreamt about him beforehand – and on their very first meeting, she calls her mother and tells her she met the man she's going to marry. This from a very level headed girl who's never even been close to being engaged. And lastly, we have to admit that what follows is just short of miraculous. Within weeks, Mallory finds him the perfect job – and, suddenly, he's the golden boy. His speeches are making front-page headlines across the country. Talk about a transformation! Add to that the fact that fifteen years earlier Bernadette got Brit's name from a voice at night, and the entire story qualifies for *Ripley's Believe it or Not* if you ask me."

"I have to admit," Bernadette agreed, "it's as if we've slipped into the twilight zone," and she turned towards Samuel.

"Okay," he conceded, "let's go with the hypothesis that this is all about Brit and Mallory. Why not? We don't have a better one. I have to admit the way this entire situation is coming together is almost too perfect to believe."

"I agree," Julia piped in. "But we can't deny that it's happening. What we don't know is if any of this could be more than just chance.

Quite suddenly, Bernadette sat up straight in her chair. "Something just dawned on me. This mysterious Trillium Group who's hired Mallory and Brit. Their logo coincidentally – or not," she said pointedly, "happens to be the fleur de lys, which has always been connected in some way to the Merovingian bloodline. And remember, according to my daughter, she never sought employment with them. They mysteriously sent her a letter requesting she apply. I don't know about you, but I find that a little strange, maybe even suspicious."

"I forgot about that – and then there's the added coincidence that they agreed to hire Brit, who had no experience in that field, and immediately recognized his hidden talent of speaking," Julia added.

An infectious silence fell upon the group.

Samuel's momentum when he stood surprised the two women. "I think it's time for us to take a serious look at this Trillium Group," he growled.

CHAPTER 48

Lenzi's coded email came as a surprise: *They have Alain DeBuine. Can you help?*

Staring at the computer screen, Philippe tried to control his feelings, his slender hands fretfully running across his tuft of white hair. Lenzi had forgiven Alain. Why was he having such a difficult time? He could only think that because of the vanity of this one man, their entire project had been jeopardized. Now he was being asked to risk his life to save the egotistical traitor. His first thought was: *Alain is expendable, why bother?*

Philippe decided to share his feelings with Lenzi and the council. "Is it worth putting two others in harms way to free one?" And he hit the send button with more force than was necessary.

Lenzi's reply was quick: "Would you be more willing if I was the person held captive? Your feelings towards Alain are understandable. He behaved badly, but trust me in this, he has paid the price. Everyday has been a sentence for him – worrying about what might happen to his wife and young children, having to face his friends in Paris who are aware of his disloyal actions, and now as a captive, the fear for his own life. He has already paid for his mistake tenfold."

"Philippe, I ask you to remember that just as there is no degree in miracles, there is also no degree in mistakes. Big and small are human judgments. When a mistake is made, there is need for a correction, but not punishment. However, if you feel that you would prefer to decline, we will make other arrangements, and there will be no judgment of you."

Feelings of pettiness washed over Philippe as he read Le Perfector's message. He knew she was right. How would he feel if everyone held him responsible for every mistake he made in his lifetime?

"We will do whatever we can," Philippe sent back. "What about Alain's family? Will they try to abduct one of them if Alain escapes their grasp?"

"His wife and children are already here, safe with us. You will need to keep Alain with you until the time is right for him to travel. Expediency is important. Alain's condition, both mental and physical is waning. I'm not sure if he is capable at this point of breaking from them. You may have to enter the farmhouse."

Mon Dieu, Alain's mental and physical conditions are bad – and I wasted time oscillating as to whether I could find it in my heart to help!

Now Philippe understood completely the reason for running into Alain unexpectedly at the restaurant with the bright orange roof. At the time he believed it was only so they would know Alain had betrayed them, but now he realized the purpose was twofold. It was also so he could follow the vehicle transporting Alain, so he would know where Alain was being held.

Moving with cat-like precision, two men silently placed a canoe at the river's edge. A thin-figured woman appeared out of the dense brush, and the three quietly pushed off into the fast-flowing waters. Their expressions were somber.

When Francois first made the suggestion that Mari join them, Philippe rejected the idea, but later reconsidered, deciding a feminine presence would add to the illusion of an innocent outing. Cassarra was left to drive the car to a predetermined point downstream.

Still full from the heavy spring rains, the swift moving water presented more of a challenge than expected. Philippe's expertise with the paddle was immediately tested in the raging current, which was strewn with obstacles of rocks and debris that had been washed downstream. At the speed they were traveling even the slightest contact could rip a hole in its side or tip the canoe, plunging them into the ice-cold waters.

Mari was given the job of scanning the bordering properties with binoculars, as the men stayed focused on steering the canoe through the powerful current. Because of the dense foliage that bordered the banks, it was difficult to see what lay beyond, and occasionally they were forced to pull into shore for a short reconnaissance up the riverbank to get their bearings. Francois, being younger and more agile, did most of the scampering. This time, when he came down, he flashed the victory sign.

"The house is about 100 meters from the river," he whispered. "Two men are patrolling the perimeters. They seem quite lax."

Philippe nodded, placing a discreet marker for their next expedition. Once in place, he motioned for Francois to get back into the canoe, and the threesome made their way swiftly downstream to the prearranged spot where Cassarra was waiting.

That night in the office of The Trillium Group the lights burned late as Philippe and Francois huddled over their maps, putting together a workable plan. They knew one attempt was all they had. Their strong military backgrounds would serve them well.

"Le Perfector implied that Alain might not have the strength to help in any way. That presents us with a more difficult problem. I'm thinking a diversion at the other end of the property will draw everyone to the northern boundary. That would allow us to slip in from the river and get out quickly before the commotion is over." Philippe looked over his glasses meaningfully. "Our timing must be impeccable. There is no room for error. I think you understand the consequences if we're caught.

The younger man nodded grimly, his dark moustache emphasizing the downward curve of his mouth. He understood fully that they would be tried for espionage.

CHAPTER 49

The sun crested over the horizon in a burst of color as Cassarra started the rental van. Her signature chestnut hair had been pulled up under a baseball cap that was pulled low on her forehead. The canoe was securely fastened to the rack on top. Mari was in the passenger seat, her small case of natural herbs tucked neatly beside her. Well versed in the healing arts, Mari understood from Le Perfector's messages that Alain's condition might need immediate attention. They had folded down the seats in the extreme rear to make room for a small pallet to lay him on.

The tense tones of Philippe and Francois, as they rehearsed their plan, hung heavy inside the van, adding further to the drama of the moment. In an attempt to neutralize the atmosphere Mari and Cassarra began to sing in French. In their years together they had learned to harmonize quite well and their soothing tones slowly began to diffuse the apprehension of the men.

Quand il me prend dans ses bras,
Il me parle tout bas
Je vois la vie en rose

They drove for an hour through the flat farmland before they reached the country road that designated the northern boundary of the property where Alain was being held.

"Stop when you get to the mailboxes on the right hand side," Philippe directed.

Cassarra cautiously pulled the vehicle onto the shoulder, and Mari quietly opened the door and slid out, her hazel eyes darting across the landscape in cautious scrutiny. She was carrying a covered picnic basket that effectively hid seven homemade bombs. Cassarra then proceeded to make a U-turn, parking the car on the opposite side of the road. Francois kept his eyes glued to Mari until she disappeared, a walkie-talkie held tightly in his hand, while Philippe scanned the property with high-powered binoculars.

Fifteen minutes later in a voice constricted with emotion Francois croaked, "What's taking her so long?"

Philippe responded without removing his eyes from his binoculars. "It's all right my friend, she's taking the time to be cautious. She understands well the importance of what she is doing."

"Here she comes now," Cassarra reported, and as soon as Mari entered the van, the foursome drove off.

They conversed little on the next segment of their journey other than to briefly go over their assignments for phase two. They knew how crucial their timing must be, so watches were synchronized to the second.

As the two men placed their canoe in the swift moving river, Cassarra and Mari drove the van to the designated spot downstream. Mari stayed focused on her watch. At exactly 8:00 o'clock she pulled out the cell phone she purchased two days earlier under an assumed name, dialed 911 and, with feigned emotion, reported an explosion at the farmhouse. "We will need fire engines and several ambulances," she reported in a breathless voice, making sure to disguise her accent.

They had done their homework. They knew it would take thirty minutes for the emergency vehicles to reach the remote farmhouse. The first bomb was scheduled to go off five minutes before they arrived and the second, twelve minutes after their arrival. The next five would go off at varying intervals and places so as not to establish a pattern.

Philippe felt certain that by the time the third bomb went off, most of the men in the farmhouse would be out towards the road. Each bomb should start a fire large enough to command the attention of the men staked at the farmhouse, but not too big for the firemen to handle. Mari had been sure to place the bombs far enough apart and in an erratic pattern to create ample confusion. Their hope was to keep the men holding Alain diverted by the commotion, allowing them to slide in from the river undetected.

This time they were mentally prepared for the rapid current. While Philippe struggled with the river, Francois' eyes searched for the marker they had discreetly placed on the bank.

When they reached the farm, Philippe and Francois deftly pulled the canoe out of the water and waited in the bushes. They heard the first explosion, and seconds later, yells from the farmhouse, followed by footsteps running towards the front of the property. Sirens could be heard in the distance. When the second explosion erupted, Philippe motioned for Francois to follow him as he scampered up the bank. More sirens could be heard in the distance, along with voices shouting at the north end of the property as the third bomb detonated. Their hope was, by now, only one or two men were left guarding Alain. There were still four bombs left along with the small fires that had already been triggered.

Entering the farmhouse cautiously, Francois held a handgun tight in his right hand. His hope was that his Marshall Arts expertise would deem its use unwarranted, however, he was prepared to do whatever was necessary. Philippe waited outside, ready to alert Francois if any of the men returned. They each had a walkie-talkie type device connected to their ear with a wire, leaving their hands free.

Francois's back was tight against the wall as he slid through a back utility room towards the living area. Peering in, he could see two men standing next to each other at the front window, watching the fires smoldering out front.

Francois pondered. *If I put my gun in its holster, it would free both hands, allowing me to grab each one from behind, knocking their heads together. But what if there's a third or fourth man in the house?* He listened carefully. No noise was detected from any other area. He could see the swarm of men outside in the distance. He checked his watch. He knew the fourth bomb would detonate in seconds, and there wasn't much time left. His military instincts told him that all the others were out front. He decided to go for it.

Moving quickly, he attacked from behind, surprising the two men who were engrossed at the window watching the commotion outside. The only sound they made as they hit the floor was a thud.

Francois spun, ready to take on any other adversaries, but he found himself staring into a vacant room. He quickly noted that there was only one door off the main room. With slow precise moves, he pulled his gun and quietly made his way over, where he listened a moment before kicking it open. Alain's body, which lay limp across the bed, went rigid at the sound of Francois' entrance.

"I have him," Francois reported, then awkwardly slung Alain's lanky body over his shoulder. "We're approaching the back door. I'll need help."

Philippe knew that meant he would have to help carry Alain to the canoe. Their hope had been that Alain could maneuver his way to the river on his own. Although he was a slender man, his height would make it difficult for Francois, who was strong, but short, to carry him alone.

Philippe quickly moved to the back door and picked up Alain's legs. He was semi-conscious, and disoriented. Not realizing he was being saved, he began to twist and turn making it difficult for Philippe to hold on to him. Philippe tried speaking to him in French, but to no avail. Francois, who was fifteen years younger, took charge by slugging Alain, knocking him unconscious. He then winked and smiled at Philippe, who by silent consent became an accomplice in that small act of revenge. The two men slid down the bank with Alain between them just as the fifth explosion went off. They were right on schedule.

Philippe's knowledge of canoeing continued to serve them as they maneuvered through the treacherous current for their five-mile trip downstream where the van was parked with the engine already running. They had wisely selected a spot where the road was level with the river, making it easy to transfer Alain's limp body, which they had draped with a blanket, into the vehicle.

As they drove off, they could see the smoke from the fires at the farmhouse bellowing in the sky behind them.

CHAPTER 50

"Get your ass over here, Henry," was all the voice said before the connection went dead, leaving the vice president riveted to his seat. He knew that tone all too well. It meant there was trouble in River City, but now what? Nervously, he pondered the possibilities as he drove to Maryland, trying to prepare himself for the unforeseen. Not knowing was always the worst sentence for Henry. The anticipation almost drove him over the edge, and his pills barely helped anymore. He needed to talk to his doctor about prescribing something stronger. Turning the air conditioner up, he cursed. *Damn heat wave wasn't helping any.*

Before leaving the car, he threw two more pills into his mouth, telling himself that whatever it was, he could handle it. He always did. Every problem had a solution, one simply had to stay calm and find it. But the knot in his stomach only tightened, and the minute he opened the car door, the heat hit him like a dense wall. He hoped it wasn't a forecast of things to come as he plodded up the marble steps. When he reached the top he pulled himself erect and assumed a feigned air of confidence before ringing the bell.

Henry watched as the veins on the swollen face opposite him bulged, punctuating the fury behind the spoken words.

"An hour ago the Frenchman escaped," the raspy voice proclaimed in the manner of a death sentence, "and there's no trace of him."

Henry's face tightened in disbelief. "How the hell____!"

"That's what I want *you* to tell *me*. Can't those damn CIA agents do anything right? All they had to do was guard one middle-aged, pansy-pants Frenchman. And they messed that up royally."

Henry gulped. "This guy didn't vanish into thin air. There must have been clues." He knew the condition the Frenchman was in, hardly a state to escape. His concern was they were going to kill him before they got any information out of him. Escape was the last thing he expected.

"Oh there were clues all right. Seven bombs that exploded at intervals all over the front of the property. And apparently whoever did it called 911 requesting fire trucks and ambulances so they all arrived minutes after the first bomb went off. I'm told the place was swarming with people. It was pure bedlam." The puffy face pointed his cigar at the vice president. "And this wasn't some amateur operation. The bombs were very professional. The whole damn thing was well planned and their diversionary tactics worked very well. Most of the goddamn agents ran out front, while the Frenchman was retrieved from the back of the house."

Henry was stunned. *Bombs! And how the hell did they find him in that remote farmhouse?*

The raspy voice continued. "They found footprints leading to the river where it's presumed they had a boat waiting and probably a car somewhere downstream. He could be anywhere in the goddamn state by now."

Henry sat speechless, his mouth ajar.

"We know he had at least three accomplices, the woman who made the 911 phone call and the footprints of two men from the river."

The vice president jumped when the raspy voice unexpectedly slammed his fist on the end table. "You realize this means he has ties in this country. What the hell kind of an organization are we dealing with here, Henry? Are there Americans involved? And how the hell did they find him? We whisked the Frenchman off the streets of Paris and brought him here on a military plane. He hadn't passed through any customs checkpoint. Where the hell are they getting their information - to be able to track him to that isolated spot in Virginia?" The raspy voice stopped short, and his eyes pierced through the vice president. "This situation is getting out of hand, and my gut feeling is telling me it's an inside job, somebody very close to us." There was a long, uncomfortable pause. "I think one of our boys is working with one of the CIA agents at the farmhouse. It's the only thing that makes sense. Only our small group knew about the Phoenix Project and the Frenchman. Nobody but me, you and a handful of CIA agents knew where we were holding him." The puffy face stared at Henry. "Yep, it's one of the CIA agents working with someone from our group."

Henry's mind raced ahead, his southern drawl attempting to soothe. "It's definitely beginning to look that way. Keep in mind we still haven't cleared Michael and Pete. The Frenchman *did* come back with the information we gave to them."

The expression on the face across from him turned dark. "You had that information, too, Henry, and you knew where the Frenchman was being held," and the bulbous face froze in a broad smile, underlying piercing eyes that held a challenge.

An uneasy silence ensued, as the two men stared at one another.

"So did you," Henry finally retorted, mirroring the smile. *Two could play that game.*

The puffy face exploded with laughter, temporarily easing the tension, however, a seed of mutual mistrust had been decisively planted.

CHAPTER 51

Henry drove a short distance before he abruptly pulled off the road. He reached for the cell phone tucked in the pocket of his neatly folded suit jacket.

"Why wasn't I notified directly about the situation with the Frenchman?" his angry voice demanded.

"We tried, but we couldn't get through to you."

"You have my direct line damn it. The minute that first bomb went off someone should have notified me."

"I apologize, sir, but it was pretty frantic around here, what with bombs going off and fires needing to be put out."

"In the future I want to be the first person you call, do you understand?"

"Yes sir."

"Still no leads?"

"No sir, we've combed the area numerous times."

"Have you checked with immigration to see if any French nationals have come into the country recently?"

"We have a long list, and we've started wading through it."

"Well, get more men on it. I want this situation resolved and soon."

"Yes, sir."

"And another thing."

"Sir!"

"Check to see if there are any French based environmental groups operating out of the State of Virginia or any of the surrounding states. In fact, expand that list to include anything on the East Coast. And I want a copy of all the videotapes you have of the Frenchman while he was in custody. Have them delivered to my home immediately."

"Right sir."

Henry leaned his head against the back of the car seat and closed his eyes for a minute, but the voice echoing in his head wouldn't give him a moment's peace. *"You had that information, too, Henry, and you knew where the Frenchman was being held,"* the raspy voice reverberated in his ears.

Connolly dumped the videotapes delivered by a CIA agent onto his bed - five days of every move the Frenchman made at the farmhouse. According to the agents, the Frenchman hadn't said anything that made sense. Henry was about to see for himself. Maybe they missed something. Apparently he kept mumbling about a group of highly evolved beings who used remote viewing and mental telepathy to give him the information on the Phoenix Project. But that was *after* he was already delirious. Besides, he couldn't even tell them the most basic facts about these so-called evolved beings - where they operated from, their names, nothing. The only name he had was Le Perfector. They all assumed this was gibberish due to his delirious condition, and Henry was inclined to agree. Evolved beings were totally beyond the limits of his concepts. Mental telepathy and remote viewing, maybe. He knew his own government had spent millions developing the possibility of using those theories against the Soviets during the cold war, but their success was limited. He had met that Israeli, Yuri something or other, some years ago who claimed to have some success with it, but Henry's personal opinion was that he was a charlatan. If Henry had to bet his life between evolved beings and an informer, he'd go with the informer.

After all, the Frenchman *did* come up with both sets of information given to Michael and Pete, the two men from his group who he considered suspect. And he did give them the code name The Rock.

Slipping into something comfortable, Henry braced himself for a long night, hoping he would get some clue – anything - from the tapes. Many hours later, blurry eyed and exhausted he fell into a troubled sleep. Nothing new had surfaced.

The following evening a frustrated Henry Connolly slipped out of the White House earlier than usual, his face set with the determination of a man with a purpose. The dossiers of the agents stationed at the farmhouse were tucked in his briefcase, securely out of view of the many eyes that were always watching at the White House. The Frenchman had been weighing heavily on his mind all day. It was hard to believe that no clues had surfaced. There had to be something, damn it! Time was becoming a precious commodity in this situation.

Hours later, when the hands on the designer clock facing him had long passed midnight, the reading lamp over Henry Connolly's bed was still projecting shadows on the walls. The list of CIA agents lay loosely in one of his hands, the dossier containing their personal histories scattered across the bed. A faint smile lingered on Henry's face as he rested, his glasses pushed back on his forehead. His search hadn't been in vain. A very suspicious connection turned up – quite a plausible one – and, interestingly enough, it connected back to Michael, one of the original suspects in his group. His name had a possible connection to the code name The Rock. Now, here was a second connection pointing to him. A CIA agent who was stationed at the farmhouse with the Frenchman had years ago worked as an investigator for the insurance company that Michael's family owned. In Henry's mind, that was a direct hit.

The next morning he made a phone call to that stately mansion in Maryland before he left for the office.

"I think I might have the answer."

The voice on the other end was flat. "I hope so, because there's still no sign of that son-of-a-bitch. What do you have?"

"We need to talk in person."

Henry's solitary figure hastened up the marble stairway with an air of urgency, creating a sharp contrast to the peacefulness of the surroundings. A thick dossier was gripped tightly in his left hand. After presenting his findings to the bulbous face seated in the leather armchair, his eyes projected a triumphant gleam, though the professional nonchalance of his drawl masked his excitement.

"Interesting conclusion. So you think Michael is our man?"

"It appears that way. The question is, what do we do now?"

"This is a pretty serious accusation, Henry. My association with Michael goes back a long way. Longer than my association with you."

Henry eyed the puffy face across from him. *Was he being challenged again? Best to take the safest road.* "I know how you feel. It's hard for me to believe that Michael or anyone in our group would do this. Perhaps I've jumped to a hasty conclusion in wanting to put a lid on this as quickly as possible."

A stubby arm reached out. "Hand me those files. Maybe different eyes will see it from another perspective. After all, weren't you the one who hand picked those agents?"

Henry handed over the dossier with a forced smile. *Was he becoming paranoid, or was the finger being pointed in his direction for a second time?*

Later that evening, as he walked down the marble steps to the sweeping circular driveway, he was oblivious to the magic that filled the air with perfumed fragrance from the century old magnolia trees framing the property. His only thought was that the walls around him were beginning to crumble, and for the first time in his life, he didn't know which way to jump.

CHAPTER 52

Philippe kept the small apartment where he and Francois were temporarily housed immaculately clean. He believed that a cluttered space made for a cluttered mind. Seated in a high back recliner, his frame appeared smaller and more fragile than it actually was.

"Alain's mind may never be the same," he declared to the small group, his features reflecting his concern. "He lives in fear they will find him again."

Mari nodded in agreement, her feet moving restlessly. She was wearing sturdy hand-made leather sandals that added to her earthy appearance. "That's understandable, considering what he's been through. I was able to heal his body, but the mind is another matter."

"What are we to do with him?" Francois asked. "We can't keep him here forever."

"I've hesitated to ask Lenzi that question," Philippe confessed, "although it's been weighing on my mind. I've kept her apprised of his condition, and I assume, when the time is right, she will tell us what the next step is. Clearly, he's not mentally ready to travel, particularly under the guise of a false passport."

"No doubt the American Government has his home and all airports under surveillance," Francois said matter-of-factly. "Where would Lenzi send him?"

"His family is still with Lenzi and the council. I assume they would take him there, and that's probably where they'll stay until this is over."

"Is the end close?" Francois probed.

"I think so. Apparently Alain told the CIA agents everything. Although Lenzi suspects they didn't believe him. American belief systems don't stretch that far normally, so it's likely they suspect Alain was merely playing with them. However, Lenzi knows the information will eventually be passed on to someone who has a deeper knowledge of extra sensory perceptions, and they will escalate their agenda. Lenzi and the council advised me this morning that it would promote our cause at this point if we leaked the information about the Phoenix Project to the press," Philippe announced casually.

Mari was leaning against Francois on the sleek modern love seat, their arms entwined. "Do you think the American press will give it the attention it deserves? We know how tightly controlled it is by those in power."

"Our challenge will be to find the right sources. At least three or four different ones, so the story won't die due to lack of interest. Unfortunately, the American public has been programmed to have a very short attention span. But as you're aware, there has been a wave building of those who can look past their individual circumstances to the bigger picture, and this group has become well informed about many topics. It is to them we will speak."

"Will Brit be addressing the issue of the Phoenix Project in his future speeches?" Cassarra asked.

"Yes, that's our hope. I realize we'll have to have a serious talk with him and Mallory soon about their designated roles for the future. What do you think, are they ready to hear what we have to say?"

"I believe it would be best if we prepared them slowly. Dropping things casually on a weekly basis may serve our purpose better, rather than sitting them down and divulging everything at once. That might be overwhelming," Cassarra responded, her face glowing with an innocent child-like quality while her eyes reflected the wisdom of a wise sage.

"An astute observation. Do you think they're beginning to see our true purpose?"

"I think they have their suspicions."

Philippe swirled the wine in his glass before savoring a sip. Pinot Noir had always been his favorite, and recently, it had regained its popularity, making it easier to find. "And the President, your relationship with him continues to develop?"

"Yes, very nicely. It's now a daily ritual for us to have a long chat. I can tell he looks forward to it and senses my opinions are in his best interest."

"He's been guided by a very strong ego for a very long time. Have you been able to connect with his spirit?"

"Only for short moments. As you said, his ego has dominated for a long time. However, when his world comes crumbling in on him, like most, he will turn to his true spirituality."

"Hopefully you'll be there to guide him at that moment."

Cassarra's smile reflected confidence. "I suspect there will be no one else to turn to. Politicians, by nature, lack loyalty. They follow the flow of money and power. He'll seek me out when he finds there's no one else. Currently, he's wrapped in a cocoon of false allegiance."

"That will soon change."

"Yes," was Cassarra's only response, but it was said with the confidence that comes from those who read well the winds of time.

CHAPTER 53

Although the day was sunny, a sharp wind had unexpectedly raised its precocious wings, bringing with it swirls of leaves and dust that mischievously bounced through the wooded New England landscape.

"Looks like an early autumn," Samuel declared, as he shot a glance at the outdoor thermometer that hung right outside the window. "Fifty-eight degrees and falling," he announced to the women.

Julia responded by slipping into the rust colored sweatshirt she had earlier thrown over the arm of her chair. It accentuated the strawberry blonde color of her hair. "If this keeps up, there won't be any leaves left on the trees to turn color."

Bernadette made a face. "I was so hoping for an exceptional fall season. It's been so long since I've experienced one."

"Right now I'd say the chances of that happening are slim," Samuel stated flatly, "but then you know what they say about the weather in New England. If you don't like what's happening, wait an hour."

"It does tend to be rather unpredictable, but then I have to admit, there's something exciting about that. California weather is so predictable, it's boring," Bernadette retorted.

"I wouldn't mind trying boring for a while," Samuel chuckled, as he carefully slipped a coaster under his mug of coffee, and then running his hand over his perfectly groomed sandy hair, he eagerly changed the subject. "I had an interesting revelation this morning." Pause "It's regarding the name Mallory. This is just a thought I want to throw around," he confessed, "as it's rather out there."

The two women looked at each other and rolled their eyes.

Ignoring their response, he continued. "If you remember, the original protagonist in the Grail stories was Percival, and then somewhere along the line the focus was shifted to King Arthur and the cast at Camelot, thereby making Sir Percival a secondary character." He looked up, a gleam in his eye. "From my investigations it was Thomas Malory who was responsible for that shift when he wrote his *La Mort D'Arthur*."

The faces in front of him were blank, and a somewhat disinterested Julia began working on the needlepoint in her lap.

"Don't you get it? It was a Malory - spelled differently, but pronounced the same - who took the emphasis off of Percival, and it's *your* Mallory who's bringing Percival back as the main character."

"And exactly how is she doing that?" Bernadette asked dubiously.

"Okay, bare with me here, because I'm finding my own way. In the original versions written in the 12th century, Percival was often referred to as the 'son of the widow lady'. A noteworthy description, because it was often used by secret societies to identify their prophets - including Jesus."

Samuel paused to sip his coffee. "We're all aware that in the original Grail stories an enormous emphasis was put on lineage. It also seemed to encompass a more personal quest, where Percival finally realized he was supposed to ask the right question, which was something to the effect of 'Who one was to serve with the Grail,' and when he finally asked that question, he transcended from a selfish, simple man into a highly evolved man who was able to heal the ailing Fisher King - who mysteriously turns out to be his uncle or grandfather, depending on the version you read, which again weaves the saga back to lineage."

"Thomas Malory took that story and changed it into a more grandiose epic, rather like a modern-day action film. He brought in lots of characters and took the emphasis away from lineage and put it onto chivalry." Samuel's eyes were clear as they shone with excitement. "Keep in mind that the chivalry of King Arthur's court was always entwined with fair maidenhood - again a balance. Sir Malory put a much needed emphasis on the feminine role, at a time when the male warrior was dominant,"

Samuel stretched his arms like a huge cat. "Perhaps it's now our Mallory's role to bring back the subject of lineage."

Bernadette smiled inwardly. *When did Mallory become "our" Mallory? Was this Samuel's way of acknowledging her daughter's relationship with his son?*

"And how is she going to do that?"

"Through Brit's speeches. I'm sure we all agree that, if he hadn't met Mallory, Brit would still be living out in the wilderness."

"Hmm, I'll agree with you there, but what does that have to do with lineage?"

"I'm not sure exactly, but bare with me here, because I think I'm beginning to see how all the circles connect. To begin with we have your father who's a full-blooded Hungarian, who keeps referring to Pleiades as your constellation. And your mother, also Hungarian, who was born on Halloween, a time when the ancients believed the veil between the worlds was opened and that spirits were allowed to enter. Then, a voice wakes you up in the middle of the night so you could hear that, somehow, there is a connection astronomically between Pleiades and Halloween as well."

Bernadette ventured, "And so___?"

"Wait, I'm not finished," and he began flipping through his notes. "Okay, the next piece is that many Native American Indians believe that Pleiades is the home of their ancestors. And then we find out that many modern-day channelers claim that the Pleiadians are related to the dolphins, which of course would make them aquatic – and not just aquatic, but aquatic mammals," and he looked up from his notes to make eye contact to emphasize his point.

"That is an interesting point," Julia broke in, looking up from her handwork. "Dolphins being mammals would make the transition to human much easier genetically, wouldn't it?"

"I would think so," Bernadette agreed. "And let's not forget there have been many stories throughout history of how dolphins have saved humans from drowning."

"All good points," Samuel acknowledged. "And all of them continue to point, in my mind, in the same direction. Add to the mix that there are other indigenous people who claim their ancestors were extraterrestrials who were aquatic, and at least one of these tribes had information about a star system before our astronomers."

Julia started to say something else, but Samuel put up his hand. "Let me finish my point here, so I don't get off tract. The next circle is the Sumerians, who worshipped gods that were half-man and half-fish. And we discovered that the Sumerian language is connected to the Hungarian language. Are you still with me?" he asked.

Julia and Bernadette nodded.

"Keep in mind," he continued, "That the Royal Dragon Court of Hungary claims that they can trace their lineage to the Merovingian dynasty, and there is a myth that the earliest Merovingian was born of two fathers, one of which is a strange aquatic creature. The Merovingians are also purported to be the bloodline of Jesus, and we know that

Jesus has traditionally been connected to the symbol of the fish." Samuel looked up and took a deep breath.

"Now back to the original Grail stories, which had references to a mysterious lineage that linked Percival to the Fisher King. Again a reference to fish without any explanation. Does anyone know why he was called the Fisher King? He didn't seem to be a fisherman."

Samuel looked at them evenly. "I think that the reference to a Fisher King might possibly be one of those clues that was sprinkled throughout the Grail stories. A clue that might be saying the King was a descendant of these mysterious amphibious gods." His voice then modulated in a prophetic tone, "Amphibious gods that came from another star system, as believed by the indigenous peoples around the world. And since Percival was called the son of the widow lady, which was also an appellation applied to Jesus, perhaps Percival was the code name for Jesus in the early Grail romances."

He looked directly at Bernadette. "Maybe this is all about recognizing that we are connected through our blood to extraterrestrials, and once we acknowledge that connection, we can again establish contact with them, which is how we'll ultimately heal our planet."

"Very interesting. And how does any of this tie in to our families?"

"It could explain the origin of the mysterious Voice that speaks to you. It could belong to an extraterrestrial."

Bernadette's finger was absent-mindedly tracing patterns on the arm of her chair. "I've actually given that very thought some consideration, especially after reading the story of Billy Meier, the Swiss farmer who allegedly made contact with the Pleiadians. Although I must confess, when I verbalize the thought, it seems bizarre."

"I understand. But just because it's not comfortable, doesn't mean it's not true," Samuel interjected. "You told me once that your father was a visionary. Maybe he was also receiving messages from ET's."

Samuel ignored the look of reluctance on Bernadette's face and pressed forward. "We've all remarked about the odds of Mallory's meeting with Brit as a mere coincidence. Is it possible that somehow, someway it was orchestrated from above?"

Bernadette stood, anxiously. "This is crazy!"

"Is it? Why would it be out of the question that you're receiving information from a strange voice in your head, and she's not? If she'd been receiving messages in that manner since she was a child, it would seem natural to her, possibly even viewing them as her own thoughts."

Bernadette plopped down, her face mirroring her confusion.

Julia put a hand on her knee. "None of us really know where our thoughts come from. Think about how often something just pops into your mind. Did it come from our own mind – or did we pick it up from someone else? And why couldn't that someone else be from another world?"

Julia continued, "It's quite possible that both Mallory and Brit have been receiving information that way all their lives. It might even explain why you received Brit's name years ago. It could have been to prepare you for their meeting, so you would be more receptive to your daughter falling in love with someone who appeared to be a recluse."

Bernadette became agitated. In a strained voice she blurted out, "Why us and our families?"

Samuel took a more solicitous approach. "Could it have something to do with the Hungarian connection to the Sumerians? Not long ago, you said that one of the things that has always intrigued you about the Holy Grail was the mysterious significance that surrounded the blood. Most scholars have equated that to lineage and stopped there. But it could be more. It could be that through our blood certain families have the gift of prophecy or the gift of telepathic communication with these star brothers," and he looked directly into Bernadette's eyes.

CHAPTER 54

As the bright blue sky began to fade, the surrounding woods were silent. An eerie silence. One that made you listen.

Bernadette walked to the large picture window. Why was she so nervous about this? She had been meditating for years. The shrill caw of a large bird – a hawk, perhaps – rang out nearby, and the woods came alive, as if a spell had been broken. A chorus of songs filled the air. It was the stuff of old Celtic tales.

Bernadette moved to the small table and lit a candle. *I can do this. The Sinclairs are right, I should at least try to contact The Voice.* And seating herself, she forced her mind to focus on the deep breathing techniques she learned in her yoga class. As she began to feel her body relax, she asked: *Who are you, and how can I reach you for guidance?* And she allowed herself to slide into a deep meditative state.

Thirty minutes later, as she was coming back to her usual consciousness, there was a firm knock on the cottage door. A moment of panic engulfed her. *Would she open the door to find the face of The Voice on the other side in response to her request?*

"Who is it?' She asked tentatively.

"It's the creature from the black lagoon," Samuel answered playfully, the anxious note in her voice amusing him.

"And the creature's lovely wife," Julia added facetiously.

"So why are you so nervous?" Samuel asked when Bernadette opened the door.

She looked embarrassed. "I just finished a meditation where I asked The Voice how I could reach it for guidance and your timing was such that I half way expected a strange man to be standing there saying: You called?"

"Wouldn't it be nice if it were that easy?" Samuel replied as the couple entered and made themselves comfortable on the loveseat.

"Maybe," Bernadette responded dubiously.

"Well, at least you had the courage to ask," Julia sympathized. "It's one thing to talk about it in the abstract and quite another to step over the line and try to make contact."

"It's what the mystics call harnessing your intentionality," Samuel noted.

Bernadette furrowed her forehead. "Harnessing intentionality?"

Samuel pulled himself erect as the two women exchanged a meaningful glance. They knew his professor personality was about to kick in, and they prepared themselves to be lectured to for the next ten minutes.

"One of the many things we learned from quantum physics is that the process of observation in some way affects the experiment. Therefore, the same experiment conducted by two different scientists could produce two different outcomes, depending on each observer's perception. Put more simply, somehow we affect matter. Of course metaphysicians have claimed this for centuries."

"And exactly how does this apply to me?" Bernadette asked in a confused voice.

"Well, I'll assume you asked with the intention of receiving an answer. If that's correct, your request will manifest. On the other hand, if you asked with the hope that you really won't be answered, that will be the end result. Or, if you were putting fear or doubt into the request, those emotions will also effect the outcome."

"I understand what you're saying, but I don't understand how it works," she admitted.

"You're not alone. Scientists are still scrambling trying to explain it, while the mystics sit back with big smiles on their faces, patiently waiting for the light bulb to go off."

"How do the mystics explain it?"

"They maintain we affect matter with our thoughts and feelings."

"But how?"

"That's what scientists are trying to figure out. If we had the answer to that one, we'd be celebrated as the Einstein of our day."

"I think I might have the answer," Julia offered timidly.

Samuel's head swung towards her, his mouth agape.

Searching Julia's face, Bernadette half expected a silly pun, but Julia only stared back at them.

"Please enlighten us." Samuel said, and his voice was sprinkled with sarcasm, surprising Bernadette. Normally he treated his wife with complete respect. Although it was often laced with humor, it never showed signs of malice.

Julia scrunched up her shoulders, her voice uncertain. "Remember that movie that was around a few years ago *What the Bleep Do We Know?*"

Samuel nodded. They had watched it numerous times together, fascinated by the information presented.

"In one segment they presented the findings of a Japanese researcher, Dr Emoto, who had discovered that the molecules in water reacted to the words taped onto the containers holding the water. If the word was positive the molecules formed into beautiful snowflake patterns, and if the word was negative, the pattern of the molecules turned chaotic."

Both Samuel and Bernadette were listening intently as Julia continued haltingly. "Then recently, I remembered something I read a while back, but it always stayed with me. I didn't understand it, yet at some deep level it rang true, and it corroborated Dr. Emoto's findings." Her right hand was nervously fumbling with her gold bracelet.

"It had to do with electrons," Julia said hesitantly, knowing she was venturing into unfamiliar territory. "They're like tiny little angels of magic energy that are charged with the quality of obedience. It's not just the molecules in water that respond to our words, but the molecules in all things – through the electrons."

"Did the book say how?" Bernadette asked.

"Yes. It had to do with our thoughts and feelings. It's more than the words, it's also the intent behind the words."

"So if I wanted to create wealth, all I have to do is say I want to be rich? That's a little hard to believe. If that were true, wouldn't we all be rich and happy, because that's what most of us want?"

"But I didn't say electrons respond to our wishes. What they respond to is our thoughts and feelings, which equates to our belief system. There's a big difference. For example, you might wish you were rich, but if your thoughts are saying: Money is the root of all evil, or the rich get rich and the poor get poorer, or no matter what I do, I can't seem to get ahead financially, then what you're really doing is pushing money away by creating a reality that's in alignment with your belief system. The unfortunate thing is that the average person isn't aware of what they're thinking most of the time. We simply let our minds ramble from one topic to another. An interesting experiment is to keep track of your thoughts throughout the day and then go back and look at them. It will show you what you really believe, and what you're unconsciously creating."

She continued breathlessly. "According to the mystics, we're creating all the time. The sad thing is we're doing it unconsciously – and what we're creating is this madness we call the world." Her voice, then, turned into a whisper of hope, "If we could only completely comprehend how we're doing it, we could do it at a conscious level and just as easily create the peace and happiness for which we're all so desperately longing."

Samuel and Bernadette said nothing at first, mesmerized by the depth of Julia's emotion. It was Bernadette who broke the silence.

"That was beautiful. You made me feel as if I could do it."

"You could," Julia whispered. "All you have to do is truly believe it, because what we believe is what we create."

CHAPTER 55

"Get me the low down on that kid," the vice president said to his staff. "I mean everything from the day he was born. And I want it by tomorrow. I have enough problems without having to deal with some crazy idealist running around convincing people we can turn this country into some kind of a utopia."

As the last staff member left his office, Henry threw his pen down on the desk and leaned back in his chair, flicking on the switch of the tape recorder sitting off to the side. Half way through Brit's speech, he hit the off button. The kid was good, damn good. He sure would like to know who was feeding him his information. Henry's gut feeling was telling him this was more than a one-man act, and he was determined to find out who was behind it. The kid worked for an environmental company – The Trillium Group, but recently Henry was beginning to suspect the Democrats were running this little dog and pony show. *Too damn bad that car incident in Pennsylvania wasn't successful. It would have alleviated the problem of this kid with one stroke.*

Henry decided to take another route to deal with the bothersome kid. He had friends in the news media, and trading favors with them was never difficult, especially with the top brass. In this case, he decided to go one step further. The majority of the ever-enlarging news corporations had become media empires controlled by individuals who realized these high level connections were not only in their best financial interest, but often determined their very survival. The administration that Henry served under had been more than generous to the wealthy. He had no hesitations in making the call.

"Chester, I need a favor," the vice president's silky voice implored. "There's a young upstart named Brit Sinclair running up and down the East Coast making speeches that aren't in our best interests. I'd like you to put a media boycott on his activities for a few months until the public loses interest in him."

"Consider it done," Chester replied. "Anything else?"

"Find some sensational story to captivate the public's attention and keep it on the front page as long as possible."

"This kid must be a real thorn in your side."

"Let's just say he's bringing up events that would be better left alone."

Chester understood he was being told it was none of his business. "By the way, we're planning a little yachting party weekend after next. Thought you might want to join us. There'll be some skeet shooting off the back of the boat and the usual."

Henry knew what 'the usual' meant - plenty of booze, attractive young women and high stakes poker. Influential crowds that included Supreme Court justices, high ranking governmental officials, and powerful lobbyists knew how to party.

"Let me check my schedule and get back to you, things are pretty busy around Washington right now, but if there's a chance I can squeeze it in, you know I will."

Later that evening Henry had his driver leave him off at the historical brick building just across the state line.

"This may take a few hours," he said, "stay close and leave your phone on, but I don't want you parking right in front," and he made eye contact with the driver to make sure he understood his meaning, then vanished up the back stairs.

Henry was the last to arrive, and he sensed the room became unusually quiet when he entered. *Had he interrupted a discussion about himself or was it his imagination?* Trying to shake off any doubts he cordially accepted a drink, but his feelings of isolation persisted.

"Henry, we're all worried about the Frenchman. Still no leads?"

"Not one," he admitted, shaking his head. "Seems the trail ended at the river, but I have my men checking out every French national that entered the country in the last six months, plus any environmentalist group that has French connections."

"And your men are checking passports of everyone leaving this country?" the raspy voice persisted.

"Here and in Canada, but nothing so far. From the condition the Frenchman was in when he was taken, it's my assumption he wasn't up to any long distance traveling. My bet is he's close at hand."

The raspy voice turned cynical. "Let's not assume anything, that's what got us into this predicament," and his words came at Henry like swift arrows, piercing his ego. It took all of Henry's effort to keep his anger in check, however, he was savvy enough never to show any signs of weakness to men such as these. The façade he presented remained neutral, adequately camouflaging his true emotions, though, now he was certain he was under attack and needed to watch his back more closely.

The evening seemed to drag on for Henry as he felt his circle of friends pulling away from him. He knew he hadn't done anything to jeopardize the Phoenix Project, but how to convince the others? Isolated and alone, his eyes were drawn to the ornate eighteenth-century grandfather clock standing in a corner of the room, and he became mesmerized by the second hand as it moved in a slow and pronounced rhythm, each tick emulating the strike of a judge's gavel.

CHAPTER 56

"That's strange," Mallory commented as she placed the morning paper on the small dinette table. She was still in her bathrobe, her tousled brunette locks falling seductively around her pretty face.

Brit looked up from his notes. He was working on his next speech.

"This was the biggest crowd ever at your rally, yet there's no mention of it in the morning paper."

He only shrugged as Mallory clicked on the television.

"Maybe it will break tomorrow," he finally said, as he watched her flick through the news channels.

"It's never taken that long before."

His smile was soft, his tanned complexion emphasizing the whiteness of his teeth. "Does it matter?" And Mallory instantly understood his meaning. She remembered him telling her how he had become disenchanted with speech tournaments in high school when his parents became too involved. *Was she becoming his mother?*

She smiled sheepishly. "No it doesn't," and she turned off the television. *But how to turn off her mind?* It hadn't escaped Mallory that Philip was scheduling Brit's public appearances to coincide with Cassarra's days off so she could come with them. And now, this was the second one of Brit's speeches that was ignored by the media. *Was she becoming too suspicious or was something going on?*

The next morning while Brit was out of the office she took the opportunity to address the topic directly with Philip.

"Yes, we've noticed the media has suddenly lost interest in what Brit has to say."

"But his appearances have been drawing larger crowds than ever. Surely they recognize that as a sign people are interested."

Philip raised his eyebrows. "Perhaps there are those who are concerned the general public is too interested, eh?"

Mallory cocked her head to the side. "But they couldn't control the entire news media!"

Philip stared at her with a knowing look, his eyebrows raised. "Have you ever heard of the name Chester Randolph?"

"Isn't he the head of one of the international news stations?"

"Not the head my dear, the owner. He reports to no one. No board of directors, no partners. And his conglomerate owns dozens of newspapers, news magazines, television and radio stations."

Mallory peered at him, her mouth agape. "Isn't that considered a monopoly?"

Philip's smile was one of indulgence. "The men who want and seize power are very shrewd, and I might add, a very tight-knit circle. Would it surprise you to know that Mr. Randolph and the present administration socialize regularly – and that includes key members of the Supreme Court."

Mallory flopped back in her chair. "I get so discouraged when I hear things like that. It makes me feel insignificant, as if I'm wasting my time trying to make changes because the cards are stacked against me."

"That was true in the past," Philip said confidently, "but a new day is creeping over the horizon. Soon the morning bird's song will awaken those that are beginning to stir in their sleep, and they will see glimpses of a world that will no longer support societies based on corruption and fear."

"You don't know how much I'd like to believe that," Mallory sighed.

"Believe it, my dear, because it's inevitable. There are powers in this Universe that are far greater than those who think they wield the power."

CHAPTER 57

The next morning the vice president received an early phone call from the CIA. "We came up with a French environmental company in Virginia, and interestingly enough, they've recently lobbied a few issues through Congress by way of the Democratic Party.

The vice president's voice was terse. "What's their name?"

"The Trillium Group."

"The Trillium Group? And you say their French?"

Henry swiveled quickly in his chair. *Bingo! That's the name of the organization that kid worked for. The one who was going around the country stirring up trouble with his speeches. So, the kid and the missing Frenchman were connected!*

CHAPTER 58

The huge potted fern behind Philippe outlined his slender frame. He appeared unusually rigid, and his deep resonating voice carried an urgent quality. "It's imperative we move Alain immediately. Lenzi says the CIA is checking all French nationals in the area."

"Where can we take him? He can't be left alone," Francois replied.

"He can stay with Cassarra and Mari for now.

Francois froze, the veins on his thick neck pulsating. *Not with Mari. Why put her in a potentially precarious situation?*

Philippe knew what his good friend was thinking. He tried to reassure him. "Mari will be safe. Le Perfector will see to that. Remember, Cassarra is an American citizen and her apartment is in her name. It's doubtful their investigation will go that deep; but if it does, we'll move him again. I have knowledge that the council is keeping a close eye on our situation. We should have plenty of warning," and his compassionate eyes conveyed confidence.

Francois said nothing. He remained standing, his feet planted firmly on the slightly worn commercial carpet. Philippe could feel his uncertainty.

"We are much closer to the next step than you think, Francois, and I suspect the next few months will test all our faith. The human ego rarely allows transition to take place easily. Be prepared for some tense times, my friend."

CHAPTER 59

The dense darkness of the moonless night had settled over the outskirts of Richmond, as one by one the city's lights were being put to rest. In the old days it was the time of story-telling around the campfire. Still, to those who understood – and even to those who merely caught a glimpse – it was the time of creativity when the starlight brings in a new awareness, if only for the moment.

The streets around the small, ordinary apartment complex were now quiet, although an occasional voice still could be heard drifting into the cool night air from an open window. In a second story apartment, a dim light shone through the closed drapes where two young women were comfortably lying on the floor in front of the television surrounded by pillows.

When the movie ended, Cassarra fumbled for the remote and flicking off the television, she slowly propped herself up on one elbow and turned to Mallory who was heartily indulging in the last tidbits of popcorn that remained in the bowl.

"That was a sweet movie. It's hard to find good romantic comedies anymore. I get so tired of action movies."

Mallory nodded in agreement and reached for her soft drink, a pensive look capturing her features. Something had been weighing on her mind for some time, and she had been waiting for the perfect opportunity to discuss it with Cassarra. She hesitated, but her concern pushed her on.

Sitting upright, she purposely made direct eye contact with her good friend. Her manner was imploring. "Speaking of action movies, I can't get the real one that we were involved in recently out of my mind. Ever since that SUV tried to push us off the road in Pennsylvania, I've had this uneasy feeling that something isn't right," she confessed in a strained voice. "I've tried to dismiss the incident as a random act of road rage, but I keep having this uneasy feeling there was more to it than that. It just didn't add up for me. We were out in the middle of nowhere. There was no traffic. Along comes a guy in a brand new SUV and tries to push us off the road. And when we go to help him after he crashes, we see a gun in the seat next to him. I don't know much about guns, but his looked like something powerful and expensive!"

Cassarra reached over and held Mallory's hand in both of hers. "Brit's speeches are causing a great deal of worry in some political arenas, and as his popularity has grown, so has the alarm in those communities."

Mallory stared, her dark brown eyes wide, "What exactly are you saying?" she stammered.

"Brit's become a fly in the ointment of those in power."

"Isn't that what we wanted? To cause change within by applying pressure from without."

"Exactly, but. . ," and the word floated on the air - *but, but, but – echoed around the room.* "But you must understand, those in power aren't going to bend that easily."

"I realize that, but if we continue to apply pressure, they'll eventually have to respond, won't they?"

Cassarra's smile was patient. "Yes, but first they'll respond by trying to eliminate the fly."

Mallory's mouth dropped open, as she stared in disbelief. She knew something was wrong, but . . .! "You're not suggesting they would . . .! Those in power would ...?

No, I can't believe that could ever happen, not in this country!"

"A government only reflects the ideas of the men behind it."

"But in America they couldn't get away with such things."

"They can and they do. Your instincts about that incident in Pennsylvania are correct. The man driving the SUV was more than just a chance erratic driver."

Mallory stared at the placid face beside her for a long moment. She had hoped Cassarra would put her doubts to rest, she never expected her to confirm them. "Do you know for a fact that man was purposely trying to harm us?"

Cassarra's only response was to silently hold the distraught eyes that searched her face.

"Does Brit know?" Mallory whispered, tears rolling down her cheeks.

"Not yet. But you mustn't worry. That's why I'm traveling with you."

"But how can *you* protect him?" Mallory's hand was clutching her chest. *The thought of losing Brit was too much to bear.*

Cassarra reached out and hugged her friend. "You must have faith. You saw that I was able to do it once."

"You did that? I mean, I know you helped by keeping Brit focused, but . . . . how?"

"I've been trained since an infant to understand the powers of the mind."

Mallory stared at her friend, stunned. Yet, this didn't come as a complete surprise. She had been sensing for some time that Cassarra had highly developed psychic powers.

"But if Brit's life is in danger, how can you watch over him every minute?"

"There are others watching from a distance as well."

Even through her anxiety Mallory's curiosity was piqued.

"How can they do that?"

Cassarra hesitated. *Yes, her friend was ready to hear this.* "There are several ways. One is remote viewing."

"Remote viewing?"

"Yes, it's the ability to see past the scope of visual eyesight. There are those who are quite accomplished at seeing things that are happening anywhere on the planet."

"That seems so . . . so hard to believe."

"Would you be surprised to know that the United States government spent millions of dollars on remote viewing during the cold war period?"

Mallory was amazed. "The United States Government did this?"

"Yes."

"Were they successful?"

"To some extent. But not to the extent of those I speak. These are truly enlightened beings whose goals are universal love, rather than personal advancement. They've spent many lifetimes developing their skills and they use them only for higher purposes."

Mallory's mind was reeling. *There really were advanced souls out there, somewhere. In one respect it was hard to believe, but then she had a perfect example right here in front of her.* She expelled a long sigh. This was all too overwhelming. She had so many questions, she hardly knew where to begin.

Reading her mind, Cassarra's velvet voice enveloped her in a veil of certainty while her words presented a challenge. "Always remember that you co-create your life by what you focus your thoughts on."

"It's difficult to maintain a Pollyanna attitude when you've just been told that a man was trying to kill you," a frustrated Mallory blurted out.

"I'm not suggesting that you see no evil, that would be foolhardy. When you step into a busy street, you must be aware of the traffic to be safe, but that is very different from stepping out into the street in fear. Do you see my point?"

Mallory was grappling with her emotions. "So you're saying I must be aware of what's happening around me without becoming an alarmist?"

"Exactly. And know there are others out there that *can* and *are* helping. Learn to tap into Universal energy."

"How do I do that?"

"By staying in the present moment with an open and loving heart. Then listen and follow your intuition."

"You make it sound so easy."

"At first it won't seem so, because you've allowed your mind to spend so much time fretting about the past – or worrying over the future. But the more you practice, the easier it becomes until it's second nature," and Cassarra's eye's reflected a belief so strong that, for the moment, Mallory didn't doubt her in the slightest.

That moment, however, was difficult to maintain.

CHAPTER 60

Mallory turned on the table lamp to better read Brit's expression. The evenings were already getting dark early.

"Did Cassarra actually come out and say that?" He finally asked.

"Not in so many words, but her implication was clear."

"You're sure you're not overreacting?"

"I'm sure. She talked about advance souls that were protecting you by remote viewing and how she saved us through mind control that night in Pennsylvania when that crazy driver almost pushed us off the road."

"Did she say how she did that?"

"Not exactly. She simply said that she had been trained in the powers of the mind since she was a small child."

"Wow, wouldn't you love to learn how to do all that stuff?"

Mallory bristled. "Aren't you concerned about your safety? If you continue to make these speeches, your life could be in jeopardy!" *And to think that I was the one who got him into all this!*

"So you think I should stop?" he asked in an incredulous voice.

Tears welled up in Mallory's eyes, and she fumbled in the pockets of her khakis for a tissue. "I don't know. It's all so confusing. This is what I wished for all my life; but if there's a chance I could lose you, would it be worth it?" she sobbed.

Brit pulled her into his arms. *Why did human relationships have to be so complicated? He had finally found his niche in life, and now he was being asked to let it go in order to keep what he believed was his soul mate. Was life always a juggling act between desires?* "Before we make any decisions, why don't we sit down with Cassarra and Philip and find out what this is all about?"

Mallory pulled away, her face contorted. "What this is all about is you're rattling the cages of some very influential people. People who don't want to change their lifestyles for the advancement of the human race or our planet. These men want to keep the status quo at any cost, and they're not going to let anyone stand in their way."

"Mallory, I think you're overreacting."

"Am I? Do you remember how you felt that night the car was swerving into us. I saw the look on your face. I saw how you slumped over the steering wheel when it was over. What if he *had* hit us?"

Brit had never seen her this way. "But he *didn't* hit us."

"Not this time," she retorted with tight fists.

CHAPTER 61

Bernadette was seated cross-legged on the white wicker loveseat, the plush green cushion hugging her curvaceous derriere. The phone was cradled against her shoulder, as she spoke in soothing tones. "Honey, every couple has disagreements. It would be unrealistic to think otherwise."

"But *we* never did. Brit and I have always seen eye to eye on everything."

"I know this seems like a major event right now, but give it a few days, and it will pass. Then, you'll look back and see how minor it was. This is not life or death. It's a little disagreement."

Mallory began crying. "But it is life or death!"

"It only feels that way, dear."

"No, I mean it mom," she sobbed bitterly. "It is life or death. They are trying to kill Brit!"

Bernadette's body stiffened as she tightened her grip on the phone. *What was her daughter saying? Someone was trying to kill Brit? Absurd!* "Who?"

"The ... sob ... government."

"Our government? What are you saying Mallory?"

Haltingly, between tears, Mallory related their experience on the road in Pennsylvania and her recent conversation with Cassarra.

Bernadette's mind was reeling as she began pacing. *You and the girl will be safe if you leave this alone, otherwise, we can't promise to protect you. . . It would be unwise to make any further contact with Samuel Sinclair . . .* Threats that made no sense when she received them suddenly had a whole new meaning. She dropped back onto the loveseat. *This is all my fault. I put Mallory in this situation – all over those damn letters.* Suddenly Bernadette realized the consequence of her actions. What had started as a family mystery had turned into a life-threatening situation. Overtaken with fear, she could feel the blood drain from her face. Lives were now hanging in the balance.

"Mom?"

"I'm here, dear," a trembling voice responded. "We need to talk. I'm getting on the next plane to Richmond."

The Sinclairs stared at Bernadette, bewildered.

"This is rather sudden, isn't it?" Samuel was studying Bernadette's face. *Clearly she wasn't herself.* "Is something wrong?"

"No, just a mother's sudden need to be with her daughter," she lied, pushing her hair nervously back from her face.

"Well, at least let us drive you to the airport."

Bernadette recoiled at the suggestion. *They would ask too many questions on the drive, and Mallory had specifically asked her not to tell them, fearing it would make Brit lose trust in her.* "Thanks for the offer, but I need to turn in the rental car."

A startled Julia gasped. "Then you're not coming back?"

"Probably not. I think you can understand I need to go home. I can't stay here forever."

"So . . . everything we've done . . . our research - you're ready to drop and move on?" *This wasn't making sense.*

Samuel pursed his lips, remembering the first time she made an about face. *Had there been another threat?*

"This is just a stab in the dark, but have you been threatened again?"

Bernadette stood motionless, her face frozen, a child caught in a lie. She had wrestled with her conscience all night, but in the end her first priority was her daughter. What she had originally seen as a blessing – her relationship with the Sinclairs – had turned into one of life's cruel little jokes. Now, in order to keep her daughter safe, she felt compelled to cut her ties with them.

Samuel walked over to Bernadette, and taking her suitcase, he led her to an armchair. "Bernadette, you know how much we both care for you and how entwined our lives have become. We need to know what's happened. If you feel a need to leave, no one would understand better than Julia and I. But don't run away. Tell us what's going on and we'll help you."

Bernadette was visibly shaken. *Where to begin?* She dropped her head into her hands.

"Did you receive another threat?" Samuel repeated, his voice solicitous.

Bernadette's eyes were teary when she looked up. "Not me."

"Mallory?" Julia ventured.

"Sort of," Bernadette stammered.

Samuel's impatience flared. "Just tell us what's going on, and we'll deal with it."

"Brit," she blurted out. "It's his life that's in danger, which puts Mallory in a very precarious position if she stays with him."

Julia's hand instinctively went up to her chest.

Samuel turned interrogator. "Who told you this?"

"Mallory."

"And what's her source?"

Bernadette expelled a long sigh. *She might as well tell them the whole story.* "There was an incident last month when a serious attempt was made by another vehicle to push them off the road into a ditch. At the speed they were traveling, dropping off the bank would have probably killed or at least seriously injured them. The man driving the other car ultimately lost control and swerved off the road. He was killed on impact when he hit a tree. When our kids stopped to help, they found a gun in the seat next to him. Later, they were told by the police that he had no identification on him."

"That's pretty bizarre. But it could simply have been some crazy out there, and they were just in the wrong place at the wrong time."

"That's exactly what *they* thought, until Cassarra, when pressed, confided in Mallory it was intentional, *and* there would probably be other attempts. She claims she averted this accident with her mind."

"Who the hell is Cassarra?"

"Philip - the man in charge of the Trillium Group in America – it's his niece. She works as a tour guide at the White House. I've mentioned her to you before. Mallory has sensed from the beginning that this girl has highly developed physic abilities."

"Yes, now I remember you mentioning her. But to be able to stop something of that magnitude . . . !"

"I know. It's hard to believe. But all of this is hard to believe. I feel like I'm trapped in an episode of a horror movie and can't find my way out!"

"Why are they trying to . . ." Julia couldn't get herself to say the word kill. ". . . hurt Brit?"

"Because of his speeches. In a very short time he has organized a huge segment of society who knew they were being duped, but didn't know what to do about it. Brit has become a catalyst for change by giving them a voice and organizing them to put pressure on their Congressmen."

"Yes," Julia muttered softly, "and the last thing those in power want is change." She looked to her husband for guidance. "What do we do now?"

He turned to Bernadette. "What's Mallory's read on all this."

"She's frightened and wants Brit to stop making speeches."

"And Brit refuses to quit," Samuel said knowingly, his tone resigned.

Bernadette's emotions flared. "I wish I had never come here, then none of this would have happened."

"You don't know that," Julia responded. "Mallory's job with the Trillium Group had nothing to do with your coming here, and it was her moving to Richmond that put her in the right place to meet our son."

Bernadette stared, then dropped back into the armchair. "You're right. So this would have happened whether I contacted you or not!"

"It's the Trillium Group," Julia accused, "They're behind all this. We were suspicious of them from the beginning." Her impetus, when she stood, startled her husband who was next to her on the couch. "I'm going to Richmond with Bernadette," she announced with conviction.

A stunned Samuel was slow to react as he watched Julia head towards their bedroom to pack. "I think I'd better join you," he announced and followed her towards the stairwell.

CHAPTER 62

Mallory was stunned. "You're all at the airport!" *What was her mother thinking?* "Why did you tell the Sinclair's, Mother, you know how Brit feels about parental interference," and her face scrunched into a deep frown.

"I know dear. I'm really sorry, but it couldn't be avoided. I'll explain when I see you. I'll call as soon as we're settled in our hotel room."

Mallory slowly sank to the couch. Overcome with confusion, she pulled her moss green sweater close around her. Suddenly it seemed very cold. She wanted her mother here for moral support – to help her through this situation, but all three parents descending on them would only compound the problem. Too many people pushing and pulling in different directions. *"What have I done,"* she sobbed, as she saw her world falling apart without any means to stop it!

Traffic seemed particularly heavy as Mallory wove her way through the downtown streets to the historic Jefferson Hotel. Hardly noticing the refined luxury of the hotel lobby, she waited impatiently for the elevator, her mind rehearsing her strategy. She hoped to convince her mother and the Sinclairs to go right back to Boston. She knew now that it would be best to deal with the situation alone, without being swayed by the opinions and fears of others.

Her knock on the door was firm.

"Oh honey, it's so good to see you." Her mother's arms engulfed her. Mallory was careful to keep herself from melting completely into them. She had to stay strong, her relationship with Brit was in the balance here.

Bernadette felt the resistance. She knew all too well how obstinate her daughter could be once she made up her mind. "Where's Brit?"

"He's at work. I took the day off." She took a deep breath, "Mom, this isn't going to work – all of you being here."

"But dear, you have to understand . . ."

Mallory interrupted. "No, Mother, you have to understand. You're going to ruin everything."

"But if your lives are at stake, we deserve as parents to have some input."

Oh God, why, did I ever tell her!

Seeing the frustration in her daughter's eyes, Bernadette reached out and took her hand. "As long as we're here, why don't you let us help?"

Mallory pulled away. "Brit doesn't even know I've talked to you about this. Don't you see? Now he'll not only be upset because I want him to quit giving speeches, but because I've betrayed his trust as well."

"Honey, sometimes we have to put our personal perspectives aside and look at the big picture – and the big picture here is your lives are at risk, and we might be able to help. Maybe it's time for Brit to let go of the past and start building a new kind of relationship with his parents."

Mallory stood abruptly and stamped her foot. "That's what he was trying to do – and now *you've* muddled it up!"

"But you asked me to come down here."

"Since when does *you* include the Sinclairs? You should have asked me before you told them," she retorted, and the fire in her dark eyes intensified.

Why are we wasting time on all these silly entanglements when lives are at stake? Bernadette shifted gears. "Samuel spent the trip down here researching this Trillium Group. We have some pretty sound evidence that they're a clandestine society possibly connected to the Priory of Sion."

"The who?"

Where to start? There was so much information that Bernadette never shared with her daughter, mostly because Mallory had scoffed at the subject, brushing it off as her mother's overactive imagination. Now it was time to reveal everything she knew. "The Priory of Sion is an ancient secret society who many believe was organized solely for the purpose of keeping the truth about the Holy Grail alive until a designated time in history – and... well, we, that is the Sinclairs and I believe – or at least suspect that somehow our two families are entwined with this, and the designated time is close."

"With the Holy Grail!" Mallory sat down on the bed, a stunned look rippling across her face. *Now her mother was going too far!*

"Mallory, the Holy Grail is not what you think. The Sinclairs and I have been researching this for a long time. Listen to what I have to say before you jump to any conclusions."

Twenty minutes later Mallory stared at her mother. There was a hint of mirth in her eyes. "Mom, can you hear what you're saying. Do you really think that Jesus was an extraterrestrial from a planet where the beings were aquatic?"

"Honey, many aboriginal people believe their ancestors came from other planets."

"Look Mom, this is so far out I don't even want to talk about it. Even if it were true," and her look said it all, "it really isn't pertinent to the situation at hand."

"But it is pertinent. Don't you remember me telling you that when I was a young girl my father, your grandfather, always told me that Pleiades was our constellation? Well, the original myths that surrounded the Holy Grail were all concerning some mysterious heritage or dark secret about lineage, and don't forget, the original protagonist in the first Grail stories was named Percival."

Mallory released a deep sigh. *Where was her mother going with all this fantasy!* "Mom, there are lots of people out there with the last or first name of Percival. Can't you see what you're doing? You and Mr. Sinclair are both very creative writers – with highly developed imaginations. I think you've taken some historical facts and a few incidents from your lives and woven them into a wonderfully creative story, which you're now confusing with reality."

Mother and daughter sat staring into the mirror image of the other, each frustrated because the other was unable to see their perspective.

Bernadette tried another approach. "Don't you think it's rather strange that you received a letter from a company on the opposite side of the country asking you to apply for a job with them – *and* it was a company that just happened to have the fleur de lys as its logo."

"The fleur de lys is a fairly common logo."

"Okay, let's leave the fleur de Lys out of it. How did the Trillium Group get your name?"

Mallory stammered. "I don't . . . I never asked them."

Bernadette handed her daughter the phone. "Well, this is a perfect opportunity to find out. Give them a call, right now, and let's see what they say."

Her daughter shriveled back. "Why are you doing this?"

"Because I love you, and I don't want anything to happen to you or Brit."

"But Brit and I both love working for this company. All I want is for them to find another position for Brit."

"This company is not what you think, Mallory. It has motives that go far beyond caring for the environment, and it's very possible that you and Brit are being used as pawns in a very complicated drama that's been going on for centuries. Many people have been murdered trying to protect or destroy the information for which secret societies have become the stewards. The only goal of these societies is to preserve this information, to them lives are expendable."

Mallory was visibly shaken by her mother's words . . . *pawns in a complicated drama . . . lives that were expendable!*

Bernadette's tone softened. "Why don't you and I sit down and talk to the Sinclairs. You have to trust me, honey, I don't want to do anything to jeopardize your relationship with Brit. I only want to keep you both safe. Maybe if the four of us talk, we can come up with a plan that will work for all of us. In the meantime, Brit doesn't have to know we're here."

Mallory's large brown eyes were underlined with dark circles, her pallor pronounced by the moss green color of her sweater. "I don't know, I can't even think right now. I haven't slept in days, and suddenly I'm exhausted," she groaned, sinking onto the bed.

Her mother squeezed her hand. "Why don't you take a nap right here?" and she pulled back the satin bedspread as an enticement. "It will give me a chance to talk to the Sinclair's alone, so they understand the game plan."

Julia balked. "I think we should include Brit on this right from the beginning. It's paramount that he understands immediately that he's in danger," she said sharply, and in frustration, she tugged at the long sleeves of her blouse. Her cheeks had turned a bright pink.

"I understand how you feel, Julia, but put it in the perspective of your history with your son. I think he'll be more than a little resistant to anything you and Samuel say. Perhaps if we wait a few days, gather a little more information, possibly even set up a meeting with someone from the Trillium Group, we'd have a better grasp on the situation ourselves. Mallory is of the same opinion that we are, which is that Brit should stop making speeches for his own safety, and she's clearly the best avenue to him. If we can keep her from seeing us as the enemy, we'd have a better chance with him."

"Makes sense to me," Samuel admitted. "So what's our next step?"

"Well, this girl Cassarra might be the key. She's the one who told Mallory that the incident in Pennsylvania wasn't an accident – that it was a deliberate attempt on Brit's life. Since then, Cassarra has accompanied them to every one of Brit's speaking engagements – supposedly as protection."

Samuel's eyebrows arched. "That's pretty hard to swallow. Is it possible this girl has delusions of grandeur and has created this entire drama to make herself look important?"

"That's a possibility. Although Mallory has talked to me about her from their first meeting and has suspected for some time now that Cassarra is unusual."

"She might be an unusually good actress." Julia offered.

Bernadette's expression was one of surprise. "I never thought of that, but it's certainly a possibility. Mallory can be very naïve at times."

Samuel spoke with authority. "I think our next step should be for us to meet this Cassarra and make our own judgment. This Trillium Group might be an organization with very high ideals - or it might be a very devious organization cleverly disguised as one with very high ideals. Either way, it seems to me they are using our children for their own purposes – rather like live bait!"

CHAPTER 63

The following evening Bernadette returned to her room from dinner just as the phone was ringing. She fumbled in the dark before finding the light switch.

"Mom, I'm on my way over there. Something very alarming has happened."

"What is it dear?"

"I don't want to talk about it on the phone, but it's very serious! Can you ask the Sinclairs to come to your room? I'm only fifteen minutes away. We need to talk."

They were all gathered around the small table in the hotel room. Mallory's dark eyes were wide in a face that was drawn with tension.

"Today, when I went to Cassarra's apartment, a very confused man came stumbling into the living room from one of the bedrooms. He was clearly afraid and was mumbling about plots and being tortured – it was pretty surreal. Cassarra excused herself and settled him back into the bedroom. When she returned, I questioned her about the man, and she said they were providing asylum for him until he could travel home. When I asked asylum from whom . . . she hesitated before she said - your government." Mallory's hand impulsively went to her stomach. "I'm beginning to think you're right about this group – there's more to their agenda then meets the eye. We've got to find a way to get Brit out of this. If it weren't for him, I'd give my notice right now."

Bernadette clasped Mallory's hand for support. "Did she say what this man did?"

"No, and I didn't ask. By that time my only thought was to get out of there. If you saw this man . . . the extent of his confusion ... he mumbled, mostly in French so I was only able to understand some of what he was saying; but the one thing that was clear to me was that he feared for his life. I didn't bother to ask Cassarra to meet with you. I made up my mind right then and there. I'm an environmentalist. Clandestine politics is not my thing," and the tears she had been fighting back since she arrived began to stream down her face.

As Bernadette consoled her daughter, Julia, feeling a need to move, began pacing nervously around the room. "I think it's time we talked to Brit," she exclaimed in an unusually high-pitched voice. "He needs to know our concerns – and that his life is in danger– before he's reduced to a mumbling idiot like the man in Cassarra's apartment!"

CHAPTER 64

Inside the offices of the Trillium Group, Philippe laid down his pen and gave the two women across his desk his undivided attention. His deep resonate voice was soothing as he spoke in their native tongue. "What you saw as an unfortunate circumstance was perhaps the Universe opening a door inviting us in," he suggested with an endearing smile.

"But had you seen the expression on her face," Mari replied, and her eyes shifted towards Cassarra for confirmation.

Cassarra nodded. "The circumstances of Alain's state alarmed her. She had already been concerned about Brit's welfare, and this incident only propelled her deeper into fear. A frightened fawn in an unknown forest of corruption and deceit, she bolted to safer territory."

"I knew keeping that turncoat with Mari and Cassarra would bring us nothing but trouble," Francois grumbled, and his tight muscular frame moved uneasily in the chair.

Philippe ignored Francois' remark, understanding his concern was for Mari's safety. "It will be our task to rein Mallory back in by making her feel secure about our goals. As you well know, we have no backup plan, she and Brit must rise to the occasion."

"Brit will bring her back into the fold," Cassarra predicted. "He can see better past the microcosm to the bigger picture."

Philippe smiled. "Yes, their roles have now reversed. First she brought *him* to us, now it is his turn to complete the cycle by bringing *her* back."

"There is another element that must be addressed," Cassarra shared, and her vibrant hair moved slightly as she spoke. "And that is the parents. I understand they've converged here in Richmond. Part of Mallory's fear has been fanned by them."

"Ah, their presence explains much."

"I only had awareness after Mallory fled our apartment. I suspected there was another element in this equation, and in meditation, I saw they had come to town with their own agenda."

"We knew we'd have to deal with the parents eventually, since they'll be instrumental in the next chapter." Philippe smiled knowingly. "Again it appears the Universe has orchestrated a grand opportunity. But, before we act, I believe a consultation with Lenzi is in order," and swiveling his chair towards his computer, he brought up his email program.

CHAPTER 65

Bernadette waited impatiently as the room-service attendant removed the Sinclair's breakfast tray. The door had barely clicked behind the young man when her voice bubbled over with excitement.

"Mallory phoned a few minutes ago, and guess what? Philip, the man in charge of the Trillium Group, asked if he could arrange a meeting with us!"

Samuel's eyebrows arched, "An appealing request. I'd personally love to meet the man and ask him a few pointed questions."

"The interesting thing is Mallory claims she never told him we were in town." Bernadette was searching their faces. "So how did he know we were here? Is he, or are *they* watching us, keeping track of our every move?"

Julia sat wide-eyed in disbelief.

In an attempt to neutralize the women's reaction Samuel offered, "It's very possible Mallory told someone in the organization without realizing it. She *is* very upset right now."

Bernadette frowned. "I suppose that's a possibility."

"Maybe that's one of the questions we could ask Philip when we sit down with him," Julia suggested.

"Good idea. In fact I think we should make a list of all our questions so we're sure not to get side-tracked," and he pulled his pen from his shirt pocket and marched over to the desk to find some paper.

The sound of heels moving rapidly across the tile floor was amplified in the dimly lit lobby of the deserted office building, as Mallory lead the small group past the interior courtyard to the elevators. No one spoke on the way up. Before they entered the office of the Trillium Group, Bernadette put her arm around her daughter and gave her a quick hug in a show of support.

Mallory's voice was shaking as she made the introductions, but the tension in the room was quickly dispersed by Philip's natural ambiance.

"I understand you have concerns about your children working for our organization," he prompted.

Samuel immediately took charge. "That's correct. It was suggested to Mallory by your niece, Cassarra, that an attempt has already been made on their lives."

"This is true." Philip hesitated. He could feel the fear in the room intensify as Julia gripped the arm of her chair. *How much should he divulge at this point? Le Perfector gave him the authority to use his own judgment.* "Cassarra also assured Mallory that they would both be protected."

"Yes, she told us that," and Samuel's voice took on a sarcastic note. "Forgive me for questioning your methods, however, we're all at a loss as to how this can be accomplished."

"There are those who are skilled at this."

"Cassarra?"

"Yes, but she is just one of many."

"And these others. Who and where are they?"

"That's unimportant," Philip answered.

Samuel's temper flared. "It may be unimportant to you, sir, but it's very important to us. How do we know we can believe you? Mallory spoke about the man she met while visiting your niece. Apparently your people weren't able to protect him, based on his condition and story."

"That was an unusual circumstance."

"How do we know our children won't be an unusual circumstance?"

"That man acted on his own volition, without our authority. We rescued him even though his goal wasn't worthy to our cause."

Samuel stared at Philip. His voice held a challenge. "Is your organization affiliated with the Priory of Sion in any way?"

"Ah yes, the Priory is getting much attention these days. But no, we know nothing of the Priory. We're an independent organization."

"Whose goal is?"

"A better world."

He's answering all of my questions, but he's not really telling us anything.

Bernadette stepped in. "How did you originally get Mallory's name? She said she received a request from you before she ever applied for a job."

Philip's smile was one of measured patience. "Perhaps it would be best to first address your main concerns. I want to assure you that Brit and Mallory's lives will be protected at all cost. They are very important to our organization."

Samuel looked unconvinced. "If you have people with highly developed psychic abilities in your organization, why do you need our children?"

Philip rubbed his chin. "First let me explain our agenda. The Trillium Group is aware that there are those in and behind the government of the United States who have secretly begun a process whereby nuclear waste will be sent to the planet Mars. This cannot be allowed. The best-case scenario is, if successful, they would continue with the process until the surface of Mars is completely contaminated, eventually causing repercussions throughout our solar system. The worse case scenario is, if the rocket crashes upon landing, it would detonate and cause a nuclear explosion, triggering a series of events in our solar system that would eventually be catastrophic throughout the Universe." Philippe's voice took on an edge. "Either way, life on Earth would be stilled, the only difference between the two possibilities would be the time frame."

The others in the room gasped at his last remark.

"There is also a third possibility, and that is if the rocket explodes during take off, it would cause and atomic explosion similar to the one in Hiroshima," and he looked purposely at them, his thick, white eyebrows accentuating his expressive eyes. "I'm sure you've seen the pictures of the aftermath of the bomb in Hiroshima." He paused. "So, you see, Brit is our instrument of hope. He's been able to capture the trust of the people and spur them into action. He could be the catalyst for change that would literally save the human race."

The women were stunned; Samuel was dubious. "Why don't you simply expose this plot through the news media?"

"Let's say we found a source that believed us and was willing to be ridiculed for printing the story. Do you think those behind the plot would admit it? None of you are that politically naïve. Those involved in this project are very powerful and influential men who have the trust of the American people. They would deny everything, and make it seem as if it wasn't possible to cover up something of that magnitude from Congress and NASA. Then, they would create lies to show that we are nothing but a left-wing group of fringe lunatics. As you can guess, these tactics have been used very successfully in our historical past, but never with the severe consequences that are presently at stake." He paused for a long moment to make his next point. "Nuclear weapons have changed the tapestry of world events."

Julia's voice was constricted with emotion. "Mr. Boule, we would love to believe you, but I'm sure you can understand a mother's concern for her child. Can you give us some evidence, some proof that all you're telling us is true? You see the thing I'm finding so difficult to understand is – well, why my son? If your niece has these great powers as you claim, wouldn't it make sense for her to be the one making these speeches and putting her life on the line?"

"Each person has a different role. Cassarra is traveling with your son. If he were in danger, then she would be as well." Philip smiled at Mallory. "You have been with us for how long now – five months?"

She nodded.

"You are intelligent and have good instincts. What has your heart been telling you about us, both as individuals and as an organization?"

"You know I love everyone here, even Frank, who, at first, I found grumpy."

"Do you think we could have fooled you for such a long time if our intentions were contrary to your own? Think of all the hours you've spent with Cassarra in intimate conversations."

Mallory's face turned scarlet. "It's just so . . . so confusing. You know I love Cassarra like a sister – and you like the grandfather I lost so many years ago."

Bernadette bristled. "Mr. Boule, our purpose of coming here today is to be assured that our daughter and son are safe working within your organization, not to have you question Mallory's loyalty. I feel what you are doing here is playing on her emotions so they'll override her intellect."

"On the contrary. I'm trying to encourage her to tap into her intuition. Emotions are the tool of the ego. My efforts are to get her to step out of the emotion of fear and guide her towards her heart and higher intellect, which are the true doorways to her spirit. From there she will know how to choose wisely."

Samuel interceded, "As much as I'm opposed to putting nuclear waste on Mars, I don't understand why it would make such a difference. We're already putting it in the ground here just as we're creating nuclear explosions on Earth by regularly testing nuclear bombs. Why would the same thing happening on Mars be so detrimental?"

"If contamination is confined, it can be somewhat controlled. However, when it begins to spread, eventually critical mass is reached and the entire structure is doomed. This is true whether it be a cancer cell within a human body or cancer cell within the solar system."

Samuel's voice contained more than a hint of distrust. "How did you obtain this information about the proposed mission, and is there some way you can give us proof?"

Philip appeared to be making a decision. "Le Perfector will be arriving in a few days, specifically to meet with you. I believe it would be in order at that time to show you a brief presentation that will help convince you of our cause. In the meantime, I suspect a meeting with Cassarra would be most helpful in assuring you that both Mallory and Brit are in safe hands. Would you be free the evening after next? We could meet here again, or we could come to your hotel suite."

The navy blue collar of Samuel's shirt outlined his jaw that was firmly set. "I'd prefer our hotel, and let's make it tomorrow evening. This charade has gone on long enough, there's no point in postponing it longer than necessary. You can let us know about the time."

CHAPTER 66

The next morning in one of the nicer suites of the Jefferson Hotel, Bernadette placed the phone back in the cradle. Her knees buckled as she groped for a chair, as a ghostly pallor washed over her face.

Julia ran to her aid. "What is it?"

Bernadette stammered through lips that quivered, "It was the voice, I'd recognize it anywhere – dear God, it's him!"

Samuel entered the room. "What's going on?"

"Bernadette received a phone call from The Voice."

Bernadette looked up into their questioning faces. "No, not *The* Voice," she answered cryptically.

They were still staring at her. "Then *what* voice?" Samuel finally asked.

Bernadette was shaking. "The one that threatened me after my father's death and recently called to first say to stay away from you and later to say it would be all right to contact you."

"What did he say?"

"He asked if it was all right . . . if it was all right if . ."

"If___?" Samuel prodded.

"If they came at 7:00?"

"What?"

"It was Philip from the Trillium Group," she gasped as she sank further into the cushion of the chair.

CHAPTER 67

"Are you absolutely sure?" Samuel asked in a surreal voice.

"Samuel, that's the fourth time you've asked her that."

"I'm sorry, but I need to know."

His wife stared at him. "*You* know. She said 'yes' three times," and she handed Bernadette a cup of hot tea as she joined her on the divan. Samuel was staring blankly at the large floral painting on the wall behind them.

Bernadette patted Julia's knee. "It's all right, dear, I understand Samuel's disbelief. I can't explain why I didn't make the connection the night we met Philip. I suppose in person one doesn't focus on a voice in the same way one does on the phone." Then, emphatically, "But, Samuel, I'm as sure as I can be."

"What do we do now?" Julia asked. "Do we still want to meet with them?"

Bernadette shook her head. "I don't like any of this."

"Now wait a minute, you two. Maybe we're finally going to get some answers."

"Do you think we got any answers the other night in his office?" Bernadette's tone was mocking.

"Not really. He was great at sidestepping every question we asked. And this Le Perfector - what the hell kind of a title is that? Talk about lofty. On the other hand, they certainly have roused my curiosity. I definitely want to meet whoever goes around calling themselves Le Perfector!"

"Do you believe all this talk about Cassarra's highly developed skills?"

"It's hard to know what to believe. I'm hoping tonight will reveal more to us than our previous meeting. I don't know about you girls, but I'm anxious to meet Cassarra to get my own read on her."

"What about Philip? Should I tell him I recognized his voice?"

"Yes, but let's not play our trump card right away. I think we should wait and see how the evening goes, and then toss it out on the table when it will have the most impact."

Although Mallory had told them Cassarra was attractive, they weren't prepared for the stunning beauty that entered. Her lustrous chestnut mane shimmered with auburn highlights and framed an oval face of flawless porcelain skin. A silk scarf in a kaleidoscope of greens and blues was artfully draped over her white tank top, accentuating her extraordinary coloring. With a humble demeanor and an incredible sweetness that immediately touched their hearts, she created a cheerfulness that radiated around the room, dispelling any doubts about her.

Philip had brought a box of chocolates and an expensive bottle of French cognac, which were immediately looked upon with some suspicion, however, his opening remark caught them all by surprise.

"So you recognized my voice," he announced, looking directly at Bernadette. "This is good. Now we can put all our cards on the table, *non?*"

Bernadette's mouth dropped open, her eyes transfixed on his. This was the last thing she expected. "How... how did you know?"

"We have been studying for many years to project our minds outward so we can see what's happening in other places. The procedure is referred to as remote viewing. When you were in my office the other night and I told you that was how we would protect your children, there was great doubt. So I felt the best way to prove our abilities was by example. There are those like Cassarra who have even greater abilities than myself, because they've been trained since early childhood."

They all shifted their focus to Cassarra, who only smiled demurely.

Philip addressed Bernadette. "You have questions?"

"Lots of them. I'd like to start with the first time you called and threatened me. Why did you do that?"

Philip's smile was completely genuine. "I'm sorry you perceived that as a threat. Our goal was to protect you. If we had allowed your curiosity to lead you without regard for caution, there was a possibility you would have uncovered information before you were ready to integrate it."

Samuel interjected, "What made you change your mind about contact with me after Bernadette arrived in Boston?"

"It was Le Perfector who made that decision."

There was that name again! "I assume you know the reasoning behind it?"

"It was based on events that were happening within your government."

"You're speaking of this project to send nuclear waste to Mars?"

"That was a major one, along with other environmental indiscretions that have been allowed by the current administration. Many of which are already having catastrophic effects on the global environment. However, there was another major concern, and that was the fact that America, a place historically set aside for freedom, had become an aggressive nation willing to use weapons of mass destruction on other countries under the guise of defending itself and spreading democracy. And we have reason to believe this behavior will continue unless there is a major change in the hearts of the people." Philip smiled in the most beguiling of ways. "As I mentioned the other evening, Brit's speeches have already become a catalyst for that change."

"Can you explain to us how or why our families are connected to this?"

"That is a subject better left for Le Perfector. My job is to assure you in every way possible that Brit and Mallory will be safe, and that our motives are of the highest ideals. I've shown you the ability to see and hear what is happening in distance places, now I'll have Cassarra give you assurance of another kind."

All eyes turned to the young girl, who blushed slightly, but maintained a look of complete confidence.

"First I must ask that what happens here goes no further," she demurred. Then seeing the apprehensive glances that past around the room, she explained. "I only ask this because often these attributes are misconstrued as either saintly or of the devil's hand by those who fail to recognize they are abilities latent in every individual." Then turning to Samuel, "Mr. Sinclair, would you mind pouring some cognac for me."

"Certainly," but when he tried to pick the bottle up, he couldn't move it. "What the___!

"That is how I stopped the car from hitting us on the road to Philadelphia," she said quietly. "Now you may lift the bottle." And Samuel easily picked up the cognac.

Still doubting, he said, "I'd like to see an example with something more substantial. A bottle of cognac could hardly be compared to a speeding car."

"Would the entertainment center convince you?

Samuel nodded, his eyebrows raised in doubt.

An instant later, the huge piece was sitting on top of the bed in the other room.

Julia gripped Bernadette's hand as the two stared in disbelief.

Samuel's mouth hung open. "Amazing, absolutely amazing," he muttered, his head shaking in awe at what he was seeing.

When Samuel finally recovered, he smiled, "Now I hope you can put it back, or we're going to have a lot of explaining to do to the hotel management," and Julia and Bernadette, still in a state of shock, only stared as the entertainment center seemed to dissolve in one place and reconstruct itself in another.

"Was that sufficient to convince you that I can protect your son?" Cassarra's question was asked quietly and with lack of any arrogance.

"But you can't be with him constantly. What about when he's not with you," Julia's voice cried out.

Cassarra's incredibly clear eyes held Julia's. "Philip showed you that we are able to see and hear even from afar. There is a group of men and women referred to as the council, who are assigned to watch Brit and Mallory around the clock."

Mallory blushed profusely. "That's not necessarily a comforting thought," she sputtered, thinking of intimate moments.

"It doesn't work the way you think. We have ways of being alerted only if there's a problem. We're not watching you every minute, we're only aware of what's happening around you. If there's something troubling, then we focus in."

The four were shaking their heads in confusion unable to truly fathom the concept that Cassarra was trying to convey.

"I know this is all difficult to absorb, but if I explained it further you still wouldn't understand. It would be like trying to teach a kindergartener calculus." Cassarra looked directly at Mallory. "That's why it was important for us to become friends first, so there would be the element of trust until you had enough knowledge for complete comprehension."

"Will we be taught how to do these things," Samuel asked eagerly.

It was Philip who responded. "Eventually everyone will be taught from birth, however, it's like any other skill. It takes practice and the proper belief system to be effective," he reminded them. "And as with other abilities, some will come by it more naturally because of genetic disposition and lessons learned in previous lifetimes. We're not all meant to be concert violinists nor are we all meant to have great psychic abilities, however, if we cultivate either of these talents, we will have enough ability to heighten our own enjoyment of life." Then, in a more serious tone, "I'm sure you understand there is a great responsibility that comes with the development of psychic skills, which is why they aren't taught indiscriminately. One must learn to expand them through study and knowledge so they're used only for the further advancement of mankind, rather than for acquiring power and personal gain."

"I'm hoping you've seen enough tonight," Philip continued, "to assure you that Mallory and Brit will be safe, and that's it's to the best advantage of your country for Brit to continue with his speeches." Then, his demeanor gripped Mallory with a profound intensity as he made direct eye contact. "Without your support, Brit's effectiveness would be greatly diminished, which would be a great loss for the human race. In spite of its conspicuous failings, humanity has begun a transformation of human consciousness that in the end will be more momentous than any revolution, and Brit has within his power the opportunity to greatly diminish the length of the purifying cycle required. There is a great possibility we will see these changes in our own lifetimes."

Tears filled Mallory's eyes as she reached her hand towards Philip. "I think I understand now. I'd like to stay on with the Trillium Group and help."

CHAPTER 68

"You're awfully quiet this morning," Bernadette said to Samuel across the breakfast table of the small local restaurant they had grown fond of patronizing. It was family owned and operated, and all the food was cooked on the premises.

"I'm still trying to come to grips with everything we saw and heard last night."

"I know how you feel. It was as if we closed our eyes for a minute, and when we opened them, we were characters in a science-fiction novel."

Samuel nodded. "What's remarkable to me is I've always believed in mind over matter, and yet, when I was confronted with Cassarra's abilities, I didn't want to believe it. I kept thinking it must be a trick of some kind."

"I totally understand. I'm right there with you," she remarked, as she patted her lips dry with the floral patterned napkin.

"I wish they had given us more information," Julia sighed. "It seems as if Philip is doling everything out in bits and pieces."

"Maybe they're afraid if they gave it to us all at once, we'd freak out. Seeing that entertainment set dissolve and then reconstruct itself on the bed nearly put me over the edge. I'm not sure I could have handled much more," Bernadette admitted. "On the other hand, I'm wildly curious about how she did it. I spent half of the night testing my own belief system."

"As did I," Samuel confessed. "And it made me realize how in many ways we've accepted two diametrically opposed belief systems about our world."

"In what way?" Julia questioned, and she pushed her empty plate off to the side.

"For example, take this table. If we looked at it through a strong enough microscope we would see that's it made up of many molecules that science tells us are rotating at phenomenal speeds, and that there is more space than matter in it. We accept that as fact, right?"

The two women nodded their heads in agreement.

"And yet our senses and minds tell us that this table is rigid and solid, and we also accept that as fact." He paused looking right at them. "So which one is it? They can't both be right, can they?"

Bernadette smiled whimsically. "Isn't it interesting that we've accepted science's conclusions without questioning our reality."

"It's more than interesting," Samuel stated emphatically, "It's baffling."

"The great mystics have always said this world is merely an illusion. It seems to me that's a pretty good description of what modern science has proved. Although, I can't say I understand it," Bernadette shrugged her shoulders.

"Yes, the parallels between modern physics and Eastern mysticism have become daunting," Samuel, agreed, and he held up his coffee mug to the passing waitress, indicating he needed a refill. "Scientists have literally turned matter inside out and upside down trying to define it, and the results are they found it to be practically non-existent. Translated, that means the very ground we're walking on is empty space!"

He added a healthy amount of cream to his fresh mug of coffee before continuing. "Think about it!" he said, his voice becoming animated. "If molecules are a form of energy and everything is made up of molecules and a lot of empty space, then if one had a really deep comprehension of that concept and that same someone had developed the powers of their mind, like Cassarra claims she has, I suppose anything is possible. Clearly something happened last night when Cassarra moved that entertainment center. We all saw it, didn't we?"

Bernadette was shaking her head. "I think I saw it. Last night I actually began to wonder if Philip had put something in that cognac that would affect our minds."

"I didn't have any cognac," Julia stated flatly, "and I saw the same thing you did."

"What if their expertise is mind control and nothing else? Is it possible they had somehow hypnotized us into believing the entertainment center moved, when in fact it never left its original spot?"

"Isn't it interesting," Samuel suggested, "That we're willing to believe this table is mostly space – and yet we're leaning on it; and we don't question that inconsistency - we simply accept it arbitrarily as fact because our scientists have told us. Yet we have trouble believing that the entertainment center was moved, even though we all saw it. And if we believe our scientists, the entertainment center is also mostly space. Assuming that's true, it could easily be moved," and he heaved a huge sigh.

"My mind's going in circles," Julia exclaimed with a perplexed look. "But I agree, this is forcing us to test our belief systems and to recognize our minds are split into accepting two opposing realties."

And then a light bulb went off in her head. "Remember the theory that I told you I had read concerning electrons, and how they obey our thoughts and feelings? If that theory's correct, it would explain how Cassarra, with that knowledge and her superbly developed powers of the mind, is able to move things. Particularly, when we consider that matter is mostly space and energy."

"That's certainly a possibility. Hopefully, this Le Perfector, who apparently is the head ducky of this organization will shed some light on all this."

"Yes, and explain how Mallory and Brit were selected for the roles they're playing. Clearly they've been watching them for years, maybe since birth."

"That's such an eerie feeling. Do you think they're watching us now?"

Samuel looked up, smiling devilishly, and flashed his third finger. "Here's to you Trillium Group."

"Oh Samuel, don't be coarse," his wife laughed.

"Well, if they're really as good as they say, they can read my mind and know I'm only joking."

"I'm just glad we can tell Brit we're here, so I can see him," Julia's voice radiated with excitement."

CHAPTER 69

Anticipation of the day made it come so slowly that when it finally arrived, it was a surprise.

"Le Perfector will be here tomorrow," Philip told Mallory and Brit, his eyes bright with expectation. "Your parents are anxious for the meeting, and I know the feeling is mutual. I'll arrange everything as quickly as possible."

Samuel was still scribbling his questions on a small note pad when the knock came on the door. Bernadette eyed Julia and took a deep breath. *Le Perfector had arrived!*

Expressions turned from apprehension to puzzlement as Philip entered, his arm entwined with an older woman's. *But where was Le Perfector?* Their puzzlement turned to shock when Philip introduced Lenzi. *A woman! The formidable Le Perfector was a gray-haired elderly woman with a slight limp! Impossible. Was this a ploy, a joke?*

Julia and Bernadette looked at each other, a mixture of surprise and relief on their faces, however, a disappointment hovered in Samuel's eyes. His plan had been to take an aggressive approach. Now he would have to temper his attack, and a part of him felt cheated. This almost seemed unfair.

Mallory's reaction varied greatly from the others. For her there was an immediate recognition at the soul level, a hint of familiarity that put her at ease. At first she attributed this to Le Perfector's grandmotherly manner, but later, wisps of other memories taunted her conscious awareness.

"I know you have many questions for me," Lenzi began, "About the role you're playing in this elusive dance that has connected us and brought us together today, but first, let me present the broader picture."

"It shouldn't surprise you to know that countries have potential destinies just as individuals have potential destinies." Her smile was embellished with much love when she turned to Philippe.

"You wondered why I mentioned your Basque heritage when I selected you for this mission."

Philippe nodded eagerly. *At last he would discover the meaning behind Le Perfector's words. Words that had been churning in his mind, haunting his peace since their utterance.*

"The Basque have in their distinct genetic makeup, above all else, a deep, almost overwhelming drive to be free and independent. Through the centuries the Basque people have guarded this trait by resisting domination from many - the Visigoths, the Franks, the Arab Muslims. They even resisted Romanization by remaining true to themselves. As we anticipated, the Basque became an acorn for democracy planted between France and Spain, fanning the flames for human rights and keeping alive the hope in the hearts of men that someday they would live free from tyranny and oppression. That seed ultimately became the source of both the French and Spanish Revolutions."

"It was our original plan that the French Revolution would be the beginning of a democratic Europe," and then a great sadness washed across her face. "However, *we* can only ignite the fires for humanity. It is their job to control the flames. Unfortunately, in this instance, that didn't happen. As the power in France shifted away from the monarchy, instead of the masses taking the momentum and moving towards a nobler cause as we hoped, they became swept away by the winds of vengeance. Like fire raging uncontrolled through open fields, their bitterness spread. The guillotine became their temporary god, and their thirst for blood became all consuming."

She then focused on Brit as if there were only the two of them in the room. "Can you see how the French citizens of that time exhausted their energy on revenge? It's important to remember for the future that when a change in leadership takes place that it's in a nation's best interest to funnel the passions of the public away from past mistakes and towards the future by welcoming all into the light. That does not mean that the previous leaders should not be held accountable for their wrong doings. But if trials are appropriate, it would be healthier for the country that they not become the main focus of the citizens."

Lenzi then shifted her attention back to the group. "But somewhere in the French psyche," she continued, "was the understanding that they failed in their mission, and that is why they gave you the gift of the Statue of Liberty. A great reminder to all that the eyes of this nation must stay focused towards a vision of equality and justice for all people. That was and is the potential destiny of the United States. The citizens of this country are – by destiny – the custodians of freedom. They have come together to build a democratic society where men can abide together in peace. A true nation of the people, by the people and for the people." Again she made eye contact with Brit and Mallory. "In order for this to happen, the citizens must come together in a common goal for something bigger than themselves. The two of you, working together, have the ability to bring this vision to the people and give them the inspiration to carry it through as intended.

Lenzi then released a great sigh and a hint of weariness passed across her features. "This same goal has been attempted before on this great planet, however, without the success that was intended. Atlantis was one such place. The Atlantean's failure was brought about by their obsession with the material world. Focusing all their attention on the pursuit of advanced technology, the Atlanteans greatly ignored their inner spirits. Technology without a higher purpose becomes the tool of the selfish lower nature. This is what led the Atlanteans ultimately to the bomb instead of the Buddha. In the end they destroyed themselves with their fascination for dominance of the false material world."

"Then there was Lemuria, a remnant of which remains in the island you call Australia," her voice continued as her eyes looked towards the past. "The Lemurians took a different road to destruction. They erred by over-indulging in self-woven dramas until their destinies became so entangled in a web of intrigue that they couldn't find their way out. As their emotions whipped them around in a sea of turbulence, they lost all connection to their spirits. This also proved fatal. In order to flourish, the soul needs to be nurtured in a calm, loving environment. The soul's very nature is repelled by strong emotions. Emotions whether positive or negative create intense electrical currents, like static, and cause the soul to withdraw." Her lips turned up into a frail smile. "I will remind you here that love and emotion are not the same thing."

Then Lenzi's smile brightened. "However, at this time in America, an ample number of souls that chose to reincarnate are from the consciousnesses of those two societies, and their purpose in coming here is to complete the task in which they previously failed."

The women sat transfixed. *So Atlantis and Lemuria were more than myths.* However Samuel, in his impatience, interrupted with a torrent of questions, "What role does the Holy Grail play in all of this?"

"As you know," Lenzi shared, "We've been keeping a record of the progress of your studies, and I would say your assessment has been quite accurate. First, your understanding that the Holy Grail is only a small piece of a much larger puzzle, and secondly, the recognition that it has to do with the balance of the male and female energies. Atlantis was of a masculine dominated energy. Lemuria was of a feminine dominated energy. At the present time those two strong consciousnesses are trying to blend and find an equilibrium within the steaming cauldron of current times."

Then she issued words of caution. "Be aware that your current belief system tends to perceive the masculine yang energy as negative. Both yin and yang are positive and negative, depending on what the individual does with the energy. The solution is to find the balance within you. Too much of either is equally unbalanced. Think of yourself as a bird. One wing is yin, the other yang. The bird can only fly when the two wings are equal."

"Was Jesus married?" Samuel blurted out.

"You're putting far too much emphasis on *if* he was married and *to whom*. The importance is that he had women in his inner circle because he recognized the value of their intellect and their goddess energy. That is what is being overlooked. Can you see how the custodians of the knowledge documenting Jesus' bloodline have been just as responsible for keeping societies off balance as those who tried to bury it?"

"How?"

"By validating the fight, which then allowed them to keep the male energy of the sword as the focus. War is a negative energy no matter what the purpose behind it. They also mistakenly put the emphasis on the messengers instead of the messages. Veneration of a personality, no matter what sex, or how evolved or enlightened is a denial of one's own powers."

Samuel was still bursting at the seams, "What about the extraterrestrial connection – was Jesus from another planet?"

"Le Perfector smiled softly. "Would it surprise you to know that all on this planet were star seeded?"

"From which star system?"

"Many, which now explains your different races."

"Would it be possible for us to meet an extraterrestrial?" Samuel asked, his voice excited at the prospect.

"Yes, many on your planet have expressed that desire. My advice is to make your peace with the many races, religions and nationalities on your own planet first. How do you expect to open your homes and share your thoughts with an alpha zentaurian, if you can't open them to a black person or a Muslim?"

"However, I remind you that even with extraterrestrials, caution must prevail. It is important not to make gods out of them. They are only sparks of divinity, such as yourselves, who developed in a different way and in a different time frame. They are your elder brothers; but just as with those in your society, some of them have also taken the lower path. They are not all of pure motives. Although those that are, can be of great assistance to you at this time. But you must ask for their help. However, I remind you that caution and discretion should always prevail, which is why you are being encouraged to develop your finer senses. So you can see through the deception and the mundane desires of personalities. Both your own and those whom you come in contact with. And this brings us back to the question of your personal involvement."

Lenzi turned to Mallory. "You saw something when I first arrived, but you haven't yet made the connection."

Mallory's voice was unsure. "Yes, there was something familiar."

"Look deeper," Lenzi urged.

All eyes in the room focused on the young woman as she studied Lenzi's face, when Lenzi moved her hand and leaned forward in a certain way.

Mallory faltered. "Grandfather?" she whispered, causing Bernadette to pull back as she looked from Lenzi to her daughter. *What did Mallory see that she didn't?*

Lenzi broke into a wide smile. "You knew he had a twin sister."

Mallory's answer was cautious, "Yes, they were separated in Hungary when very young, and he was brought to America."

"We were separated physically, but never mentally. And because of our close bond, we soon learned to meet in other dimensions."

Bernadette was watching silently, her hand at her mouth. *Her father had died fifteen years ago at the age of sixty-eight; her memory of him was of a much younger person than Lenzi.* She searched the elderly face across from her. *Now she could see the similarity. How had it escaped her earlier?* A torrent of questions rushed in.

Lenzi turned to her. "You always wondered about your name. It came from me."

"You, but . . . ?"

"When I was a young girl and became aware of my potential destiny, at my urging my family left Hungary for the Pyrenees Mountains in France where I was bathed daily in the spring where the young St. Bernadette saw her apparition. It was there I was taught the goddess energy, which I shared with Gabor."

"Gabor?"

"Yes, that was your grandfather's name in Hungarian, and he was wisely named. It means the strength from God."

Mallory's face brightened. *Gabriel, the strength from God - how appropriate for such a special man.*

Feeling slighted by the lack of attention, Samuel asked, "What about our family's connection?"

"Julia and Bernadette have already sensed their connection in their instant bond of sisterhood. Although they don't thoroughly understand it yet, it will continue to reveal its many facets as they explore it. Your connection, Samuel, is one of previous experiences – or lives as you call them – that brought you to this point, both in Atlantis and Lemuria. You were very determined to pull it together this time and you haven't disappointed the cause. You chose to come into a family with the Sinclair name because of the vibration it brought with it. Julia was naturally drawn to that vibration."

Bernadette, still visibly shaken, managed to ask, "What about the Hungarian connection?"

"As I mentioned, all countries have a destiny. Because of its location Hungary was the bridge between the East and the West, a melting pot so to speak of the two cultures and races. The Romans invaded, then the Huns, then the Franks, then the Magyars followed by the Hapsburgs. Can you see the pattern? Occidental, oriental, occidental, oriental. What better way to lose our suspicions of a race then to intermarry? A commingling of blood and consciousness, hopefully to take the best of each."

"And Hungary's connection to the ancient land of Sumer?"

Le Perfector's smile was one of a teacher for a student who has shown great promise. "Yes, the Hungarians originally came from the same star system as the Sumerians, hence their language has many similarities. It was important for you and Julia to hear the sounds of that language."

"Why?"

"All language has been sound coded. One can learn a great deal from the sound of words."

"But neither of us can speak Hungarian."

"That was by design. The meaning of words has become too concrete. One can better receive the coded messages in the sounds behind them when not focusing on the meaning."

Samuel pressed. "Here's what I don't understand. If those in your organization have developed powers far greater than the average man, why don't you simply stop those in the American government from proceeding with this Phoenix Project?"

"We could do that, and we have employed methods of that nature in the past. But can you see that in itself is a full time job? Men only find more devious ways to accomplish their self-serving agendas, which keeps humanity caught in a wheel of negativity and destruction."

Lenzi looked from one to the other before she continued. "But at present, the time is ripe to move forward in human evolution. You've all studied the original Grail stories, where Percival, a simple man, was transformed into an evolved being by letting go of his selfish thoughts and by asking whom he was to serve. This shift in focus from self, ultimately allowed him to heal the King, who was the link to his bloodline, and ultimately the kingdom," and then she turned to Brit who had been sitting quietly taking it all in. "It will be Brit's job to help shift that focus in the masses. However, first he had to find Mallory, his symbolic Lost Bride, because within the male/female relationship lays all the potency of the finished product. Brit and Mallory wisely understood that pooling their resources has created a balanced intention behind Brit's speeches. One that is free from personal attachment and pointed towards a higher goal."

Julia smiled affectionately at her son, but Samuel's intellect was not satisfied. "Since you've already shown you can put thoughts into other's minds by mental telepathy, why not simply put good thoughts into the minds of those in power?"

The light in Lenzi's eyes seemed to flicker a moment. "If you only knew the countless hours we've spent sending loving thoughts throughout the Universe, but you need to understand, Mr. Sinclair, even the greatest of masters must bow to the free will of man. If men choose to look the other way, we can't force them to accept our thoughts of love and peace."

"I don't understand why not, if it's for the good of all."

"We are not here to change minds. We are here to change hearts. If a man hasn't changed in his heart, ultimately his darkness will surface and drive him again towards the negative, and the world will continue in the same old cycle of pain and suffering. Can you not see that religions have tried to force restrictions on the negative aspects of the human nature? The result has been widespread neurosis. Governments on the other hand, have tried to legislate morality, with similar results. Morals cannot be successfully forced upon humanity; they must come from within to be effective. It is education, not legislation that promotes permanent progress in men. If you'll recall, the only thing Prohibition did was to produce speakeasies and create an environment in which gangsters could prevail."

Samuel looked wary. "If Atlantis and Lemuria both failed, what makes you think this time will be any different?" he quipped.

Le Perfector's face was filled with kindness. "What makes you think that Divine Intelligence doesn't have the power to draw a line in the sand and say, 'enough'? Although the line is not rigid by your definition, it is there nonetheless."

"I would love to believe you," Samuel confessed, "But when I look around I'm not seeing the world going in that direction."

"Really? Look at the millions who have turned out for the world peace rallies."

Samuel nodded. "I agree our numbers have multiplied, but still we've had no impact on those in power. It's discouraging."

"I know it appears that way, but have heart. Our plan is to allow institutions based on fear to continue to dominate in appearance while we quietly seep away their source of power – the fear of the masses. Humanity can only be manipulated and enslaved through fear. Once fear is released, freedom is obtained; and once freedom is obtained, the institutions rooted in fear must also change - or collapse."

Lenzi smiled at Brit and Mallory "You have both done well. When you came together your soul's immediately recognized your united purpose. Together you bring out the best in each other in the writing of Brit's speeches by allowing the inspiration to flow from one to the other. Your mutual understanding that we do not own this land, but are only the caretakers, along with your compassion for humanity has served to bring the interconnectedness of all things into the awareness of the general public. It won't be long before people realize it's in their best interest to cooperate rather than to compete with or dominate other countries."

"My father always spoke of Pleiades? Is there some connection there?" Bernadette probed.

"You've all pondered over the Pleiades connection. Are you aware that our solar system orbits around Alcyone, the central sun of Pleiades approximately every 25,000 years?"

Lenzi read well the surprised looks on the faces in the room. "We are now entering a point on that larger cycle when we are closest to Alcyone. Eastern mystics have long understood the meaning of this period. It is the time of awakening when the light from Alcyone is the brightest, influencing us in many powerful ways. It's a 2,000-year respite when we are all drawn more intensely towards Divine Love. Personal shifts towards the light are possible at any moment in time, however, there a certain moments when the shift can be made more easily. This is one of those times, and the wise will use it to advance their spiritual growth."

Lenzi's bright eyes were glowing. "Always during that period, we identify more strongly to Pleiades. But many of you have a deeper relationship. For some there is the genetic connection through the blood," she finished dramatically. Then she heaved a very long sigh. "I know you have many more questions, but I'm beginning to tire, and I have given you much to contemplate for now. Let us save the rest for another day."

CHAPTER 70

The next day the group met for the second and final time. Lenzi's demeanor had changed perceptibly, as one who understands the torch has been passed, however precariously, to the next generation.

"Mankind sits on the brink of a new way of life," she began. "And how you conduct your lives in the following years, will determine your individual futures. As I mentioned yesterday, we are about to pass into a time frame that occurs approximately every 11,500 years as we circle Alcyone. It is a glorious period that, if used to its fullest potential, allows mankind a wonderful opportunity to make a vast leap in its conscious evolution." She looked deep into Bernadette's eyes. "That is what the 'next step' that you pondered over in your father's letters referred to. It is just that – conscious evolution on the part of humans. We have great hope that during this period when you are closest to Alcyone, those on this planet will discover the secrets of conscious creation and use them wisely for the advancement of all. There is great excitement throughout the Universe of this happening – and its potential possibilities – and many have gathered to observe this awakening."

Fervent glances were exchanged around the room, however, Le Perfector ignored them and continued.

"There are now and have always been only two choices: to choose to live in love, or to choose to live in fear. Which of these vibrations a person chooses to dwell in, will determine their role in this momentous period. Only those who conquer the fears that hold them in bondage, and only those who discard all selfish desires will be given the tools to advance. Know that in recent decades the energy around this planet has been purposely amplified, making the aggressor more aggressive, and the loving more loving. This was by design to stimulate choice. Remember yesterday, when Mr. Sinclair commented that he wasn't seeing any changes. That is because as the light becomes brighter, the shadows loom larger, but this is so they are more easily recognized. The problems were always there, cleverly hidden, but at this time they are being revealed so that they might be healed. Problems must first be recognized and acknowledged in order to be corrected. This is true both with individuals and countries. But I caution you, discernment is necessary, however, it must be done with an attitude of forgiveness. Not forgiveness of the wrong action, but forgiveness of the wrong thinking." Lenzi sighed heavily. "Now before I leave you, we have time for a few more questions.

Bernadette smiled warmly at the older woman, understanding that in many ways she was involved with her upbringing. "I'm curious about this Voice that speaks to me. Can you tell me who it is?"

"Yes," and then Lenzi's tone became so soft they had to strain to hear her. "It is you."

Bernadette's expression was bewildered. "Me?"

"Yes, my dear. It is the part of you that *is all* and *knows all.*

"But it's a male voice."

"The soul has no gender, Bernadette. Your human ears gave it a male signature."

Bernadette sat dazed, and Lenzi, seeing her confusion, clarified. "We continue to look for answers everywhere but in our own hearts where our divine spirits wait patiently for our recognition. You've pondered at length over the meaning of the symbol of the fleur de lys. It is the symbol for the threefold flame that resides in your heart, representing life, love and balance – and it is this threefold flame that connects you to divinity. That is where one must seek for answers. Searching exclusively in the material world has kept humans troubled and lost, and the peace and happiness they yearn for continues to elude them." Lenzi's voice intensified. "There is but one place to look, and that is within."

Bernadette's tone was one of frustration. "I've tried to do that, but I rarely get an answer."

"Perhaps your efforts have not been of a consistent nature. If one would open a dialogue with one's higher self and maintain awareness of it throughout the day, instead of always focusing on the ego self that keeps the mind controlled with the false trivialities and glamour of the illusionary world, everything would become very clear. Remember, in order for there to be a relationship with your soul, there must first be an awareness."

Lenzi shifted in her chair, and to those who knew her well, she seemed to lean heavier on her cane than in the past. "It is important here to understand that you are not your body. The body is only the vehicle the spirit uses in the material world. But most of you have detached from your spirit by giving your entire focus to the body. You clean it, cloth it, keep it warm, keep it cool, feed it, find ways to entertain it and on and on. It's as if you got into your car to drive to the store one day, and somewhere along the way, you became your car and forgot you were the driver. Reconnect with the driver, and you will be surprised at the rewards."

Lenzi paused for a long moment. "There is only one way out of this matrix, and that is to go in. That is what meditation is all about: quieting the mind that is dominated by the personality so that one may hear the softer voice of the soul that is quietly, but persistently urging you to wake from the stormy dream of separation. Take the time to listen, and you will be surprised at what you hear."

"What are we to do now?" Samuel asked.

"First you must clear your minds, wash the slate clean of the many idle, careless and harmful thoughts of the lower desires. Then become the silent sentinel of what you allow to come in. Look up and out, away from self and the illusionary material world. Then you can use your intellect as it was designed, which is to connect you to higher planes of thought. When one unites the loving heart and the disciplined mind, the answers will come intuitively."

"As to the future, it is most important to recognize that your futures are nothing more than a blank slate with possible potentials. A slate that in the past has been filled by your uncontrolled thoughts and emotions that pushed you towards poor choices. The hope is that, henceforth, you will recognize the importance of allowing your hearts and your minds to rise above the mundane to the higher planes and connect you to your intuition, which will guide you to a new pinnacle in human evolution."

"Samuel, you and Bernadette have come together to write the story in novel form. Everyone comes to truth differently. Brit and Mallory's speeches inspire many, but there are others who can only learn from fiction. It is to them you will speak. Together you will become the Merlin of your times, weaving wonderful stories as you combine Bernadette's poetic words into the fabric of Samuel's logical mind, thereby presenting many with a wonderful and inspiring saga to bring them home again. And you, Julia, through your kind nature and humor will keep the other two balanced, as you share with them your prophetic insights to incorporate into their works."

Bernadette's voice had a woeful quality. "But so many of those in power in our country and around the world are such dark souls. And they seem to have such absolute power. It's hard to believe they will let go."

"I know it is much easier to see the face of God in an innocent child. But the souls of which you speak are also sparks of the divine, however misguided. Your forgiveness will be not of their actions, but for their wrong thinking. Cassarra has developed a deep friendship with your president. When his world comes crashing down around him, as it will, and those he thinks are his loyal friends abandon ship, he will turn to her, and she will be there to advise him. Have faith and write your dreams to inspire others."

Lenzi closed her incredible eyes for a moment and when they opened they seemed to be looking far beyond those in the room. "In leaving I remind you not to put too much emphasis on the trail markers. They are only there as a sign that you are on the right path. But often men see them as the answer in themselves. They stop their forward motion, wrongly believing they have arrived, and then proceed to turn the trail marker into a religion. You were meant to flow in the current of the river of life, not to stagnate on the shores, hanging desperately onto a signpost, no matter how valid the message painted across it."

Her voice slightly trembled when she said, "There are already those who are beginning to understand that they must look from a broader perspective in order to see the big picture. Life was not meant to be dissected into a million pieces as is being done presently. At this point in your history mankind has categorized itself into isolation, leaving him with the inability to connect the pieces and see the entire picture. Scientists - who have become your current priests, only this time in white jackets - are so busy looking for the ants, they are being stampeded by the elephants."

Light laughter spread throughout the room.

"Although there are a few who have broken through. Quantum physics brought us the realization that nothing can be understood in isolation, but must be seen as part of a network. Those who comprehend the deeper meaning behind that theory realize that the study of science and religion when combined with philosophy will result in the emergence of true wise men. Men who will live more graciously because of their recognition that we are not islands of individuality, but part of the unity of all life. They will see our planet as one large borderless country, and they will fully grasp that intolerance, whether religious, national or racial, is a deterrent to soul growth. Once this wider consciousness is reached, the realization that together we can do anything will abound. These men and women will eventually unlock the secret of the human purpose, which is the perfection of mankind. Note, when I speak of religion, I am not referring to your institutions based on fear and guilt, but as the individual search for truth in developing one's latent mystical powers."

Lenzi saw the doubt written on the faces before her. "I know this sounds like lofty idealism, especially when one looks around at the events unraveling in the world today. But there are many, like yourselves, who have dreamed dreams of a better way, and I am here to tell you we are getting very close to critical mass, at which time the change will come so fast that no institution or military power will be able to stop it."

"Do you really believe our generation has the potential to consciously create perfection," Mallory asked, her voice solicitous.

The love that streamed from Lenzi's eyes drenched them in warm sunlight. "Do you truly believe that what you are seeing presently was what the Creator had in mind for us?"

CHAPTER 71

Le Perfector departed as she arrived, with little fanfare and great sped, leaving them with many unanswered questions, yet with the knowledge that they each held the answers within themselves, and the knowing that sometime in the not too distant future there could be a world that was very different from the one before them. But they had been clearly led to understand that this better world would only come into being if individuals pressed forward towards personal evolution as well as national evolution. One could not sit back and do nothing and wait for it, because then it would never come. Nothing comes from nothing. It was necessary to create it by taking responsibility for one's thoughts and actions and comprehending how these very acts created one's future and, consequently, each country's future.

CHAPTER 72

Three Months Later:

Henry Connolly's townhouse was uncommonly quiet. He stared out his large picture window where the first rays of dawn were beginning to trickle across the landscape. Small patches of the dense early morning fog remained, creating a surreal effect.

His figure sat unmoving as a paralyzing numbness replaced the nauseating feeling that engulfed him when he received that phone call in the middle of the night. It was one of his sources warning him that the Washington Post was going to break the story about the Phoenix Project. The Washington Post had all the names of their elite little group, dates, memos. The Frenchman was their source. He had even taken the journalists to the farmhouse were he was held. They had pictures of his scars, interviews with the first responders who arrived after the bombs went off and some of the videotapes of his treatment while held in captivity. *How in the hell had they gotten their hands on them!*

He was told that Interpol made a strong statement to the press: the American government, had abducted, held captive and tortured, a French citizen. There would be an investigation, and those involved would be held accountable to the World Court.

Henry was holding a prescription bottle loosely in his left hand. He hesitated a brief moment before unscrewing the cap. He looked up at the original oil painting by one of the great Masters that hung in his living room and remembered the pride he felt when he acquired it. Not because he was a great art connoisseur, but because of what it represented financially.

He looked back at the prescription bottle. These were the stronger pills his doctor had recently prescribed when he complained the others weren't working. The bottle was full.

Hours later the phone rang, and a gruff voice left a message on the answering machine. "Henry, what the hell is going on? You'd better get your ass over here and fast." But there was no one to hear the message. Henry Connolly's body was slumped in the chair, the empty prescription bottle on the floor beside him.

For the rest of the citizens of the United States, the day began, not different from any other day. The sun rose slowly in the east, reflecting a prism of colors on the clouds that still lingered after the passing rain. A cleansing rain that washed the grime and oil from the city streets, the pollutants from the factories down the streams to eventually meet the ocean where the churning waves would neutralize them.

The usual morning sounds slowly began to creep into the air. The buzz of an electric razor, the gurgle of a coffee pot, a door closing, the footsteps of a neighbor down the hallway, a car engine.

Newspapers were being opened and read at the breakfast table, the coffee shop, on trains and buses. Americans were stunned as they read of the deception of the Phoenix Project and the massive amounts of money those behind it were blatantly scamming from the government coffers. Their coffers. How had this happened? How had they become so complacent to graft and deceit that they had forgotten to make their lawmakers, their representatives accountable? How had they allowed those in prestigious positions to become so powerful that they believed they were above the laws they themselves had put into effect?

The world sat and waited for a response while the American public, first dazed by the unraveling events, stood shaken and uncertain. But as their indignation took over, they began to demand answers. Within weeks, the climate in Washington changed dramatically as fingers were pointed in every direction. Ultimately, the infighting weakened the power of all, and the infrastructure began to collapse in on itself, starting a domino effect that even the most devious or influential politicians were able to stop.

And somewhere in a remote corner of the planet, a very old woman put down her magnificent indigo cane that was embellished with gold symbols, as she sat on the edge of her bed. She unwrapped her long braid and let her gray hair fall loose around her shoulders. Her face was lined, but her unusual silver eyes shone with the light of eternal youthfulness. A smile lingered on her face. It was a balmy night with light breezes from the east. Pleiades was just beginning to rise in the clear night sky. Yes, the new dawn had finally broken in the consciousness of humanity. Not for the first time in the history of the planet. But this time she had the greatest hope that mankind had finally reached a place in their hearts where they could wisely and justly take advantage of the sliver of opportunity that they held so precariously in their hands.

. . . for the legend promised that the restored Grail had the power to heal the wasteland.